"Hey, I'm Will. I saw you this morning at breakfast. You must be new?"

His breath reeked of coffee, and he seemed to have more energy than I was prepared to handle. "Uh, yeah. Ronnie. Got here Saturday," I answered, closing the textbook in front of me.

He smacked the table. "Man, I miss everything." Then he smiled. "Well, at least the good stuff."

I tried not to smile at the obvious pickup line. But this guy was kinda cute. I couldn't help it. Although, I feared my attempt at not smiling may have resulted in some twisted demonic mess of an expression. Ugh.

"My brother and I went home for the weekend. It was my dad's birthday."

"That's nice," I said, keeping my eyes forward. I could feel his stare. My mouth twitched; it was like I forgot what to do with it. I didn't want to smile. But I didn't want to look angry or sad either. So, I pressed my lips together in an attempt to make my mouth disappear.

"You always this polite?" He laughed. Then he sat up straight and folded his hands on the table, like I had mine, and with a goofy smile, he said, "That's nice."

I gaped at him. "Are you mocking me?"

He smiled big, and I noticed he had nice teeth to go along with his nice face. And for the second time in under a minute, I started to smile. This time I let it happen.

What We Hide

by

M. L. Stoughton

What We Hide

Contact Information: info@thewildrosepress.com

Cover Art by *Jennifer Greeff*

The Wild Rose Press, Inc.
PO Box 708
Adams Basin, NY 14410-0708
Visit us at www.thewildrosepress.com

Publishing History
First Edition, 2023
Trade Paperback ISBN 978-1-5092-4960-2
Digital ISBN 978-1-5092-4961-9

Published in the United States of America

Dedication

To Scott,
For feeding me when I didn't want to leave my desk.

Prologue

August 22

The silver vase sat in the stone cubby as if it were a trophy on display—something to be proud of. I couldn't look at it. At the moment I was overwhelmed with feelings, but pride wasn't one of them.

The pastor said his final ceremonial words and turned to my father. "You're welcome to stay while the vault is sealed."

The wall in front of us was made up of thick marble slabs, four high and at least twenty across. Each slab was a door to a vault—a cubby just like this one. And each had a metal name plate on the front. My mother was placed between the Berringer family and Thomas Kolbach. Strangers.

I glanced down at my little sister, her sweaty hand in mine, and wondered if she truly understood what was going on. But how could she? I had nine years on her and couldn't wrap my head around it—around the fact that my mother had been reduced to ash and stuffed into that silver vase. Or what'd they call it…an urn?

Two men dressed in black suits stepped up to the wall, and I braved one last look. Read the engraving:

Valerie J. Campbell

Always in our hearts

Panic, thick as a fist, lodged in my throat. I

couldn't watch them lock her in there. File her away, like old belongings in a storage mall.

I turned to my father, who held my sister's other hand. "Do I have to stay?"

"No," he answered, not looking at me.

That was the beginning of endless months of him not looking at me.

That was the beginning of my downward spiral.

Chapter 1

Friday, April 23

The crash and crunch of metal woke me with a start. Pulse racing, I casually sat up straighter in my seat and glanced around.

It seemed as if no one else heard it. Once again it was in my head—it was *always* in my head.

"How about you, Miss Campbell?" The mention of my name called my attention to Mr. Little, standing at the front of the class. "What do you think the narrator means when he says the men had 'no connection with the bread'?"

I looked down at the open book in front of me and frantically scanned the page.

"Page thirty-six," Mr. Little grumbled.

Cringing and squirming in my seat, I flipped the pages. *Thirty-two, thirty-four, thirty-six.* Yikes, I'd missed more than I thought.

"Umm," I hummed, trying to buy myself some time as I searched for the line he mentioned. But it was so hard to concentrate with the metallic clang still ringing in my ears.

Mr. Little heaved a heavy sigh. "Try to pay attention, Miss Campbell," he said, moving on and pointing to a girl with her hand in the air. "Yes, Emily, can you tell us what it means?"

My jaw clenched shut. His patronizing tone didn't go unnoticed—the fact that he called me by my last name with rigid distaste and practically sang her name. *Em-il-ly*, I repeated in my head as my lip twitched toward a snarl.

I pulled a long breath in through my nose and released it slowly. Though, it did little to ease the rising tension. I swear every nerve in my body was as taut as the strings on a violin.

After Mr. Little praised Emily for a job well done, he circled toward the back of his desk. "Okay, class, we've still got fifteen minutes before the bell. This week's vocabulary words are on the board."

All around me, students opened their spiral notebooks and worked on the assignment. But I couldn't move. At the moment, I was too focused on breathing and calming my racing heart. The *thump-thump-thump-thump-thump-thump-thump* of it echoed in my head.

I closed my eyes and prayed the feeling would pass. But then the *scratching* of pencils on paper began to fill my ears, and I knew it was too late.

It was happening.

These episodes always followed the same pattern. First, I felt shaky and anxious, then a shortness of breath and rising heart rate, followed by an extreme sensitivity to noise.

As if on cue, the clock on the wall at the front of the room grew louder. *Tick. Tick. Tick.* Then came the *tap-tap-tapping* of a pencil in the hands of a fidgeter with no rhythm.

With each sound, flashes of light and color danced across the backs of my eyelids as if I could suddenly see their vibrations. I hated this feeling because I knew what usually came next. A google search told me it was palpitations. But it felt more like beetles crawling around in my chest.

I still have a scar—three scratches below my collarbone—where I tried to claw the beetles out during a particularly bad episode.

The wheels on Mr. Little's chair screeched, and my eyes sprang open.

He was glaring at me again.

From early on, Mr. Little and I had a mutual understanding. Unfortunately, it was that neither of us liked or respected the other.

With arched brow, he held my stare and pointed to the board. Blurred patches of blue ink danced against the white background as my vision grew spotty. I couldn't make out the words on the list, much less write them down.

As my gaze turned back to Mr. Little, I could tell his lips were moving, but it was as if he were speaking in a vacuum. I couldn't make out what he was saying.

Blinking slowly, I focused on the ticking clock. At the moment it was hypnotizing. The only sound keeping a perfect tempo, like a metronome. And it represented the countdown to escaping this hellhole.

The next time my eyes blinked open, he was standing closer. Hands on his hips, mouth pressed in a scowl, and forehead pinched at the center.

"*Wah wa-wa-wa wah!*" His mouth snapped shut. The veins in his temples bulged. He seemed to be waiting for a response. A response I wasn't able to offer.

In moments like these, it was nearly impossible to

speak. The worst part was that I never knew how long each stage would last. Depending on my surroundings, the whole episode could pass quickly, without incidence…or it could go the other way.

With one long stride, Mr. Little was at my desk, posture primed for a showdown. And just like that, all eyes fell on me.

That's when the switch flipped. It was going the *other way*.

"Well, Miss Campbell?" Suddenly, his voice was the only sound in the room—his words clear and vivid. Loud. "What do you have to say for yourself? Do you want a zero for this assignment? Maybe you'd like to pay a visit to the principal's—"

"Shut up!" I cried, exploding out of my chair, my fists tight at my sides.

"Excuse me—"

"You heard me." My lips pressed shut. Air huffed noisily from my nostrils.

His eyes twitched, looking me up and down as if he might have been afraid.

I scooped my bag from the back of my chair and walked out the door, whispers and snickers followed my exit.

No sooner had the door clicked shut when I heard it open again.

"Straight to Kirkland's office, young lady," his voice boomed behind me. "He'll be expecting you!"

I flashed a peace sign over my shoulder and kept walking. It wasn't exactly the threat he thought it was.

The door slammed shut, and I ducked into the nearest bathroom. I went to the last stall, locked the door, and stepped up onto the toilet seat. Crouching there, with my feet off the floor, I popped in my earbuds and hit play on my iPod.

****

At least twenty minutes later, long after the period had ended and the next one began, I strolled into Mr. Kirkland's office.

"Hey, Stan," I said lazily as I plopped down into the chair across from him.

His eyes flicked up to me, like little daggers. He didn't say a word. He was busy rifling through a file folder. Mine, no doubt.

Mrs. Stewart, my guidance counselor, stepped in the room and closed the door behind her. She put some papers on Mr. Kirkland's desk. "Here is that information you asked for," she said and sat down in the chair on my right. She had a folder too, my name in bold print at the top.

"Veronica—"

"Ronnie," I corrected, grabbing a chunk of my long, dark hair and twisting it casually around my finger.

He continued, without missing a beat. "I've asked Mrs. Stewart to join us because we have some things to discuss and decisions to make. I've called your father at work, and he is on his way to meet with us." He sighed and went on, "At this point I don't think summer school will keep you from repeating the eleventh grade next year—"

"What?" I snapped. "That's ridiculous! Why can't I just ace the finals and show you that I know this shit?"

Mrs. Stewart took over, looking at the file in her hands. "You haven't completed a single assignment for math." She flipped the page. "Science…no assignments handed in." She flipped again. "History…same thing."

I rolled my eyes.

"And we haven't even addressed the behavioral issues," Mr. Kirkland said.

I felt like they were ganging up on me. My nose started to wrinkle, and I grabbed a piece of hair again, this time twisting with a little more vigor as I stared down at the floor. I tried to tune him out as he rambled on.

"…the outbursts in class, lying, cursing, and drinking on school grounds…we've tried to be understanding because of your circumstances…enough is enough. Detention isn't going to cut it anymore."

Wait. I stopped twisting and met his gaze. What did that mean?

"Ronnie." Mrs. Stewart had my attention now. She turned in her seat, rested her forearms on her lap, and leaned toward me. "This just isn't like you," she said, softly.

That was true. I wasn't the quiet girl, who followed rules, got good grades, and liked going to school and seeing her friends, anymore. The fact was, I'd chased all my friends away. It wasn't by choice. I just couldn't stand the pitying looks and the sympathy.

I didn't deserve sympathy.

And a long time ago, I found that people don't tend to bother if you never let them see your vulnerable side. Being the "Angry Bitch" was so much easier. The other nickname I'd acquired over the last few months was "Party Girl," and that was because I'd also found that alcohol and boys gave me a break from the constant pain.

"Come in," Mr. Kirkland said, answering a knock

on the door.

The door opened, and my dad walked in. The look on his normally expressionless face surprised me. In the brief moment our eyes met, I could tell that he was disappointed. Maybe pissed was more like it. Either way, I was surprised as it seemed he had desensitized himself to the living. It had been months since we'd had a conversation. And what little interaction we did have was tense. Or on paper. Like the note he left on the kitchen counter this morning.

We have to talk about your grades this weekend.

I'd tossed it in the trash like the others.

"Thanks for coming." Mr. Kirkland stood, extending his hand.

"I got here as quickly as I could."

After shaking hands, Mr. Kirkland motioned to the chair on my left. "So…have you thought any more about our discussion last week?"

My head whipped around, and my demanding eyes fell on Dad. "What did you talk about last week?"

Again, our eyes met, maybe a fraction of a moment this time.

"I've thought of nothing else," he answered, reaching blindly toward the arm of my chair and resting his hand on top of mine. He let out a heavy sigh and gave my hand a gentle squeeze. "I want what's best for my daughter. And I think Evergreen would be the best thing for her right now. I am just not emotionally able to deal with this anymore."

Rage thundered inside me. I shot out of my chair so quickly it squealed across the floor.

"You're not able to deal with this anymore! What the fuck is that supposed to mean? You haven't dealt with this at all!"

"Language—" Mr. Kirkland tried to interject.

"Can you even remember the last time we just talked, or watched one of our shows together, or did *anything* together?" Once I got started, it was hard to stop. "For the first time since I was ten, we didn't go to the theater to see the latest Marvel movie on opening night." My voice cracked, but I held the tears at bay, the anger overriding the pain. The truth was, I missed my father. It was as if he'd died that night too. "You think I don't notice that you polish off a six-pack every single night—"

"You're right," Dad whispered, his gaze shifting away. "I haven't dealt with it…but I don't know how. We are *all* hurting. We *all* lost her."

With my lips pressed shut, my breathing came in quick, forceful bursts. I squeezed my eyes closed, as if somehow that would erase his words. They confused me, threatened to avert my attention from the immediate issue at hand: Evergreen. I knew what that place was; it was a boarding school for the bad kids. A place where parents could lock their children away. Out of sight, out of mind.

I folded my arms across my chest. "I'm not going. You're not sending me away."

"Ronnie." He almost raised his voice but caught himself. Let out a breath, slow and steady. "I have to think of your sister. A seven-year-old shouldn't be exposed to this kind of behavior. You know how much Tori looks up to—"

"I'm not going!" I screamed as loud as I could. But it didn't feel loud enough.

I swiped the name plate and other knickknacks off

the front edge of Mr. Kirkland's desk. Then spun around, kicked my empty chair out of my way, and burst out the office door.

Ignoring the demands to "stop" and "get back here," I ran out of the school. I wasn't sure where I was headed as long as it was away from here. I darted between the cars in the student lot, weaving my way farther into the sea of metal, hoping to go unnoticed by watching eyes.

Then I came across Josh's car. I opened the passenger door and slid in.

My throat hurt, my head was pounding, and I couldn't breathe. I reached down and yanked the lever, reclining the seat. Then habit had me reaching for my iPod.

"Shit!" I'd left my bag in the office.

My hands shook. I needed my iPod like an addict needing a hit. My ears itched for the buds that worked like an IV line, piping loud music directly into my system. It was the only way to keep my own destructive thoughts from taking over.

When school let out, forty-five minutes later, the parking lot flooded with kids. Josh saw me before he opened his car door. He didn't look happy. Clearly the senior was regretting his involvement with me.

"What are you doing in here?" he asked as he rolled his eyes.

"I had to get outta there, and I didn't know where else to go."

"Fine. I'll take you home."

"No! I can't go home. Can't I just hang out with you until Beeve's party tonight?" I didn't like begging.

"Don't you have any real friends you can go to?"

Ouch. That hurt. I thought Josh was my friend. But apparently, he's only my friend when there are benefits. "No, as a matter of fact, I don't."

He may have griped and groaned at first, but at least he let me hang out until it was time to go to the party. On the way, he stopped by Steve Harder's, where we picked up two more passengers.

Josh made it very clear to his friends that I "just needed a ride."

I moved to the back seat so Steve could take the front. I didn't know the other guy's name. He kept eyeing me sideways. Finally, he faced me head-on. One brow arched, and his nose wrinkled with disapproval. "What are you, like fourteen?"

"Sixteen," I snapped. "Like it's any of your business." *Jerk.*

Beeve's party was packed. His older brother was a freshman in college, and the two of them had the house to themselves for the weekend.

Sometime around midnight, Josh stopped me on my way to the keg. "You don't look so good. Have you eaten anything?"

I tried to shake my head, but it made the room spin even more.

"Come on." He dragged me into the kitchen where we found four empty pizza boxes on the counter. He opened the nearest cupboard. "We have to find something to put in your stomach besides alcohol," he grumbled.

"Why are you being nice to me, now?" I asked as I opened the freezer and spotted a carton of ice cream. I took it and went to the table. "I thought you weren't my friend."

"I didn't say I wasn't your friend," Josh argued, closing the freezer behind me.

While he grabbed a bowl from a pile of clean dishes and a spoon from the drawer, I leaned against the table, hugging the Heavenly Hash like it was a security blanket.

"Here." He set the dishes in front of me.

I removed the lid and grabbed the spoon, jamming it into the half-eaten carton. The spoon bent as I scooped it out and brought it straight up to my mouth.

Josh pulled a chair over. He spun it around and straddled the back. I could hear the condescending tone before he even opened his mouth.

"Look, Ronnie, you're a nice girl. I'll be your friend, but I'm not into babysitting."

Not even the ice cream could shield me from that low blow. I dropped the spoon.

"What the fuck is that supposed to mean? Did you feel like my babysitter last week when you had your tongue down my throat and your hand up my shirt?"

The chair tipped over, slamming to the ground as I jumped to my feet. I had to get the hell out of there.

I remember that.

The rest was kind of a blur.

Chapter 2

A band of sunlight hit my face, waking me with an instant headache.

My eyes felt too large for their sockets and the lids too thin to block out the light. I rolled to my side and curled into a ball, trying to tuck my entire body into my sweatshirt for both warmth and darkness.

I tried to go back to sleep, but I could hear voices.

Who the hell is talking so loud?

Snippets of last night popped into my head, and my eyes painfully sprang open again.

I was in the back seat of my dad's car. It wasn't the first time I'd hidden there when I came home too late and too drunk.

I tried to sneak a peek to see who was outside, but the windows were fogged over. For once, I found myself grateful for my dad's ancient Pontiac Grand Prix with crank windows.

One crank at a time, I slowly opened the window until the cold morning air began streaming in. It wasn't long before I could see enough to know who was out there.

Two police officers were at our front door, talking to my dad.

Shit. Wonder what that's about?

I waited until the cops were long gone, then circled around to the back of the house. Entering the door into the kitchen, I found the coast was clear. With two hands, I eased the door shut and worked the knob to avoid the possibility of a click. Then, releasing my held breath, I turned into the room and stopped short.

"Where were you last night?"

I didn't want to get into it with him right now, but he was blocking my way to my room.

"At April's," I answered. She used to be my best friend, though we hadn't spoken in months. However, he didn't know that. I took a step, hoping he'd move aside. But he wasn't budging.

"Well, I have something here that says differently." He held up some papers before reading from them. "This says you were at one-forty-two Sycamore Street, at a house belonging to John and Renee Beevers."

I felt my nose and brow wrinkle. I couldn't hide my confusion.

"It's a complaint for property damage." He cleared his throat, before continuing. His voice grew louder and angrier with each word. "Dishes, wall hangings, a chair, and a picture window!" He lifted his eyes to meet mine. "Do you have any idea how much this is going to cost me?" He crumpled the paper, drew his arm back, and threw it to the floor like he was skipping rocks. "Start packing. You're going to Evergreen!"

His thundering voice had me trembling, which a year ago would've been cause for surrender. Now it only fueled the rage that was always ready just below the surface.

My head began pounding even harder as my pulse raced out of control.

"Like hell I'm going!" My nails bit into the palms of my hands. I couldn't squeeze my fists any tighter. "I hate you!"

Feeling trapped, I grabbed the closest thing within reach—the glass coffee carafe—and threw it across the room. It hit the floor and exploded.

I expected a fight from him, but he said nothing. He wouldn't even look at me. As I stared at him, he seemed more shocked and focused on the mess I'd made.

Then a quiet gasp—barely a peep—pulled my attention from his face.

I hadn't seen Tori walk in from the other doorway to the living room.

She stood stock-still, just a few feet from where the carafe hit—directly in the splash zone. Shards of glass lay sprinkled at her feet. Brown liquid stained her pink princess nightgown, and red drops of blood dotted her bare legs. And while tears rolled down her tiny face, that wasn't the worst part.

No.

It was the look of fear on her face: her eyes the size of saucers, her mouth downturned, and bottom lip quivering. Other than the hitch in her breath, she never made a sound.

A cold rush washed over me as my father scooped her up and sat her on the counter. He grabbed a dish towel and turned on the faucet, then began cleaning her up.

"I'm sorry," my voice squeaked as I took off toward my room.

Locking the door behind me, my gaze roamed over my deep purple walls. I wondered if this would be my last night in my own room.

Bile gurgled up into my throat. I climbed onto my

bed, taking deep breaths and fighting the need to retch. With my legs tucked under me, I folded myself over, burying my face in the covers.

I never meant to hurt her.

I recalled my father's words from the day before. "*A seven-year-old shouldn't be exposed to this kind of behavior. You know how much Tori looks up to you.*" They hit harder this time.

As the tears came, my body began to rock back and forth of its own accord.

I couldn't remember the last time I actually cried.

I don't know how much time had passed. Could've been minutes or hours, for all I knew. The sickness and panic had faded, leaving me drained. But I heard my dad talking in the next room. I lifted my head to try to listen. Darkness clouded the edges of my vision, and it took a moment for my eyes to adjust to the light.

It sounded like he was on the phone as I only heard one voice. The instant I heard him say my full name, I knew who he was talking to, and the panic began again.

I didn't want to leave my room, but I felt like my bladder would burst if I didn't.

Opening the door just a crack, I peeked out and scooted quietly down the hall.

When I left the bathroom several minutes later, my father was waiting for me at the end of the hallway.

I stopped in my tracks and held my breath.

"We leave at three," he said abruptly, then turned and walked away.

Without a sound, I ducked into my room and closed the door, leaning my back against it as I struggled to catch my breath. I didn't want to leave my home—enter a world of unknowns.

I thought about running away…

But where would I go? I didn't have any money and I didn't have any friends who'd help me. I didn't even have a cell phone. I used to, but I'd destroyed it during one of our fights, and my father refused to pay for another. Hence, my older-than-dirt iPod.

Dread rolled painfully through my body. Change was coming, and I couldn't stop it.

After several minutes of panicked pacing and several more sitting at the edge of my bed and staring off, I grabbed a large, black duffel bag from my closet.

Though I had no idea what to take.

Do I bring my own clothes? Or will I be issued an orange jumpsuit?

Why did my brain insist on torturing me?

Eventually, I packed as if I were going on a long vacation. Then zipped the bag closed, sat on my bed, and waited.

At three o'clock on the dot, there was a knock at my door.

"Time to go," Dad announced from the other side.

My bag hung heavy off my shoulder as I left my room and found him waiting by the front door. As he reached for his keys hanging from a hook in the entryway, I noticed my gray canvas hobo bag on the bench below. I was relieved to see it had made it home. I never went anywhere without that bag.

I looked around, waiting. "Where's Tori? Isn't she coming?"

"She's next door with Mrs. Kelly," he said curtly, then opened the inner, wooden door. "Now, let's go. It's a long drive, and I'd like to get back before dark."

I swallowed hard and planted my feet. "I want to

see Tori before I go—tell her I'm sorry and say goodbye."

"I think for Victoria's safety, I need to limit your contact with her." He pushed open the glass storm door and held it with one arm.

"So I'm not allowed to see my own sister?" I could feel my pulse rising.

My father didn't speak. He just waved his arm, gesturing for me to cross the threshold.

It was obvious he wasn't going to listen to anything I had to say. I shouldn't have expected more, but I did. I expected some sort of response—a lecture, or maybe a scolding about what a horrible person I was. *That* would've hurt less.

Because *this* felt like he was done with me for good.

My lips parted, ready to give him an earful. But for the first time in months, I didn't want to fight with him. That didn't mean I didn't want to hurt him.

"Fine. I can't wait to get out of this place," I said, snatching my hobo bag from the bench as I slipped by him and went to the car.

The trip to Evergreen took over an hour—seventy-three minutes to be exact—and neither of us said a word. That's a lot of quiet for my thoughts to fill. Mostly, I spent that time wondering what to expect. And if I'd ever see home again.

The car turned off the main road, passing the sign slowly:

Evergreen Boarding School

"For a Brighter Future"

With disdain, I pictured myself as a tour guide using a sickening sweet voice and announcing, *next stop, Juvie.*

The long and twisted driveway sliced through the woods, adding suspense to trepidation, not to mention an immediate feeling of isolation. But at least I didn't see any tall prison fencing with coiled razor wire along the top.

Finally, the forest opened up, offering a glimpse of the Evergreen campus. We followed the path, passing a small house and a maintenance shed before pulling up to a building with a sign marked: *Main Entrance*.

My father stopped the car right in front of the door and turned off the ignition. As he got out and circled around, I remained frozen in the passenger seat.

With my nose to the glass, I stared up at the massive old building. It hovered over me like a stone and mortar paddle. And with the afternoon sun glimmering off the windows like fire, I was afraid it would smack my ass all the way to hell.

Slowly, I pulled the handle and opened the car door. But it took me a minute to bring myself to get out. In the meantime, my dad grabbed my duffle from the back seat and started toward the front door of the building.

Once I was at his side, he pressed the button under the sign that read: *Ring bell*.

Moments later the lock released with a loud click, and the heavy wooden door creaked open.

"You must be the Campbells?" a gray-haired woman asked. She had a large frame and wore a gray dress with the buttons done all the way up to her neck. Clunky, black orthopedic shoes completed her matronly look.

"Yes, I'm Robert Campbell," Dad answered, "and

this is my daughter, Veronica."

The woman glared. "I just got the message that you were on your way. We weren't expecting you 'til Monday."

"I'm sorry—" he began.

The woman interrupted. "Come in. I'll call Mrs. Brown and let her know you're here." She turned and walked away.

"Are we supposed to follow her?" I whispered, but I think my dad was just as confused. Neither of us moved.

The massive corridor stretched equally in both directions, lit only by single-bulb brass pendants hanging from the ceiling every twenty feet or so. Everything about this place looked cold and hard, from the overly waxed black-and-green checkered asphalt floors to the shiny wood walls and the portraits that adorned them. Nothing about this place said 21st century. Heck, it barely said 20th century.

"Well, come along," the woman ordered before disappearing through the second door on the left.

By the time we caught up to her, she was already hanging up the phone. She handed my father a clipboard. "Start filling out these forms. Mrs. Brown, the Head Mistress, is on her way." Then she looked at me. "Bring your bags and follow me. I'll show you to your room." And with that, she was gone again.

"I'm Mrs. Trumble, the House Mother and school nurse," she said as she clomped back down the corridor, the way we'd come.

I hurried to keep up. For an old woman, she sure moved fast.

Opposite the main entrance was a wide staircase. It

was pretty much the fanciest one I'd ever seen. It went up half a flight, to a midway landing, and then split in two—one to the left and the other to the right—both winding around to the second floor. Dark wood handrails decorated with carved posts and finials lined every bit of the grand staircase.

At the top, she went to the right.

"Bathroom is here," she said as we passed, just before she took another right at the end of the hall.

I had yet to see another person. "Where is everyone?"

"Out," she answered, stopping in front of the third door on the right. Room 203. "You will be staying with Amanda," she said as she opened the door and flipped on the light switch. Two long fluorescent tubes clung to the high ceiling, flanking an ancient, low-hanging fan; they sprang to life and flooded the room with enough light to feasibly do surgery.

My eye began to twitch.

The room in front of me had two of everything. The beds and nightstands jutted out from the wall on the left. One tall dresser sat to the right of the door and the other on the wall opposite the beds, between two narrow doors.

"You're the bed closest to the window," the woman said as she crossed the room. She opened the second narrow door. "This is your closet, and this is your dresser," she added, tapping the wooden top. Leaving the closet open, she headed back toward the door. "Start getting settled. I'll have someone retrieve you when the Head Mistress arrives." And with that, she was gone.

Well, I knew one thing for certain: Mrs. Trumble

was a woman of few words.

I heaved my bags onto the bed and started wandering around the room—snooping, was more like it. But I wanted to get a glimpse as to what my roommate was like. The poster of *NightShade* hanging on the wall was a big sign that we didn't have the same taste in music. I liked emo, but that band was a little too dark, even for me.

The top of her dresser was cluttered with hair and makeup products. I got the impression my new roommate was high maintenance. I didn't have a good feeling about this matchup.

I crossed the room and pulled back the heavy, off-white curtain. Like I suspected, I was nowhere near the front of the building—there was no sign of the driveway, or our car. But I could see now that the back of this place was shaped like a big squared-off U, and my window overlooked an empty courtyard in the middle. I scanned the windows across the way and noticed that every curtain within my view was closed tight—just a bunch of cream-colored rectangles. This place definitely didn't give off a warm fuzzy feeling.

I turned back toward the room, at the space assigned to me. With its bright light and dim asphalt floor, and its pea green walls and beds in a line, it was dreary and sparse. Institutional.

Oh my God. I can't do this.

I grabbed my bags off the bed, ran for the door, and yanked it open and almost mowed down another girl.

Poised to knock, the girl swallowed a gaspy breath. She had thick bangs and wide eyes behind her dark-rimmed glasses.

Both startled, we just stared at each other for a

moment.

"Out of my way!" I snapped as I dashed past her. I didn't have time to waste.

****

From the top of the stairs, I could hear my father's voice below. It sounded like he was leaving.

"…thanks again for understanding."

How could he leave without saying goodbye?

"I'm just glad it worked out and we had the room ready," the woman, who I could only assume was Mrs. Brown, said.

"Wait! Dad, wait!" I yelled as I flew down the steps, dropping my bags at the base of the staircase and rushing to where he stood near the main entrance. "I don't want to stay here. I promise I'll—"

"No, Ronnie," he said pointedly, throwing his hand up and shaking his head. "You have to give this a chance." He sounded spent.

"But, Dad, coming here was a wake-up call. I can't do this. I know I said I couldn't wait to get out of there, but I didn't mean it." Tears welled, and my throat constricted. It hurt to breathe. My eyes darted up and down the corridor; it looked massive when we first arrived, but now seemed to be closing in around me.

"Please!" I begged, flinging my arms around him. "I want to go home."

I felt his hesitation, the stutter as his arms went up to embrace me. His touch was light at first. Reserved. Guarded. As if he was afraid of me. But then he squeezed tighter, and I hoped it was a sign. The first sign of a father and daughter mending ways.

But it wasn't.

"You'll see. This is going to be really good for

you," he said into my hair.

"What?" My voice was just a whisper as I pulled away and looked up into his eyes.

He said nothing more, just turned toward the door.

That's when the rage hit. Again.

"You blame me, don't you?"

"Okay. Settle down." Mrs. Brown stepped between us.

"I knew it! That's why you can't look at me!" I lurched after him. But strong arms wrapped around me from behind, pinning my arms at my sides and holding me back. Still, I raged. "You blame me, don't you? Say it. Tell me the truth. You blame me for everything!"

And no matter how much I fought and wiggled, I couldn't get free.

I was stuck there, watching my father walk out the door.

Never looking back.

Chapter 3

My mind was quiet. My body, heavy and sluggish, as if my heart rate had slowed too much. But, as I stared at the painting on the wall in front of me, I didn't much care.

It was beautiful. The painting. And so peaceful and realistic. I wanted to go there. To that cottage by the lake and listen to the sounds of the forest around me, while I stared at the brilliant autumn colors reflecting off the glassy, still water. I could stare all day.

A woman, probably in her early thirties, with strawberry-blonde hair and kind eyes, stepped into my view. "Would you like some water, Veronica?" She held a plastic cup in her hand.

"Um, yeah," I answered, blinking a few times to redirect my focus as she handed it to me. I took a long sip, pulled the cup from my lips, and drew a breath. Ever since my mother died, I didn't like to be called Veronica. "I prefer Ronnie."

"Okay. Ronnie, it is." She lowered herself into a bright red wingback chair, and my gaze fell on the autumn painting again. It hung just over her shoulder.

The thick, dark wood frame was a nice contrast to the soft, creamy yellow walls. The whole room was bright and cheerful, nicely decorated. And with healthy green plants in colorful pots and the sun pouring in through the tall windows, I had to wonder if I was still at Evergreen.

I didn't remember getting there.

My gaze dropped to the side, and I placed my hand beside me. I stroked the velvety soft fabric of the overstuffed couch beneath me. *I don't remember sitting on this couch.*

The woman spoke again.

"How are you feeling now?" Her voice was soothing.

"Okay," I managed.

"My name is Dr. Olivia Swan. I'm a psychologist here at the school." So, I was still at Evergreen. "Have you ever talked to a psychologist or a therapist before?"

I went to a counselor once. I didn't like her, so I never went back.

I nodded.

"Part of the policy here at Evergreen is meeting with me on a regular basis. Our goal is to help you learn to overcome obstacles in order to live a safe and stable life." She paused a moment. I think she was waiting for a response. I didn't have one.

After a beat, she stood and circled around behind her desk. She opened a drawer and looked inside. "Red, blue, or purple?"

I shrugged. "I don't know…purple, I guess."

She pulled out some sort of book with a purple cover and bumped the drawer closed with her hip. Circling back over to me, she said, "This is for you. For when you don't feel like talking." She handed it to me. "It's a journal. I'd like you to give it a try. Write as much or as little as you'd like. Even if it's just one word." She sat back down across from me and smiled. "Sometimes just acknowledging our feelings—even if it's on paper, for no one else to see—can be quite therapeutic."

Lips pursed, I kept my eyes on the journal in my hand and nodded.

"Do you have any questions for me?"

I looked up, meeting her gaze. "Yeah. How long do I have to stay here?"

"Well, that depends entirely on you." Dr. Swan hesitated with a friendly smile. "We'll work together to set some goals and see if we can't get you home by the start of the next school year."

I felt sick to my stomach. The start of next school year was four months away. It seemed like a lifetime.

"I'm hungry. How about you?" Dr. Swan asked. The thought of food made my stomach pang again, and it occurred to me that I hadn't eaten anything all day. Maybe food would do me some good. I nodded, and she looked at her watch. "We have about fifteen minutes. Why don't we get you settled in before dinner?"

****

Dr. Swan helped me put my things in the dresser. As I pulled stuff out of my duffle, she'd open the drawers for me. First a stack of jeans. Then a stack of shirts. Before closing the shirt drawer, she held up a purple one with black lace. "I love this," she commented. "I bet it looks so pretty with your dark hair."

"That's my favorite." The words spilled from my lips. I pressed them closed and bit down. I felt like my mouth had betrayed me.

"It is?" she said with a big smile. "Oh, I know we're going to have a lot of fun getting to know each other."

I felt myself actually wanting to smile back. But I fought the urge. I scooped up an armful of socks and underwear and dumped them in the top drawer.

I peeked to see if Dr. Swan was watching. And while her eyes were busy wandering the room, I grabbed the framed picture from my bag and tucked it under my socks and closed the drawer.

Lastly, I put my cosmetics and toiletry bag on top of my dresser, in front of the standing mirror, and tossed the duffel bag in the bottom of the closet, along with a pair of slides and black ankle boots.

I looked around the room again. It wasn't much, but I guess it would do. *Fingers crossed, my roommate isn't irritating.*

Dr. Swan gave me a brief history and tour of the building on our way to dinner.

"The main building was built in 1905 as an all-girls finishing school. In the late sixties, with the addition of the gymnasium and the boys' dorms, the school went co-ed," she said, adding, "This floor is girls only. You'll notice most of them have their names decorated on their doors. You're welcome to make one too. The floor is broken up into two wings, the north and the south. They're laid out the same. Each has a dorm leader. Your room is in the south wing, so your dorm leader is Kerry. Their room is here." Dr. Swan gestured to a door on the right as we turned the corner. Room 213. A small whiteboard beside the door had the name Kerry and in parenthesis "they/them" at the top. There was a note scribbled underneath: *Out now. Will be back after dinner.*

"Kerry is a college student, so they have classes during the week just like you. But they're usually around nights and weekends. They're pretty good about letting you know when they're out. I left a message saying you were here early." Dr. Swan continued down the right side of the hallway. "And here you've got the laundry room. Next, is the common room—or lounge, if you will—there's a TV and a couple couches and chairs, and at the other end is a small kitchenette area, where you can keep your own drinks and snacks. Just make sure you label them. The whole floor shares the common room, so be respectful," she added with a smile.

I nodded, obediently.

With the grand staircase behind us, we turned, and Dr. Swan gestured to the doors flanking either side. "Each wing has its own bathroom. Just a word of warning," she said, bringing her gaze back to me. "Your wing has twenty-four girls and three shower stalls, so keep that in mind when you're planning your day."

"Okay."

"The school supplies the towels. There should be plenty on the shelves. By the way, curfew is at ten on school nights and eleven on Fridays and Saturdays. You just need to be *in* your room by curfew," she added as an important afterthought. "Monday morning Mrs. Brown will go over everything with you…the school schedule, mealtimes, dorm rules, and stuff like that."

We made our way down the stairs, to the first-floor corridor. From where we stood, Dr. Swan did a quick run-through of everything to the right: Mrs. Brown's office, the library, the gymnasium through the double doors at the end, and all the classrooms around the corner.

We went left.

"And here we have the security office," Dr. Swan said, gesturing toward the first room to the left of the front entrance. It had a window beside the door, looking out into the corridor. "If you don't see the officer roaming the halls, then he's probably in here watching the monitors." I swallowed hard, remembering the man from earlier. The idea of security officers hovering over us was a little unsettling.

I peeked through the window. The room was small, barely big enough for the desk and chair. Three monitors sat in a semi-circle on the desk. Each screen was broken into a grid, showing six camera views.

Dr. Swan's voice pulled me back. "And continuing on this side, we've got my office. Then Mrs. Trumble's, which doubles as the nurse's office. She may have told you already, she's not only the House Mother, but also our school nurse. She and her husband live on the grounds—Mr. Trumble is our maintenance and groundskeeper."

At the end of the corridor were a pair of double doors, identical to the ones at the opposite end. The bottom halves were made of dark stained wood, and the top halves were frosted glass. Only these doors had a large metal panel with a keypad below the handle.

"Where do those doors go?" I asked.

"To the boys' dorms," Dr. Swan answered. "Which is off-limits—you need a pin to get in and out. And everything is monitored through security, so we know every time someone passes through those doors."

With raised brow, I gave a nod, and we kept moving, following the corridor to the left.

Straight ahead was another set of double doors,

leading to the dining hall. We entered a door just before it, on the right, marked cafeteria. We went through the line, filling our dinner trays, then exited to the dining hall. The room was large; it had tall ceilings, crystal chandeliers, and fancy drapes that were tied back with thick, gold cords. Although dated, it was formal and vastly different from the lunchroom in my old school. The tables were the biggest improvement. Instead of the long, skinny, white tables with molded plastic chairs, the tables here were round with tablecloths and eight wooden chairs.

There were just seven of us in the dining hall. Thankfully, there wasn't an orange jumpsuit in sight.

Dr. Swan and I sat at a table near the door. The others sat together at a table in the back corner. There were three girls and two boys. The girl with the dark-rimmed glasses was amongst them.

"Is it always so empty?" I asked as I pushed the food around my plate.

"Weekends are usually like this. Sometimes the students go on field trips or go home to their family, or they just come to dinner later. It's pretty relaxed." Dr. Swan took a bite. She swallowed and added, "I think they had a trip planned for today—sometimes they'll go to the mall, or the movies, or even some other fun places."

My brow pinched. "Really?" I was surprised we were allowed such luxuries.

Dr. Swan smiled. "I think you'll find that it isn't so bad here. Most even like it. It'll just take some time to adjust, that's all."

If everyone is as nice as Dr. Swan, then maybe. But the image of Mrs. Trumble popped into my head, along with her gruff manner. I tried to keep my thoughts from showing in my expression.

We ate in silence for a few minutes, then she asked, "What do you think of your dinner? Pretty good, right?"

"Mhm," I answered with a mouth full of mashed potatoes.

"I have yet to hear a complaint about the food here," she said with a smile.

After dinner, Dr. Swan and I left the dining hall. She stopped near the grand staircase, and I felt it coming—the goodbye—and for some reason, it bothered me.

"So, what do you think so far? Do you have any questions before I take off for the night?"

I felt weary, and my lips pursed.

She put her hand on my shoulder. "I'll be around tomorrow. I'm coming in to do some paperwork. Feel free to stop by and see me," she said, giving my shoulder a pat. "And why don't we plan on meeting after classes on Tuesdays?"

"Okay." I nodded.

"Okay. I'll see you tomorrow, then. Good night, Ronnie."

And with that, she was gone. It felt strange parting ways with her. I suddenly felt so alone, wandering the desolate halls back toward my room.

****

The light from my small bedside lamp didn't reach much farther than the nightstand it sat on. But I preferred it to the harsh brightness and the institutional feel of the overhead lights.

I crashed on my bed and popped in my earbuds. I

was in for an exciting Saturday night. Not. Rolling to my side, I noticed the purple journal on my nightstand. I picked it up and unwound the attached elastic band that held the cover neatly closed. Tucked inside was a purple pen.

Maybe I could give the journaling thing a try. But I wouldn't even know what to write.

A couple of songs played on my iPod while my thoughts went back to Dr. Swan. I pictured her from earlier, holding up my shirt. *"I bet it looks so pretty with your dark hair."* I felt a connection with her, on a level I hadn't felt with anyone since my mother…

When the next song came on, I closed the pen in the book and turned up the volume. "Stars" by Grace Potter was one of my mom's favorite songs. If only she knew how important it would come to be for me.

My eyes fell shut as I hummed along.

I wanted to believe there really was a heaven and it was up there amongst the stars, just like the song said.

I felt a rumbling in my chest. It hurt to breathe.

Suddenly, the overhead lights came on.

I opened my eyes, squinting against the bright light.

A girl with dark auburn hair and black-lined eyes stood over me, her nose wrinkled and mouth flapping. I pulled the buds from my ears.

She had one hand on her hip and the other was waving a pointy finger. "You better not have touched my stuff!"

"I didn't touch anything," I spat back. I put my buds back in. There was no way I was going to listen to this girl bitch. I tried not to pay attention as she stormed around the room, seemingly checking inventory.

When she left with supplies for the bathroom, I got out of there.

I didn't want to chance running into her again, so I wandered down the stairs to the first floor. There were several groupings of leather armchairs—like the ones at my local coffee shop—lining the edges of the wide corridor. I thought about taking a seat in one of them. But as there were a few people coming and going, I opted for more privacy and ducked into the library.

A lamp at the main desk was on; between that and the little bit of light that streamed in from the corridor through the long, narrow, transom windows near the ceiling, it was fine. I wasn't there to read.

I passed by the tables and chairs in the front and made my way to the farthest corner. It seemed like the best place to lie low.

Easing myself to the floor, I popped my earbuds back in and rested my head against the wall behind me.

As my current playlist neared the end of its second run, my iPod chirped. The screen lit up with the message: *battery 10%.* It was only 10:34. I still had twenty-six minutes, and I planned to savor my peace and quiet for every second of those twenty-six minutes.

I turned off my music to save the last of my battery and pulled the buds from my ears. Then, hugging my knees, I put my head down. I was so tired; the stress and lack of sleep was catching up with me.

I believe I had started to drift off when…

"There you are!" Startled, I looked up to find the girl with the dark-rimmed glasses.

Brow wrinkled, I looked up at her with confusion.

"Come on." She waved her arm, gesturing to follow. "Kerry is looking for you."

"Why? What's wrong?"

"Oh, thank God, you found her," the voice greeted us as we stepped into the corridor.

I shook my head, confused by all the commotion.

"I'm sorry. I'm Kerry, your dorm leader," they said, expression softening. "We didn't mean to scare you—it's just that, curfew is at eleven, and we weren't sure…"

I glanced at my iPod: 10:55.

Kerry responded to my check of the time. "Like I was saying, we were just concerned—"

"We?" I didn't mean to interrupt, but I was, what's the word…befuddled.

"Oh, well, I stopped by your room to check in on you, and when you weren't there, I asked your roommate Amanda if she had seen you, and she told me you had disappeared and that she hadn't seen you for over an hour, so…" Kerry finally paused to take a breath. Then laughed. "I thought we had a runner. I guess we were worried for nothing."

Yeah. I'm sure *Amanda* was really worried.

We made our way out of the library, and I noticed a different security guard standing in front of the main entrance as if on high alert.

Then Mrs. Trumble's gruff voice caught my attention. "I hope this isn't going to be a recurring problem with you—disappearing like this," she said as she descended the staircase.

"I wasn't—"

"We'll talk about this tomorrow. Off to bed now, all of you," Mrs. Trumble said, turning toward a group of girls peering down from the midway landing. A pretty blonde girl rolled her eyes. My roommate stood beside her, and the smirk on her face confirmed my suspicion—the bitch was trying to start trouble.

The girls seemed disappointed by the lack of excitement as they begrudgingly went back up the stairs to their dorms.

Meanwhile, the girl with the dark-rimmed glasses stayed by my side.

"Don't let Mrs. Trumble scare you," she whispered. "She always sounds angry. That's just the way she is. I swear she can make 'have a good day' sound like a threat."

Keeping my eyes forward, I quietly snorted.

Whoever this girl was, she seemed nice. Even though I'd snapped at her, broken down in front of her, and ultimately sent her traipsing all over the school looking for me…still, here she was. Offering a friendly face and kind words.

I kind of wanted to talk to her. To say *something*, but I couldn't bring myself to speak. I just wanted this day to be over.

"Good night," she said at the top of the stairs as we parted ways.

Chapter 4

When I opened my eyes the next morning, it took me a moment to remember where I was. *Damn, I was hoping that was a bad dream.*

The first thing I did was look over to see if Amanda was still sleeping. Her bed was empty. She was already gone.

The clock on my nightstand said it was 8:47.

I threw the covers off and sat up, my bare feet hitting the cold tile floor. Another harsh reminder of where I was. Tomorrow, I'd be better prepared and have my slides next to my bed.

As I sat on the edge of the mattress, I let my eyes roam the room. My lip curled. I couldn't find a single redeeming quality. But by far the worst was the color on the walls. It reminded me of split pea soup—but not like straight from the can, more like the soup had been consumed, partially digested, and thrown up.

I moved to the window and pulled back the heavy curtains. The sun poured in and made the room a little less dreary, but unfortunately, the green walls were even uglier in the morning light. Maybe that was why no one else opened their curtains.

My stomach rumbled, and I sighed. It was time to face the public.

After changing out of my sunbathing penguin shorts and pink tank, into gray gym shorts and a graphic tee, I left my room and headed for the bathroom first.

Aside from the clanging of the water pipes, this place was unbearably quiet.

A few minutes later, as I made my way down the stairs to the cafeteria, the sound of conversation and laughter began to ease my nerves slightly. Although I knew it meant soon I would have to interact with people.

Going through the line was easy enough. Everyone was focused on getting their food. But as I entered the dining hall…that was a different story.

There were more people this morning, compared to last night's dinner crowd. And as I stood in the doorway, holding my tray, I felt every one of them staring. Checking out the new girl.

My hands started to sweat. I made a beeline for an empty table.

Within seconds, normal activity resumed. Thank God for short attention spans.

I scooped a bit of egg onto my toast and took a bite. It tasted so good. I hadn't had anything other than cereal for breakfast in probably six months. As I scooped my next bite, the girl with the dark-rimmed glasses stepped up beside me, a breakfast tray in her hands.

Why does it seem like this girl is always around?

She smiled down at me and shoved her glasses high on the bridge of her nose.

"Good morning, Veronica." She had a wide-eyed meekness about her that was rather endearing.

It was too early in the day for endearing.

"Morning." I looked back down at my plate, to the egg-covered toast I'd just prepared. "Call me Ronnie," I added as I took another bite.

"Okay. Mind if I sit, Ronnie?"

Even though I wasn't ready for conversation, it was hard to say no to her. With my mouth full, I waved a hand toward the empty chair.

You'd have thought she just won a holiday ham by the look on her face. She plopped her tray down and slid into the chair next to me. "I'm Evelyn Gardner, but everyone calls me Eve."

I passed her a tight-lipped smile and swallowed.

"So, don't worry about last night," she said as she pulled her bowl of oatmeal front and center.

"Ugh," I grumbled quietly, rolling my eyes.

I took another bite of my breakfast and watched as Eve meticulously rearranged her tray. A plate of toast went to the top left corner and a glass of orange juice to the top right. Knife and spoon, in that order, and perfectly parallel to one another, went to the right of her bowl.

"It takes a while to get used to Mrs. Trumble's icy personality." She spread her napkin across her lap.

Her oatmeal is going to be cold by the time she gets to it.

I crammed another bite of toast and eggs into my mouth, chewed, and swallowed hard. "Mrs. Trumble isn't the one I'm worried about. I just wish those girls weren't there to see." I'd noticed earlier that two of them were sitting nearby.

Eve followed my gaze. "Oh, don't worry about them. They're cool. That's Sam and Cheyenne." Eve scooped a spoonful of oatmeal. She lifted the spoon toward her mouth, but paused to add, "Cheyenne is the one on the left. She's new too—only been here a couple of weeks. They're roommates," she added, finally taking her first bite.

I glanced back at the girls, memorizing their names. Sam had pale blonde hair and coloring, although her messy bun was dyed bright pink. And Cheyenne had dark, flawless skin and a head full of long, twisted braids.

Then a voice I recognized rose above the din.

"Don't call me Mandy, bitch!"

And there she was, my monster of a roommate.

I moaned and shook my head. "Is she always like that?"

"Not *always*," Eve answered with a timid shrug. I enjoyed her candor. "Amanda has spent half her life in and out of foster homes. You could say she's a bit bitter."

"Who's that with her?" I asked of the girl with long, golden hair, who walked with perfect posture. She might've been a dancer or an athlete. Or maybe she just had a stick up her ass.

"That's Greer. She's my roommate," Eve answered.

The girls crossed to the table where Sam and Cheyenne sat. Greer put down her breakfast tray and pulled out her chair. Then her gaze happened to fall on me. Indignation registered on her face when she spotted Eve at my table.

"Eve!" Greer barked with arched brows and a stern tone.

With her back to Greer, Eve's mouth curled to one side. She gave a sigh and stood, picking up her breakfast tray. "I've gotta go. I'll talk to you later," she said with a smile, turning and scurrying over to join her friends at their table. It was clear that Greer was in charge of their little group.

Last night I was worried I wasn't capable of making friends anymore. But with Eve, it seemed like it might be easy. And maybe a friendship with someone like her was just what I needed right now—at least this place might feel a little less lonely.

I hadn't realized I was staring until Kerry stepped into view, averting my attention.

"Good morning." Kerry took the seat Eve had just vacated and placed some papers on the table. "I just wanted to touch base with you and give you a copy of the list of some of the stuff we have going on. There isn't much going on today, but you're welcome to hang out with me. I'll either be in my dorm or the common room."

"Okay." I was grateful Kerry wasn't here to talk about last night.

"Great." Someone entering the dining hall caught Kerry's attention. They perked up and waved. As the girl, about Kerry's age, approached, Kerry made the introduction. "This is Brandi. She's the other dorm leader." Then Kerry gestured toward me and added, "Brandi, this is Ronnie. She got in last night."

Brandi smiled. "Hi, nice to meet you, Ronnie."

"You too," I answered out of habit.

"I'm going to grab a cup of coffee." Kerry stood.

"That's where I was headed," Brandi chided and turned to me. "Do you want anything?"

I forced a smile and shook my head. They seemed nice, reminded me of the camp counselors at Lake Hiawatha.

A few minutes later, I got up and returned my tray

to the kitchen window. As I turned to leave, I spotted Kerry headed my way.

"Wait up. I'll walk out with you." Kerry took a couple of quick steps to catch up, then slowed to take a sip from a paper cup with a lid. "Mmm, that's the stuff." I wasn't much of a coffee drinker, but darn, it smelled good.

We headed down the hall and turned to the main corridor toward the grand staircase.

"So, I was thinking you could do your name for your dorm room door," Kerry said. "I've got colored pencils, markers, and paint…you're free to use whatever I've got."

"Okay, thanks."

We passed Dr. Swan's office. Her door was open. I could see her sitting at her desk. I didn't think she saw me.

"Ronnie? Is that you?"

I stopped in my tracks and flashed a glance at Kerry.

"Go ahead. I'll be upstairs. Come find me when you're done."

I turned back and stepped into the doorway. "Did you want to see me?"

"Yes, do you have a minute?"

"Sure." Unfortunately, I had nothing but time.

Dr. Swan rose from her desk and met me by the door. She flashed a hopeful smile. "Kerry told me what happened last night."

My shoulders fell. *News travels fast around here.* "I didn't—"

"It's okay," she said, touching my arm. "Kerry said it was just a misunderstanding and that Mrs. Trumble went a little hard on you." I nodded, and she said, "So I wanted to let you know that I'll talk to her and try to smooth things over."

For a moment, I wasn't sure what to say. It had been a very long time since someone—especially an adult—had given me the benefit of the doubt.

"Thank you." I felt like a weight was beginning to lift.

"No problem. You'll get used to how things work around here in no time." She gave a nonchalant wave and crossed the room. Stopping at the water cooler, she grabbed a mug from the top and placed it under the spigot. "Classes start at eight o'clock in the morning, but you'll go to Mrs. Brown's office first. She'll give you your schedule," she said, looking over her shoulder as the water filled her cup.

"Okay."

Dr. Swan moved to the front of her desk. Resting against its edge, she took a sip from her mug, then added, "And don't forget, I'd like you to come see me after classes on Tuesday."

"Okay."

She put the mug on the desk beside her as she took a deep breath. "So…how did it go with Amanda?"

There was something about the way she asked, maybe it was in her voice or the slight hesitation, but I got the idea Dr. Swan wasn't expecting Amanda to be all that welcoming.

"Not great," I answered, trying to keep the acidic words I had in mind to myself. *Hey, look at that. I'd call that personal growth.*

Dr. Swan sighed. "I think she was getting a little too used to having her own room for the last month.

She wasn't all that happy to hear she was getting a roommate, so I bet when she came back last night and found her new roommate was two days early"—she cocked her head and shrugged—"well…I bet that didn't go over well."

It sounded like a good excuse, but I think Amanda's issues went a lot deeper.

Chapter 5

Nerves had my stomach feeling off Monday morning, being my first day of classes at Evergreen. And of course, having to meet with Mrs. Brown, the Head Mistress, only added to my stress. Unlike Dr. Swan, Mrs. Brown was extremely intimidating, and her office reflected that in every way. Hard wooden chairs replaced overstuffed furniture.

Maybe in her late fifties, Mrs. Brown seemed the rigid type. This, I assumed after my first meeting, being that she was called in on a late Saturday afternoon and arrived in a skirt suit and heels, not a hair out of place.

Sitting in front of her now, I could say that I assumed correctly.

Again, she wore a skirt with matching suit jacket and sensible closed-toes heels. Her brown chin-length hair parted a little to the side was thick and smooth, and rolled under at the bottom. She wasn't one for makeup, didn't try to hide her crow's feet. She didn't have smile lines, to speak of, but she did have a deep crease that split her brow, giving her a constant scowl.

She wore glasses with tortoise shell frames. She'd tuck her chin and look over them when she addressed me.

"Normally, we would go through everything when you first arrive, but your situation was a little unique," she began gruffly, the moment I sat down. "Dr. Swan tells me you've been given a tour of the living areas and apprised of some of the basics."

After an awkward pause, I realized that was a question. "Yes," I answered, with a wide-eyed nod.

"Evergreen is a unique school." Mrs. Brown sat back in her chair and rested her laced fingers across her abdomen. "We are not an elite private boarding school, and we are not a juvenile detention center. We're right in the middle. We provide a safe environment and an excellent education in an alternative setting—this is where you're given second chances. And since we're not run by the state, we don't have to give you a third. We can be selective. So, if you follow the rules, we won't have a problem."

I put my hand on my knee to try to stop it from bouncing.

She slid some papers across the desk and had me follow along as she went over the rules.

- Drugs and alcohol are strictly prohibited on school grounds.

- Bullying and violence will not be tolerated.

- Please refrain from use of obscenities (verbal or otherwise).

- If staff deems your attire as inappropriate, you will be required to change.

- Boys are not allowed in the girls' dorms. Girls are not allowed in the boys' dorms.

- Security cameras are in use, in the buildings and around the grounds. Assume you are always being watched.

- All social media sites have been blocked from the school computers. You are allowed to use the internet, but know that everything is being monitored.

- All landlines require a security code to make an outgoing call.

- No cell phones, laptops, or tablets (anything with access to the internet) are allowed. Music and reading-only devices are fine.

"Now…your father has assured me that you are not in possession of these items. Is that correct?" I nodded, and she continued. "Upon arrival, every student undergoes a one-month probationary period. If you complete probation without any incidents or violations, you earn privileges. Such as use of the landline, field trips, and what have you. Any questions so far?"

"No."

Before we moved on to the next page in her packet, Mrs. Brown had me sign a paper saying that I'd read and understood all the rules.

"Moving on…there is always a security officer somewhere on the property. Monday through Friday, it's Joe. You'll see him wandering the halls and monitoring activity between classes and during lunch. We have a few different officers that cover nights and weekends."

Next, she went over the meal schedules, curfews, and the rules about leaving the building.

"After a recent incident, all students are required to check in and out with security before leaving the building," she said. "We sit on one-hundred and seventy-five beautiful acres along the Otowae Gorge, and we'd like you to be able to enjoy the outdoors and some of our trails. We currently have eighty-six students to account for, so we need to make sure everyone is safe."

Then we went over job duties and activity options,

along with their schedules and where to sign up. Each week we were required to take at least one fun activity and to help out around the school.

"You don't have to choose right this minute," Mrs. Brown said. "But don't wait too late in the week, or I'll decide for you. If you find something you like, you can stick with it each week or try something else.

"Now, for your schedule." She handed me another page. This one had my name at the top. "Here, at Evergreen, we only take grades ten through twelve and our classrooms are multi-level…meaning our classes aren't necessarily divided by grade, only by subject. Language Arts is a good example, you'll have students of all ages in one class, but each student might be working at a different level and at a different pace. We believe this type of curriculum greatly benefits the students, as everyone has a different way of learning. And we try to cater to that."

Giving my schedule the once-over, the first thing I noticed was that there were only six periods. *Can this be right?* My old school had nine. But then I noticed the times. It didn't mean that the day was shorter, just that the classes were much longer and there weren't any study halls or extra periods for labs and such.

"Any questions?" she asked after a minute.

"I don't think so."

And with that, Mrs. Brown sent me on my way.

Classes had already started twenty minutes ago, so the halls were empty as I made my way to my first class. I hated the idea of walking in late. Not because I was all about being prompt, but because there was absolutely no way "The New Girl" could slip into class unnoticed.

I stopped in front of room 105, Algebra with Mr. Santori, and took a deep breath to prepare myself.

As expected, every head turned the moment I opened the door.

“Take a seat anywhere,” I heard the teacher say.

I quickly spotted an empty seat and made my way to it, while somewhere between fifteen to twenty kids stared.

Mr. Santori called their attention back to him as I slid in behind a desk and made myself as small as possible.

“All right, class, it’s not polite to stare. There’ll be plenty of time to meet our new student later,” he said. He tapped a marker against the whiteboard, pointing to a problem they were working on. “Eyes up here. Let’s get back to our discussion.”

Once he had their focus again, I relaxed in my chair and tried to follow along. He had his back to us as he wrote out what he was saying on the board.

Then he turned to the class. “So what would *y* be in this equation?”

The answer fell out of my head the moment my eyes landed on Mr. Santori. I hadn’t really gotten a look at him before now. But he had to be one of the hottest teachers I’d ever seen. He was the epitome of tall, dark, and handsome.

Realizing I was the one staring now, I peeled my eyes away and dug through my bag for a pen and a piece of paper.

About an hour later, the bell rang, and the class began to empty. Mr. Santori met my gaze and waved me to the front.

“Ronnie, is it?”

"Yes."

"I wanted to take a moment to introduce myself. I'm Anthony Santori," he said, flashing a bright white smile. He was even prettier when he smiled.

"Hi."

"Maybe we could chat before class starts tomorrow and go over some material—make sure you're comfortable with where we're at. Sound good?"

"Yeah, sure."

"Grab a spiral notebook. You'll need it for my class." He pointed to a shelf in the corner behind his desk. "I check notebooks periodically to make sure everyone is doing the work. Generally, I hand out a worksheet for quizzes and tests that you would be graded on. But, uh…other than that, just let me know if you have any questions or need any extra help on anything. Okay?"

"Okay, thanks." Mr. Santori seemed nice. But also, kind of tough, like he was all business and didn't put up with anyone's crap.

I grabbed a notebook on the way out the door.

I had Language Arts second period. The teacher, Mrs. Oliviera, explained her syllabus for the current semester and gave me the option of deciding where to begin. Which was pretty cool. And the best part, we could choose our own reading material. We were required to read, at least, three books, and write a detailed review. We could choose anything from her shelves. But if we had a different book in mind, we could bring it to her for approval first.

I could tell this class was going to be a breeze. I actually liked to read. It was Mr. Little who was ruining it for me—insisting we read aloud and together in class.

Biology was next. The room had two rows of tables. Each table sat two students. There was one science teacher, Mr. Erickson, for all grades. So, the room had everything from frogs in formaldehyde-filled jars, to rocks and minerals, and projects displaying the laws of physics.

Mr. Erickson looked up from a textbook. “Hi, you must be Ronnie?”

“Yes,” I answered, stopping near his desk.

“Welcome. Go ahead and sit anywhere.”

There were only two other kids in the room, sitting at a front table. I went to the back, taking the seat nearest the window. Two textbooks sat in the middle of the table. I pulled one toward me and flipped through the pages, looking at the pictures. Some of it looked familiar. I wondered what section they were on.

A boy slid into the seat next to me, catching me off guard.

“Hey, I’m Will. I saw you this morning at breakfast. You must be new?”

His breath reeked of coffee, and he seemed to have more energy than I was prepared to handle. “Uh, yeah. Ronnie. Got here Saturday,” I answered, closing the textbook in front of me.

He smacked the table. “Man, I miss everything.” Then he smiled. “Well, at least the good stuff.”

I tried not to smile at the obvious pickup line. But this guy was kinda cute. I couldn’t help it. Although, I feared my attempt at not smiling might have resulted in some twisted demonic mess of an expression. Ugh.

“My brother and I went home for the weekend. It was my dad’s birthday.”

“That’s nice,” I said, keeping my eyes forward. I

could feel his stare. My mouth twitched; it was like I forgot what to do with it. I didn't want to smile. But I didn't want to look angry or sad either. So, I pressed my lips together in an attempt to make my mouth disappear.

"You always this polite?" He laughed. Then he sat up straight and folded his hands on the table, like I had mine, and with a goofy smile, he said, "That's nice."

I gaped at him. "Are you mocking me?"

He smiled big, and I noticed he had nice teeth to go along with his nice face. And for the second time in under a minute, I started to smile. This time I let it happen.

"There it is! I knew I could get you to smile." I felt myself blush. He leaned in close and looked up at me from under his long, dark lashes. "So, what're you in for? I'm unruly."

"Oh, you are, huh?"

"Yep! Can you imagine that?" He eyed me quizzically and ran his hand through the brown spiky hair on top of his head.

I laughed. "Well, I'm a bit unruly myself."

"All right, class, let's get started," Mr. Erickson said, grabbing our attention. I looked around the room and noticed that all the tables had filled up. "Open your books to page two-twenty-one. Genetics and Heredity."

As I opened the textbook, Will leaned in close.

"What activities and job duties have you signed up for?" he whispered.

"I haven't picked yet."

"You should sign up for yard work. It's better than getting stuck inside doing bathrooms or something…plus, it's what I do." He waggled his dark, bushy eyebrows.

"Oh my God. You're ridiculous," I whispered.

"Thanks," he said, grinning from ear to ear.

A laugh squeaked out, and Mr. Erickson shot me a look.

"Sorry." Then under my breath, I added, "And I didn't say ridiculous was a good thing."

"Trust me, it's a good thing."

I wanted to laugh. But I didn't. "You're gonna get us in trouble."

"I can't help it. I'm unruly. Remember?"

I pressed my lips together to hide yet another smile. Maybe Will was right. Maybe ridiculous was a good thing, because it had been a very long time since anyone had made me feel like this. Whatever *this* was?

I was starving by the end of the period, and grateful that it was time for lunch. As I was getting up to leave, I spotted Eve at the front of the class. Our eyes met. Hers widened.

"Ronnie! I didn't know you were in this class." She smiled.

"Yeah." I smiled back. "I have lunch next. How about you?"

"Yep, everyone has fourth period lunch."

"Oh, well, that's cool." I glanced at Will as he walked by. *Cool, indeed.*

Will's gaze met mine. "See ya later, Ronnie."

"Bye," I answered and looked back to Eve, trying not to blush again.

Eve watched him disappear around the corner. Then she turned back to me, her expression a little more serious. "FYI, Greer likes Will, so I wouldn't go near him if I were you."

"Oh. Yeah. I'm not interested in him *that* way"—I shrugged like it was nothing—"he was just being nice." Suddenly, I wasn't hungry anymore. I was sick to my stomach and stuck with this fucking ridiculous smile on my face. "So, what do you have fifth period?"

"Art, today. How about you?"

I feigned joy. "Same."

And with that I turned my eyes forward, letting the conversation wither. I didn't have the strength to pretend anymore. I wanted to disappear.

Eve and I got separated going through the cafeteria line. I had greatly underestimated the chaos of the lunch rush and fell back as kids reached over and around me, grabbing the plates of food as fast as the ladies put them out.

I'd probably been there a good five to seven minutes, when I noticed Greer buzz by. Apparently, her entitled ass "didn't do lines." Or so I heard her say after someone complained.

Curious where she'd slipped in, I peered around the line in front of me and spotted her beside Will. It sucked seeing them together, her touching his arm and leaning into him. He seemed so nice. How could he be with someone like her?

By the time I entered the dining hall, Greer was seated at the table with Eve and the others. I hated that so far, my only friend was so tight knit with them.

I scanned the room for an empty table. None were completely empty, but there was a table in the back corner, near the windows, with only one girl, and she had her nose in a book.

I approached the chair across from her. "Mind if I sit here?"

She looked up briefly, not even meeting my gaze. "Go ahead," she answered and went back to reading.

Perfect. No drama.

I quickly found myself wishing I had a book too, something to occupy my mind. I felt awkward, sitting on one side of the large table, all by myself. Out in the open. Like I was on display. Soup turned out to be a good choice as I could hunch over the bowl and keep my head down.

Lunch period was more than half over when an outburst of laughter caught my attention. A group of boys a couple of tables away seemed to be having a good time. One boy, with his back to me, got up from the table. Opposite him, now in full view, sat Will.

His eyes fell on me, and he smiled.

Shit. I quickly looked away.

I waited a moment, then gazed nonchalantly in Greer's direction, and sure enough, she was watching.

A year ago, I would've been equally mesmerized and intimidated by a girl like her. But a lot had changed since then. I wasn't the timid girl, worried about what others thought of me, anymore. I wasn't afraid to stand up to her kind anymore. And I didn't take anyone's shit anymore.

Although…

I looked around, remembering where I was—and why I was here.

Dr. Swan's voice echoed in my head. *How long you're here depends entirely on you.*

However, Mrs. Brown's words hit even harder. *This is your second chance, and we don't have to give you a third.*

By the end of the day, I was so tired. And I wasn't

quite sure what to do with myself. So, I wandered up to my dorm room, hoping to hide away until dinner.

My nose wrinkled at the sight of my name on the door. While everyone else's looked like they'd put a lot of work injecting personality into theirs, I pretty much did the opposite. You could tell a lot by how someone wrote and decorated their name, and I wasn't ready for these girls to know the real me. Heck, I didn't even know the real me anymore. So, I went as plain as possible, outlining block letters in black marker and painting the inside with a medium blue.

I opened the door and stopped in my tracks. Amanda stood at her dresser, pulling leggings from a drawer. While Sam sat on Amanda's bed and Greer sat on mine.

All eyes turned to me.

Amanda huffed, "Do you mind? I'm trying to change here."

I wasn't sure how to play this. *Do I assert myself and stake claim to my side of the room, or do I let Amanda and her friends continue to mark their territory?*

Amanda huffed again. "In or out?"

I decided I didn't have the energy today. Spotting my charger, I came up with an excuse on the fly.

"Calm down. I'm just here to get my charger." I crossed the room and swiped the white cord off my nightstand. In silence, they watched my every move.

Back at the door, I walked out and pulled it shut. But not all the way. The devious side of me wanted to have a little passive-aggressive fun.

I wasn't more than six feet down the hall when I heard the door slam.

And there it is. I smiled.

Chapter 6

I spotted Greer and Amanda leaving the dining hall as I was arriving for breakfast Tuesday morning. They didn't notice me, and I was glad for that.

Out of the group of five, I could tell Greer and Amanda were the tightest. They also seemed like the most difficult to get along with.

I heard my name called.

"Ronnie!" It was Eve, sitting at a table with Sam and Cheyenne. She waved me over.

Eve patted the seat next to her as I approached. "Sit with us."

Whoa. Didn't expect that. And from the look on her friends' faces, I don't think they did either.

"Uh…" Struggling for an excuse, I glanced toward the table in the back corner near the windows.

"You don't mind, right, guys?" Eve eyed her friends.

Sam flipped her pink hair over her shoulder and rolled her eyes, regarding Eve. "I think she'd rather sit with her nerd friend, Taylor. The Reader," she added, like it was a bad thing.

But Eve, in her ever-present perkiness, smiled and ignored her friend's comment. "Have you guys actually met yet?" None of us were chomping at the bit to respond, but Eve continued anyway, barreling through what I thought was an obvious lack of interest on everyone's part. "Sam, Cheyenne…this is Ronnie." She pointed to each of us as she said our names.

I smiled, awkwardly. I had to at least try. "Hi."

Cheyenne smiled back. Sam attempted—but it seemed more like a sneer as she looked me up and down.

"Sit. Sit." Eve patted the seat again.

"Okay." I caved.

The moment I sat down, Sam reached for her tray and pushed her chair back. "Come on, Chey."

I honestly don't know what was worse: having to sit at the same table with those two, or their obvious diss.

Eve and I shared an awkward look.

"Sorry." She shrugged with a lopsided grin.

Now I felt bad. "It was nice of you to try."

"Well, we definitely have to sit together in Bio today," she said with more enthusiasm. "I'll get there early to save us a table."

"I hope this doesn't come off the wrong way, but you don't really seem like you belong at this school. How did you end up here?"

Eve smiled. "I'll take that as a compliment."

"You don't have to answer if you don't want to."

"No, it's okay," she answered. Eve shook her head and began nonchalantly, "It's stupid, really. My little sister was getting picked on at school, so I threatened the kids. I was just trying to scare them, but the whole thing got blown out of proportion."

"Wow, that really sucks. But I'm glad you're here," I said with a grin.

True to her word, Eve was holding a table for us when I walked into Biology third period.

As I headed her way, my gaze met Will's. He was at a table in the back, and the chair next to him sat empty. He passed me a smile and raised his hand—a friendly greeting, an unspoken invitation.

I gave a tight-lipped smile and took a seat next to Eve.

A few minutes later, I found myself glancing back at him. The last thing I wanted to do was hurt his feelings. But I had to keep reminding myself of two things. One, I didn't plan on being here long. And two, getting into it with Greer would lessen the chances of that happening.

When the bell sounded at the end of class, everyone was quick to jump up, eager to get to lunch. But I took my time, packing up my things.

"Are you coming?" Eve asked. Over her shoulder, I noticed Will lingering near the door.

"No, go on ahead. I have to talk to Mr. Erickson."

"Everything all right?" Mr. Erickson asked after the classroom had cleared.

"Yeah," I answered as I stood and met his gaze. "I just didn't want to get caught up in the rush to the cafeteria."

"Ahh," he said with a slow nod. His mouth quirked on one side. "It's tough being the new kid, isn't it?"

I rolled my eyes and swung my bag over my shoulder. "You have no idea."

"Chin up. It'll get better," he said as I left the room.

He was really nice for trying. But seriously, chin up? Ugh. That was as bad as someone telling you to "smile" for no reason other than your resting-bitch-face was making *them* uncomfortable.

Apparently, I should've given everyone more of a head start, because the hallway was still full of kids. I noticed Will up ahead, just before Greer stepped out of another classroom. In one fell swoop, she was beside him, hooking her arm with his.

My shoulders tensed. I wasn't sure what to do. I wanted to move closer to hear what they were saying, but at the same time I wanted to run away. Why did I feel so threatened?

Greer tugged at his arm and walked on her toes to whisper in his ear. Prickly heat rose up my neck. What did she say to him? Then to my horror, she glanced over her shoulder, straight at me, and smiled smugly, making it quite clear she was staking her claim.

I slowed my pace, attempting to put more space between us.

When I got to the cafeteria, the line was almost out the door. But I didn't mind. I just kept to myself and slowly inched forward with the crowd.

First chance I got, I grabbed a turkey sandwich and a small plate of fries and got out of line. I picked up a bottle of apple juice on the way out of the cafeteria and headed straight toward the table in the back corner, near the windows.

"Hi again," I said as I set my things down and pulled out the chair. The girl glanced up, and I said, "It's Taylor, right?"

"Yeah," she answered skeptically. I don't know if she wasn't sure of her name, or she wasn't sure if she should be talking to me.

"I'm Ronnie." I smiled and pulled a book from my bag. *The Alchemist*. I'd gotten it from Mrs. Oliviera's shelf today.

Taylor noticed the book and grinned. I'd obviously gained her trust.

Later, during gym class, Will tried to summon me from the bleachers to join his "winning" team in a game of kickball. He literally stood in the middle of the gymnasium and called my name.

Ugh. Dude, you're killing me.

I waved him off and glanced around, spotting Amanda on the opposing kickball team. And Eve was trying to get in on a game of basketball on the other side of the gym. With no sign of Greer, Sam, or Cheyenne, I understood it to mean they had gym alternating days. Which was a huge relief. The less of them I had to deal with them at a time, the better.

While I listened to rain pound against the metal roof above, I watched the activity down on the floor.

I felt movement on the bleachers, heard the footsteps coming toward me from the side, and I tensed.

"Hi there," the approaching voice said.

I breathed a sigh of relief when I realized it was Mr. Thomas. I'd had him for World History last period yesterday. "Hi."

"So, as you can tell, I wear a few hats here at the school." He smiled and sat down next to me. "Besides history, I run the gym classes and the after-school sports activities." I nodded with a pressed-lip smile, and he continued, "Now, you don't have to participate in the group activities, but you can't sit on the bleachers all period."

My shoulders slumped. "Okay."

"I've got a bunch of stuff in my equipment room over there," he said, pointing. "You could grab a basketball or a tennis ball and racket. Or if you want to just walk laps around the gym, that's fine too."

"M'kay, I'll find something."

"When the weather's nicer, we won't be stuck inside," he said as he stood. Then, before he took off, down the front of the bleachers, he added, "You might even like to walk some of the trails around the property."

I made my way to the equipment room.

There were metal baskets filled with every kind of ball imaginable, and bats and rackets hung on hooks. I took my time deciding, picking up a couple different types of balls and checking their bounce. Finally, I grabbed a tennis ball and racket and turned toward the door.

Will stood between me and my exit. "Hey, what's up?"

"Not much." My eyes shifted to the open doorway over his shoulder.

He huffed. "Did I do something wrong?"

"What?" My gaze flashed to him. "No. We're cool."

He grabbed a basketball and spun it in his hand. "Then why does it seem like you're avoiding me?"

I shrugged with an ambiguous smirk. "I don't know what to tell ya."

He opened his mouth to speak, but Eve walked in and interrupted.

"Hi, guys."

"Hey, Eve, what's up?" I said.

Will kept his eyes on me, refusing to turn and acknowledge her. He seemed slightly irritated. And when she didn't respond right away, he glanced over his shoulder.

"Did you need something?"

"Oh," she stuttered. "I, uh, just came to get a basketball."

"Here ya go," Will replied, with an obvious tone of dismissal as he chucked her the ball in his hands.

"Thanks," she said, before turning her attention to me. "Come join us."

"Okay. I'll be out in a minute."

Eve took off, and I returned the equipment in my hands. When I met Will's gaze again, his brow was furrowed.

"Is everything all right?" He passed a glance out the door and back, cocking his head. "Because it kind of looks like she's got you on a short leash."

I narrowed my stare. "What's that supposed to mean?"

Expression softening, Will waved his hand. "No, no. I just meant she seems like she's trying to hog all your attention."

"Eve is just trying to make me feel welcomed," I said, brushing past him. "I'll see ya around."

Stepping out onto the gym floor, I slowed. When all I wanted to do was run.

The interaction with Will made my lunch churn in my stomach. He was so nice and cute, and I really thought I could like him. But how could I when I had Greer and her friends watching over me like a hawk? And that made me wonder if Will was onto something. Was Eve really trying to be my friend, or was she trying to keep me close so she could keep an eye on me?

****

After my last class of the day, I went straight to Dr. Swan's office for my first session. Her door was open, but I knocked anyway.

Her desk was at the far end of the room, facing the door. She looked up and waved me in. "Come on in. I was just looking through your file."

I wandered in, slowly. While I felt like we'd connected the other day, I wasn't ready to start talking about what was in my file, or my feelings.

"Sit wherever you'd like," she said as she crossed the room and closed the door behind me. With the folder in hand, she waited patiently while I checked out the pictures and knickknacks on the shelves along the wall to the left. The back of the couch was on my right, situated in the center of the room across from a large, red, cozy-looking chair.

"Okay," I answered, half-listening. An adorable sculpture of an owl with oversized eyes caught my attention. He held a sign that said, "*Who* do you love?" One side of my mouth curled up.

"How are you settling in?"

"Fine, I guess."

"Do you need anything? Or have any questions?"

Finally, I turned to face her, resting my hands on the back of the couch in front of me. "Not really," was all I could muster. I know she was trying, but I couldn't seem to drop my guard today. Hence the couch between us.

"Have you made any friends since you've been here?" There was so much hope in her voice.

"I'm not good at friends."

"Why do you think that is?" she asked as she lowered herself into the red chair.

I glanced down at my finger tracing the seam on the top of the couch cushion. "I don't know."

"I'd like you to think of *me* as a friend—someone you can talk to. And anything we talk about stays private between the two of us. Think of my office as a safe place. Nothing leaves this room."

" 'Kay."

She crossed her legs and sat back in her seat. The folder rested on her lap. "Are you ready to start?"

That was my cue to sit. I circled around to the front of the couch and plunked down, pulling a decorative throw pillow onto my lap. I held on to it, like somehow this flimsy pillow would offer me protection.

"That water is for you." She gestured to a plastic cup sitting on a small coffee table between us. "Tell me about yourself. Do you have any hobbies?"

"I used to take dance classes. Don't anymore." I shrugged. "I don't know, I guess I like to read, sorta. I like music."

"Play any instruments?"

"Clarinet in third grade. Hated it."

Dr. Swan chuckled.

"I tried clarinet in elementary school too. I was *not* good," she joked. "So, what else do you do to keep yourself busy?"

I shrugged again. "I like TV."

Dr. Swan shifted in her seat, uncrossing one leg and switching to her other. "I know you've been having a rough time in school these past few months, but how are things at home?"

"I thought you were looking at my file. I'm sure it's all in there." That might have come out nastier than I intended.

"I don't care what they have to say. I want to hear it from you."

I played with a tassel on the pillow, untangling and smoothing the threads. They were green and silky. The fabric on the pillow was bright and colorful. Big orange flowers, with yellow, red, and green. It was a pretty print. It made me think of summer. Then summer made me think of family and camping, swimming, and trips to the beach. Damn. I could feel it coming. My eyes blinked and widened as I looked away and started playing with my hair. That was the nice part about having long hair. I could hide behind it.

Dr. Swan peeked under the file cover and said, "If I remember correctly, you have a little sister?"

A vision of Tori popped into my head, from the last time I saw her. Blood trickling down her legs, standing in a pool of hot coffee and broken glass. A lump formed in my throat. I swallowed it down and struggled to keep my voice steady.

"Yes, Tori. She's seven." Suddenly, my mouth was achingly dry. I grabbed the cup of water and took a drink.

"What's your relationship like with her?"

"Fine. She can be kind of annoying. But I figure that's normal for a seven-year-old."

Dr. Swan smiled. "Yeah, you're probably right."

"How about your father? What's your relationship like with him?"

"Fine," I mumbled.

"What was that, Ronnie?"

Feeling I had control, I looked Dr. Swan in the eye. "It's fine. I'm not being abused, if that's what you want to know. I love my dad."

"But," she prompted.

"But what?" My brows creased at the center.

"It sounded like there was a 'but' coming."

Maybe there was. I turned the pillow in my lap and worked on the next tassel. I love my dad, but A) He'd be better off without me. B) I'm a huge disappointment. C) I destroyed our family. The answer is D: all the above.

I felt my lips lock shut, though the tiniest groan escaped. My head cocked to the side and met with my stuck-in-the-middle-of-a-shrug shoulder.

Dr. Swan examined my posture. "How about when you were younger? Were you and your father close?"

"Mm-hmm."

Dr. Swan was silent a moment. "But you aren't now?"

I shook my head.

"Did your relationship change before or after the accident?"

"After." I kept my head down, focusing on the tassel.

"I know this may be of little comfort right now, but what you and your family are going through is quite common. Everyone grieves differently, and sometimes this causes conflict between family members as each one of you deal with your own personal loss. The family dynamic has been disturbed, and roles and responsibilities are shifting as you all find your new normal. But I want you to know that we can work through it, and in time, your family can heal."

I wanted to believe her.

After another moment of silence, Dr. Swan leaned forward, resting an elbow on her knee. "Ronnie." Her voice seemed softer than ever. "Tell me about the day of the accident."

I closed my eyes and pulled what seemed like all the room's air in through my nose. And I held it there. I'd been asked this question before—by the police, therapists, a few friends, and even some nosy strangers. But I'd never told my side of the story.

Strangely, the one person I wanted to tell never asked.

"I know this is hard—"

"I don't want to."

"Dealing with a loss is one of the hardest things you'll ever have to do, and you shouldn't have to do it alone. Especially a loss like this." She paused, before adding, "It's not uncommon to have feelings of fear, anger, and even guilt."

My gaze flashed to hers. My body tensed, and my fingers dug into the pillow. "But I *am* guilty. It's all my fault."

"What is?"

"The accident. The reason my mom is dead." I took another sip.

Dr. Swan inhaled deeply, thoughtfully. Then she said, "Ronnie, why do you feel you're responsible for your mother's death?"

"Because I am." Clutching the cup with two hands, I rested my forearms on my knees and hung my head.

My gaze fell to the water, and I found myself entranced by the reflection of light distorting with the subtle movement from my shaking hands.

"No, Ronnie. You're not." Her voice was calm.

But it wouldn't help at this point.

It seemed the more I tried to calm myself, the further from calm I got and the more the water moved.

Ripples turned to swirls.

Around and around.

Faster and faster.

Edging closer to the rim. Rising, like the tension inside me.

It was as if I was connected to that small vortex in my hands, and eventually it would swallow me up or destroy me.

I couldn't breathe.

I sprang off the couch. Darkness clouded my vision. I couldn't catch my breath. I wanted out. Out of this room. Out of my own skin.

The cup slipped from my fingers and plummeted to the floor, splashing water every which way as I took off for the door.

"You don't understand. I'm the reason my mother is dead!" I cried and whipped the door open.

Eve, Greer, and Amanda were in the main corridor. They all stopped and looked at me. Eve flashed me an awkward smile while the other girls looked at me with judgment in their eyes.

I took a step back and closed the door. Stared at the back of it.

I was trapped.

I didn't want to turn around and face Dr. Swan. And I sure as hell didn't want to leave the safety of this room. There were literally sharks waiting for me out there.

My hands shook. My face and ears burned. I spun to face Dr. Swan.

I was surprised to see her sitting calmly in her chair, as if my outburst hadn't fazed her at all.

I wanted to scream. But I didn't. And I'm not sure why.

I sucked in a deep, needed breath.

My eyes fell to the puddle on the floor and back to Dr. Swan.

Still, my hands shook, and my heart raced. "I'm sorry. I didn't mean to…"

"That's all right. It's only water." Her voice was soft and elegant. Why wasn't she angry with my behavior? There was something about Dr. Swan that was really different. I had this feeling, like I didn't want to let her down. I had to make things right.

"I'll clean it up." I scoured the room, in search of paper towels or tissues. Anything. "I didn't mean to make a mess. I promise it won't happen again. Sometimes I just get so overwhelmed, and it's hard to think and hard to breathe, and things just happen. It's like I don't have any control. I don't know what's wrong with me—"

"Ronnie, stop." Dr. Swan appeared in front of me. She put one hand on my shoulder.

I stilled and met her gaze.

"Take a breath."

Holding her stare, I did as she said.

"Now, another. Big breath in through the nose…" I followed as she went through the motions. "And slowly blow it out."

We did it two more times.

"Better?" she asked as I started a third.

At that point, I felt my heart rate slowing. I blew out the last breath and nodded.

I stared into her eyes, mine welling with tears. My chin trembled. "I don't want to feel like this anymore."

"I know." Dr. Swan wrapped me in a gentle hug. "It's okay. Everything is going to be all right."

Chapter 7

I was the first one to Biology on Wednesday. I took a seat at the table in the front—the one Eve and I had sat at the day before.

The tables were quickly filling up when Eve appeared in the doorway. But before she could take another step, Will darted around her and slid into the seat beside me.

Eve glared at him as she approached. "Move it. I was going to sit there."

"You snooze, you lose."

I tried not to smile. I didn't want Eve to be mad at me. But he was so damn cute. And there was no way I could kick him out of the seat.

Eve scanned the room. "Come on, Will. I want to sit with Ronnie, and there's nowhere else for us to sit."

Will propped his elbows on the table, cradled his chin in his hands, and shrugged, looking up at her with a silly grin. "Maybe you'll have better luck tomorrow."

"Ugh. You're such a child." Eve spun away and sat at the table across the aisle.

Will kept his head propped up with one hand and turned his body toward me. He sighed happily. "I thought she'd never leave."

I bit my lower lip, once again fighting a smile.

"Hey, I'm sorry about yesterday. I didn't mean anything by what I said. It's just that..." He sighed.

"You know what, never mind. I'm glad Eve is making you feel welcomed."

I flashed him a curious look. "Thanks, but what were you going to say?"

He shook his head. "Nothing."

"You don't like Eve, do you?"

Grimacing, he shrugged. "It's not that I don't like her. I just don't trust that little group of hers."

"Well, that's a weird thing to say, considering…"

"Considering what?"

"You know what," I said with a sneer. "Never mind."

With perfect timing, Mr. Erickson stepped to the front of the class and demanded everyone's attention. He spent more than half the class reviewing the chapter we'd started yesterday, then he placed a stack of worksheets on both of the front tables.

"Take one and pass them back." Then he addressed the class. "I want these handed in by the end of the period. If you don't finish today, you'll have more time tomorrow."

I grabbed the papers, kept two for us, and handed them to the girl behind me.

She took them and asked, "What if we finish early, Mr. E?"

Mr. Erickson smirked. It seemed like he was familiar with the question. "Then you can leave early for lunch."

"Yes," she hissed happily.

I too was motivated by this incentive. So, I picked up my pencil and quickly got to work.

I was the fourth to hand in my worksheet and leave for lunch.

And what a relief it was to get my food and be seated before the swarm.

The rest of the afternoon was sure to be a breeze since it was an art day and Will took Wood Shop instead.

****

Against my better judgment, I signed up for yard work. It was kind of a no-brainer after I found out that the "girls" avoided the job like the plague. Besides, it didn't mean I had to work directly with Will.

Yard work was scheduled twice a week: Wednesdays and Saturdays. Mr. Trumble was in charge of the group as he was the school's groundskeeper. I wondered if he was as delightful as his wife. I was told to be in front of the maintenance shed at four o'clock.

I let security know where I was headed on my way out the front door and straggled behind three boys headed in the same direction.

Will and two other kids were already at the shed, bringing an assortment of rakes and a wheelbarrow out. An older man, who I assumed was Mr. Trumble, stood nearby.

Another kid came up behind us and joined the group.

"Great, it looks like I've got eight of you today," Mr. Trumble said. "We're going to start in front of the main building, doing a general spring cleanup. I'd like all the leaves and twigs raked into small piles for pickup." He paused, assessing the group. "Okay, let's have…Robert, Drew, Sean, Tommy, Chase, and Damian on rake duty."

They began grabbing rakes and dispersing.

"You got it, Chief," one said.

"Okay, Chief," said another.

Mr. Trumble turned to me. "Ronnie, is it?"

"Yes."

"Welcome aboard. I'm Ed Trumble—but everyone calls me Chief," he added. I'm guessing it had something to do with the fact that he wore a blue baseball cap with a ship and gold letters: *USS NITRO*. "I'm going to have you and Will handle the wheelbarrow." I didn't mean to, but I caught myself throwing a glare Will's way. "You two go around and pick up the piles. Then everything gets dumped into the compost bins behind the maintenance shed. Will can show you what to do."

Chief walked away, and my eyes landed on Will once again, my arms crossing over my chest.

"You set this up, didn't you?"

"Yeah, but only because I wanted to talk to you—"

"Whatever." I spun away, rolling my eyes. I was determined not to get caught up in his charming personality, or the drama that surrounded him. "I call wheelbarrow."

I grabbed the wooden handles and took off ahead of Will, steering toward a kid who already had a good pile started.

Will sighed behind me. "Oh. So that's how it's gonna be?"

"Yep!" I yelled into the wind.

Will caught up as I reached the first pile.

"This isn't a race, ya know?" he said, looking up with a grin as he hunched to scoop the pile of leaves.

As soon as the debris hit the bucket of the wheelbarrow, I took off.

"I just want to know what I did to make you mad at

me," he said.

I got to the next pile, parked the wheelbarrow, and looked back.

Will was wandering my way at a leisurely pace and stopped to look at something on the ground. He bent and examined whatever it was that had captured his interest.

I huffed under my breath, shifting my weight from one leg to the other.

Finally, he picked up his find and straightened.

It was a leaf. A fucking leaf. One of thousands we were tasked with gathering and taking to the compost.

Holding it by the stem, Will raised it up for me to see. Spun it between his fingers and smiled.

I threw my hands on my hips, narrowed my eyes, and cocked my head. "Come on."

Will started toward me again, this time at a slug's pace, humming happily.

Why was he still so good-natured when I was trying so hard to be a bitch?

Now it was a matter of who would break first.

I saw the glint in his eyes and quickly glanced away. He was enjoying this.

When Will got quiet, I turned back. He was sitting in the wheelbarrow with a huge grin on his face. The sunlight revealed flecks of green in his brown eyes. I wanted to like him so much it hurt.

My pursed lips pulled to the side. *I will not break.*

"What are you doing?"

"Trying to get you to talk to me."

"Ugh," I groaned, grabbing the wood handles. "Get out."

"Not until you tell me what you meant when you

said my not trusting Eve's group was"—he held up air quotes—"weird, considering."

"I shouldn't have to explain it to you." I lifted up on the handles and attempted to balance the awkward weight as I began steering toward the next pile.

I didn't get very far.

The front wheel hit a dip in the ground and came to a sudden stop, almost toppling my "load." I thought about letting it happen. But instead, I parked the wheelbarrow and took a step back, shaking out the cramps in my arms.

"Why is it so important that I talk to you?"

"Because it just is," he answered, looking up at me, eager and earnest. "That first time we met, I thought we were really hitting it off, but something changed, and I want to know why."

A moment of silence lingered between us. Then, looking from beneath his lashes, he slowly cracked a smile. "I like you, Ronnie."

"You don't even know me," I shot back.

"I know enough." He shrugged, quirking his mouth to the side.

I bit my lower lip. *Awkward.* Then heaved a sigh. "Look, you seem like a nice guy an' all, but I don't want any trouble, so…"

"What are you talking about?"

"You and Greer."

"Me and Greer?" His face scrunched. "Uhh, I don't think so. Where did you hear that?"

I hesitated, confused.

Mouth gaping, he nodded as if he understood. "Oooh, it all makes sense now. That's why they've been especially weird this week."

"So you're not—"

His brow shot up. "No. There is absolutely nothing going on between me and Greer—and there never will be. I wouldn't go out with her if she were the last girl on earth."

"Really?" I smirked. "Not even if the two of you hooking up was the only way to save humanity—essentially, the world?"

He flashed a devious, lopsided grin. "Let it burn."

My mouth deceived me, curling up into a smile.

And when I caught myself staring into his beautiful brown eyes again, I flicked my gaze away, trying to control my composure. "Well, maybe you should tell her that, because she seems to think otherwise."

"Fine. Maybe I will."

"Fine. Will you get out of the wheelbarrow now?"

"Nah." He fluffed the leaves around himself. "It's comfy in here."

I pressed my lips together and groaned. He was both adorable and infuriating.

I grabbed the handles and flipped the wheelbarrow on its side, dumping Will to the ground. His howl, that began midflight, turned to a full-out belly laugh as he lay amongst the debris.

I joined him in the laughter. Laughing so hard that my side began to cramp. My knees buckled, and I fell to the ground beside him.

Eventually, I had myself under control and let out a long cleansing sigh. "I haven't laughed like that in a long time," I admitted as I lay flat on my back, gazing up at the sky.

"Really?" he asked as he sat up and began pulling leaves from his hair.

I shook my head, affirming with a grunt.

"Well, you have a great laugh. You should do it more often."

Beyond Will, I caught a glimpse of Chief looking our way. "Uh-oh," I warned.

Will glanced over his shoulder and turned back with a wide-eyed smirk. "We better get back to work," he said, getting to his feet. He offered me a hand and pulled me up. Then he stuck his hand in his pocket. "But before we do…I have something for you."

"You do?" I watched with anticipation.

He pulled a leaf from his pocket, the one he'd flaunted earlier.

Yeah, I was confused.

"For you," he said. "Look, it's a perfect heart."

When he placed it in my hand, I finally saw it and realized why it had caught his attention. This perfectly formed leaf still held a tint of red and had somehow survived the winter untouched.

"It's so pretty." I met his gaze and smiled. "Thanks."

He smiled back, a slight pinkness spreading over his cheeks.

"Are we friends now?" he asked, raising his brow.

But I couldn't let him win that easily.

Grinning, I shrugged. "We'll see."

Chapter 8

By Thursday morning, I was feeling more settled. It helped that Amanda spent as little time as possible in our room—literally only sleeping there the last couple of nights. And luckily, the more Amanda avoided me, the less I saw of Greer. Those two were always together.

I was getting comfortable with my classes as well—even beginning to enjoy them.

Aside from gym, none of my classes had more than twenty students; add to that the longer periods, the lessons became less reading and lecture, and more of a discussion. The teachers were great too. Approachable. If you needed something explained further, they sat down with you and talked it out.

I witnessed it happening in first period with Mr. Santori.

It brought back a memory from early in my freshman year.

I told my math teacher I was having a problem understanding functions. She told me she could meet with me during zero period, a week from Monday. I didn't even know there was a zero period. But basically, I had to get a parent to take me to school an hour early. That meant I had to be there by six thirty in the morning. This made no sense to me when I was standing right in front of her asking for help. The best part, she never showed that morning, so I had to reschedule.

When I walked into third-period Bio, Eve was already sitting at a table.

Eyeing me, she patted the seat beside her. "Sit with me." I had to give her credit for being persistent.

I sat down, and Eve happily chatted my ear off before class started. It wasn't a bad thing, but I think she said more words in four minutes than I'd said in four months. I just smiled and tried to keep up. Maybe with some time, her positive energy would rub off on me.

After class, as we walked to lunch together, I finally worked up the courage to ask about what happened on Tuesday. I kept my gaze toward the floor. "Hey, um, when I was coming out of Dr. Swan's office the other day—" I felt her eyes fall on me, and suddenly I had second thoughts. I looked up at her, feeling my nose wrinkle. Warily, I continued. "Did you, um…*hear* anything?"

She eyed me sideways as if she needed more information.

"Like…" I let the word linger on my tongue. "What Dr. Swan and I were talking about?"

Her brow pinched. "No, why?"

"No reason." I released a mental breath.

A smile spread across Eve's face. "I love your earrings."

"Thanks." I absentmindedly touched a finger to one.

I was relieved that Eve didn't question me further. Even though I didn't care for the company she kept, I thought she could end up being a good friend. And maybe the key to me fitting in around here.

Is this what optimism feels like? I smiled to myself.

"If you ever want to borrow my earrings—"

Without warning, something slammed into my shoulder from behind, lurching my body forward. I stumbled a couple of steps but managed to keep myself upright.

"Sorry, didn't see you there," Greer said snidely over her shoulder as she passed on by, Amanda and Sam by her side. They all snickered as they continued toward the cafeteria.

Heat rose up the back of my neck, embarrassment colliding with anger. Everyone was staring. I turned my gaze back to Eve.

She pursed her lips and said nothing.

My stomach knotted. I really wanted to be friends with her, but I had to wonder about her loyalty to Greer's group. They were roommates after all, and they had a history together.

Eve and I proceeded to the cafeteria without a word.

Joe, the security guard, stood near the entrance, his feet spread, and arms folded across his chest. With his biceps bulging beneath his dark blue polo and his head shaved to perfection, he was the epitome of security. And why was it always that they're never in the right place at the right time?

Eve got in line first, and as we moved our trays down the metal rack, I slowed, letting a few kids go ahead, quietly putting space between us.

Today's warm lunch choice was a chicken parm sandwich and french fries. I grabbed the next plate served up, and as I lowered it to my tray, another tray snuck in behind mine.

"Hey, how's it going?" Will asked with a smile as he squeezed his way into the line.

Before I could answer, his attention turned to the woman behind the counter.

"Hi, Kathy, how's my favorite lady?"

"Can't complain," she answered, passing him a plate. "How about you?"

"I'm super." He reached for the plate with one hand, while the other rubbed his belly. "Really hungry today, though."

She gave him a wry smile, pulled the plate back, and piled on a few more fries. "I should've known you were just sweet talkin' me for more food," she said with a chuckle.

Will's smile widened. "Thanks, Kathy. You're the best."

"Mhm." She narrowed her eyes, in mock disapproval. "Try to stay out of trouble, Mr. Tucker."

"Anything for you."

I was so caught up watching him pour on the charm that I hadn't noticed the line move forward. I moved quickly, passing the wrapped sandwiches and stopping at the desserts to grab a dish of chocolate pudding.

"Sorry." Will said, sidling up to me again. "So, what's up? You seem kinda down."

"Obviously, you missed what happened on the way to lunch," I grumbled.

"I guess so. What happened?"

I slid my tray down the line, rolled my eyes, and sighed. "Greer slammed into me and caused a big scene." I still couldn't believe the nerve of her.

"Are you kidding me?" he griped, leveling his stare. "I'm going out there right now to let her have it for—"

I shook my head. "No, it's fine. She just caught me off guard," I said, trying to calm him. "I'll be better prepared next time. I can handle her."

"Are you sure? I mean, I feel kind of responsible for the situation she's put you in."

"I'm sure." I picked up my tray and turned toward the door.

"Hey, wait." Will grabbed his tray and came up beside me again. "Wanna sit at my table today? It's just a bunch of guys, but we have a lot of fun."

While I would enjoy nothing more, I thought maybe that would be asking for trouble. "Thanks, but maybe another day, when Greer isn't already on the warpath," I joked.

"Okay, yeah, anytime," he said with a shrug and headed out to the dining room.

I stayed back a moment, putting space between us so we didn't walk into the dining room together.

The moment I crossed the threshold, I felt I like I was being watched.

I glanced toward Greer's table, and sure enough, her eyes were on me. By the conniving grin on her face, I could tell she was proud of herself for that little play she'd made in the hallway.

My shoulders tensed, and I gripped the tray tighter. I wanted to slap that grin right off her face.

And I knew just how I was going to do it.

Will didn't see me standing over him until the kid next to him gave him a nudge.

He perked up in his chair and smiled. "Oh, hi."

I smiled back. “I changed my mind.”

“Cool,” he replied, jumping up from his seat. “Move over, guys.”

As the boys made room at the table, Will grabbed an empty chair from nearby. He dragged it over and whipped it into place. “Here ya go.”

“Thanks.” I set my tray on the table and sat down.

Will took his seat. “Hey, guys, this is Ronnie.”

There were six sets of friendly, curious eyes on me, including Will’s. I gave an awkward tight-lipped smile and half a wave.

Then Will went around the table with introductions. “That’s Damian, Sean, Drew, Robert, and this is Chase—my roommate,” he said, finishing at his other side. Every one of them smiled or greeted me in some way.

“What do you think of Evergreen so far?” Chase asked.

“Not too bad, I guess.”

Another boy, I think it was Sean, said, “Bet you were expecting worse. Everyone always does.”

“Yeah, I’d definitely heard some horror stories,” I answered and stuffed a french fry in my mouth.

I couldn’t believe how nice they all were. It was exactly why I always got along better with boys; they didn’t tend to get caught up in the drama.

The guys went back to their conversation, and Will turned to me.

“So, where did you go to school before?” he asked.

“Crestview.”

“Oh, do you know Chloe Vandermark?”

“Yeah.” I tried not to look jealous. Of course, I knew Chloe. She’s only the prettiest, most popular girl at Crestview.

"She's my cousin."

"Oh." I exhaled with relief and smiled. *I see their family comes from a good gene pool.* "She's a senior, so I don't know her well, but she seems super nice." I took another bite of a french fry. "What school did you go to?"

"West Corners."

I nodded. "Oh, so we're not that far from each other."

"Nope."

"How long have you been at Evergreen?"

"Just a few months," he answered. "I started here in January."

"Didn't you say you have a brother who goes here too?"

"Yeah, Wes," he answered.

"Wes," I repeated. The name didn't sound familiar. "Which one is he?" My gaze wandered the room around us.

Will stretched his neck, looking over and around me. "Table by the wall. Ugly, mean one in the red shirt," he said, going back to his sandwich.

I chuckled at his typical sibling response. I didn't know if Wes was truly mean, but he wasn't ugly.

"I've never seen you two together. Do you ever hang out with him?"

"Not if I can help it." Again, I had to chuckle.

"Is he older than you?"

"Yeah, a year older. We don't really get along. In fact, part of the reason we're here is because of our fighting." He smiled. "Basically, he's a jerk. I'm the nice one."

"I'll have to take your word for it." I smiled back.

"My word means everything," he said intensely and took a bite of his sandwich. As he finished chewing, he added, "If I give you my word, you can trust me to stick to it."

"Okay. Good to know." I stuffed another fry in my mouth. "So, you've mentioned your dad before. What about your mom?"

Facing forward, he brought the sandwich to his mouth, held it there, elbows resting on the table. "Yeah, she died when I was six," he said before taking a bite. Will stared at his sandwich as he chewed.

An awkward silence hung between us. I worried I had opened an old wound. But at the same time, I felt more connected to him. We'd both experienced a great loss. That was something a lot of kids our age didn't understand.

My heart pounded slow and hard in my chest. My throat ached. "My mom died last year." My voice was so low I barely heard the words myself.

But he did.

Will's head turned. His eyes found mine. And for one long moment, we focused on nothing else. That exchange said more than words could ever say.

How strange that, for so long, I'd been afraid to say those very words. Like somehow, saying them would make it real. Like, if I kept denying it, it wouldn't be true, and I'd wake up from this nightmare. But now, for once, I felt like I was going to be okay.

My eyes wandered away from his, accidentally landing on Greer. I'd been so enthralled with my conversation with Will that I'd forgotten about her. But she hadn't forgotten about me.

I felt like the intensity of her glare could start a fire—not that I expected any less. And since my intention was to wipe that smart-ass grin off her face, I'd say mission accomplished.

****

At the end of the school day, I headed to Dr. Swan's office. After Tuesday's session, she decided we should meet twice a week.

Her door was open, so I walked in. "Hi."

Dr. Swan looked up from her laptop. "Oh hi. I guess I lost track of time. Have a seat. I'll be right there."

I made myself comfortable on the couch while Dr. Swan finished typing and closed the lid. Grabbing her mug, she went to the water cooler. "Would you like some water?"

"No, thanks. I'm good."

"You seem a little more relaxed today," she said as she walked around to her red chair. "How are things going?"

"Pretty good, I guess." I leaned toward the arm of the couch and started to pull my feet up, but I caught myself. "Oh sorry."

Dr. Swan smiled. "That's all right. I don't mind as long as you take your shoes off."

Using my toes, I slipped my sneakers off and pulled my legs up, tucking my feet under me.

"So yeah," I began again. "I think I'm getting used to the routine, and I like my teachers."

"That's great. How about dorm life? Is that getting any easier?"

"A little." I shrugged. "I'm just not sure what to do with myself sometimes."

"The common room is a good place to hang out—there's usually someone around, or something going on."

My nose wrinkled. "I don't think I'm ready for that kind of social interaction."

"Okay, well, take your time," she said. "And check out the activities board. You can sign up for as many things as you'd like."

"I'll keep that in mind."

"So, I wanted to talk more about what happened on Tuesday." Dr. Swan shifted in her seat. "What you were describing to me—feeling like you can't breathe, like you're losing control—that sounds a lot like a panic attack. And they can be scary. Especially one as severe as what you described."

I pressed my lips together and nodded.

"I've experienced one or two in my life"—she put her hand to her chest—"and I remember feeling like my heart was racing so fast that it was going to explode…it was horrible."

I suddenly felt so validated. The fact that she understood made tears well in the corners of my eyes.

"Panic attacks like the one you exhibited can be linked to PTSD, and I noticed that when your mother's accident was mentioned, it triggered an attack." She put out a steady hand. "I promise, we don't have to talk about *that* today. But I would like to talk about your relationship with your mother."

It had been a long time since I'd talked about my mom, and I rarely allowed myself to think about her. It hurt too much. I missed her desperately, and it was my own fault she was gone.

"How about you start by telling me a little about

her," Dr. Swan said, her voice soft and soothing. "Did she work?"

I emptied my lungs quietly between my lips and relaxed my shoulders, thinking back to lunch with Will. *I can do this.*

"Yes, she worked part-time from home, doing medical transcriptions."

"Oh, nice." Dr. Swan smiled. Glancing down as she made a note. "Did she like it?"

"Yes," I answered.

"I hear that's pretty flexible. I bet that was a nice perk."

"Yeah," I agreed. "She liked being at home in the morning to see us off to school, and in the afternoon when we got out." Dr. Swan was good at easing into the conversation and getting me to talk. Relaxing a bit, I went on. "She made sure we started every day with a decent breakfast. 'It's the most important meal of the day,' she'd say." Mom's voice echoed in my head at the thought.

Dr. Swan smiled. "Aww, that's really special. Not many kids get that these days. So many moms have to work outside the home."

"She was always there for us," I said with resolve. "If one of us was sick, or if we had a school event or something, she'd be there. Work could wait. Or if one of us needed something, she did her best to make it happen." A memory popped into my head. "You know, one time she went shopping to get herself some winter boots—because hers were so worn they leaked—but instead, she came home with a new backpack for me and an outfit for Tori. She said she could just wear two pairs of socks under her boots." Tears welled in my eyes once again. "Tori and I always came first."

After a moment of silence, Dr. Swan said, "So, it sounds like you were close."

I nodded in agreement and found myself smiling, for the first time, at the thought of my mother.

Chapter 9

By nine o'clock Friday night, I was exhausted from the week, but also feeling pretty good about things. Especially since I hadn't heard a word from Greer or her pals all day. Not a grumble, a gripe, or even a dirty look.

I thought my bold move with Will must've worked.

I grabbed the purple journal Dr. Swan had given me and crawled into bed. Even though I had yet to write a single word in it, it had been useful for something. Opening the book at the center, I stared at the heart-shaped leaf and smiled.

Then I flipped back to the first page and wrote my first entry.

One week down. It's not so bad here.

A strange feeling came over me. It wasn't my initial intention, but I felt like I was writing for my mother. Like, this was the equivalent to when I'd call home from summer camp at Lake Hiawatha to tell her how it was going. Some years there were homesick tears, and others were made in a rush between fun activities. The thought made me smile.

I slid my hand over my written words and whispered, "Good night."

I woke up Saturday morning feeling refreshed and excited to see Will. We had yard-work duty at ten.

I didn't see him at breakfast, but judging by the

way he looked when he showed up for duty, it was obvious he'd just woken up. Not everyone could pull off bedhead like he could.

It was a little disappointing when Chief split us all up to work on different tasks today. I was stuck pulling weeds from along the front steps and adjacent flower beds.

It was almost noon when Chief came around, telling us to finish up what we were working on and return our equipment to the maintenance shed.

I stood and gave my area a quick once-over. With my bucket overflowing, I compressed and secured my spoils the best I could before carrying it to the compost bins behind the shed. Then I took my bucket and hand tool around to the front to return them where they belonged.

As everyone crowded in to return their supplies, Will's voice rose above them all. "Lunch time!"

Which was met with various cries of starvation from the others.

As a group we made our way toward the courtyard at the back of the main building. It was the quickest route to and from the maintenance shed.

Will and I naturally gravitated toward each other.

"So, what did Chief have you doing?" I asked.

"He had me breaking down branches and limbs into firewood. How about you?"

"Pulling weeds." I held out my filthy hands. "I can't wait to wash up."

"Me too, my hands itch," Will said, rubbing his palms on his jeans.

As we passed through the back gate, I was surprised to see that the courtyard had come to life while I was out front today. Tables and chairs now dotted the sides, and a circular firepit in the center had been cleaned up and emptied out. Firewood was stacked neatly off to the side.

We entered the school through a door near the library. I went right to the girls' bathroom to clean up. The boys did the same. Being the only girl in the group, I was done in a flash. But I walked slowly to the cafeteria.

"Hey, wait up!" Will called from behind.

I felt my cheeks warm, my chest quiver. Trying to contain my giddy smile, I stopped and turned.

"You wanna sit with us again?" he asked as he picked up his pace.

"Yeah, sure."

"Cool," he answered as we continued, side by side, to the cafeteria.

Cool. I chomped down on my bottom lip.

Between the handful of kids who went home on Saturdays and the school bus trip to the mall, the dining hall was especially quiet for lunch today. Of Greer's group, only Sam had stayed behind.

Maybe I was just paranoid, but I suspected she was delegated to surveillance duty. At least it felt that way because I kept catching her looking my way.

I did my best to ignore her and enjoy the antics of Will and his friends.

At the moment, I had no idea what they were talking about.

"I definitely prefer this generation," Chase said.

"Whatever." Robert shoved his glasses higher on his nose. "Classic Red and Blue is still my favorite."

"No way," Will argued, throwing his head back.

"You're only saying that to sound cool."

"Look at me." Robert grinned, opening his arms wide. "Do I look like I'm concerned with *sounding* cool?"

They all laughed.

Then Damian tossed Robert a criticizing look. "Dat 3D camera though!"

As Robert shook his head in denial, Chase jumped in again, agreeing with Damian. "Yes! The 3D camera—"

"Well, I don't care what any of you say," Sean interrupted. "Black and White is by far the best gen, hands down."

"No, no, no," Will protested, slapping his hand on the table. "I agree with Chase, this generation."

After a few more minutes, there was finally a break in the conversation.

"What are you guys talking about?" I asked Will.

"Oh, sorry." He smiled. "Pokémon."

My mouth made a big, silent O. A yellow character named Pikachu was the extent of my knowledge on the subject.

"Do you play any video games?"

"You're probably going to think I'm pretty lame." My nose and shoulders scrunched. "I like Mario Kart," I answered with an embarrassed snicker.

"That's not lame! I love Mario Kart." Will laughed, then gulped down the last of his water from the bottle. "So, what are your plans for the afternoon?"

"Painting with Kerry."

"Cool." Will nodded. "We're going to the gym for a little two-on-two basketball." He elbowed the boy next to him and added, "Chase and I are gonna kill it today. Right?"

At that, Chase's face lit up. Like something ignited in him. "Yeah! You guys are going down!" he warned, bringing both arms up in a wide arch and pointing to the ground.

The entire table burst with excitement as they all began dissing each other and throwing out challenges. I couldn't help but laugh. These guys seemed like a lot of fun to be around.

Will finished his sandwich and wiped his mouth with his napkin. He threw it on his tray and leaned back in his chair. "Hey, we're doing a gorge hike tomorrow. You should come," Will said. "My dorm leader, Ashton, is leading it."

"Yeah, that sounds fun," I answered with less enthusiasm than I intended. But I was slightly preoccupied. Sam was staring again.

After lunch, I went upstairs to change. I wanted to get out of my jeans and long-sleeve shirt and into something more comfortable. Yoga pants and a T-shirt would do just fine for an afternoon of painting.

Sam was the only one in the common room when I entered. She was curled up on a comfy armchair, talking on the phone. I don't think she saw me walk in.

From this end of the conversation, all I heard were a bunch of uh-huhs and yeahs.

Then she said, "She sat with him at lunch—" Her mouth clamped shut the moment she saw me, and she leaned toward the phone's base on the side table. "Yeah. I gotta go."

Kerry walked in just as Sam hung up the phone.

"Hey, Ker," Sam chirped, jumping to her feet.

"Hi, girls!" Kerry placed a large plastic tub on the

table across the room. “We have three more coming,” they added with a smile and began unloading paints and brushes from a tub.

Kerry’s enthusiasm brought a new energy to the room. I forced myself to drop it with Sam and joined them all at the table.

Kerry instructed a group painting project—called it team building—but it was like those art studios that were popping up all over the place lately. Kerry showed us all the steps, and we painted a colorful giraffe. Of course, Kerry’s was the best, but what else would you expect from an art major.

I thought mine was actually pretty good.

And we had fun too.

Sam even dropped her usual prickly attitude.

Maybe I was wrong about the phone call. Maybe things were actually turning around for me here?

There was that annoying twinge of optimism again.

****

Eve returned just after dinner and talked me into joining her in the common room. We were hanging out, watching a show on Animal Planet about “big cats” when Sam popped her head in.

“Hey! Greer wants to show you something.”

“Okay,” Eve said as she rose from the couch. “I’ll be right back.”

“No, both of you,” Sam corrected.

“Greer wants *me* to come too?” My voice dripped with skepticism.

“Yeah,” Sam answered very matter-of-factly.

Eve and I looked at each other, curiously.

I had serious reservations, but I followed as Sam led the way.

I hadn't ventured to this wing yet, so I curiously checked out the names and room numbers on each door. We passed Sam and Cheyenne's room on the right: room 218. A little farther down, Sam stopped in front of room 225. Eve and Greer's names hung on the door. She opened the door and waited for us to enter first. The lights were off, but the yellowish glow of candlelight flickered and bounced off the walls. Amanda, Greer, and Cheyenne sat on the floor in the middle of the room, one half of a circle.

Expressionless, Eve asked, "What's going on?"

"Come. Sit down," Greer said in a welcoming voice that had me suspicious.

Sam closed and locked the door behind us. Then she scurried over and sat next to Amanda. That's when I noticed the wooden board lying on the floor in the center. Even in the dim light, from across the room, I knew immediately what it was by the alphabet written in bold letters in an arch.

I'd never seen a Ouija board in person before. Just being in the same room with it made me nervous. I remained planted near the door.

Eve seemed nervous too. There was an edge to her voice I hadn't heard before. "What are you doing, Greer?"

"Chill out. We're just having a little fun," Greer answered.

My first instinct was to leave, but I wondered if taking part in Greer's little game would help her welcome me into her group. So reluctantly, I joined the circle. Not Eve. She folded her arms across her chest and plunked down on her bed, staring at the opposite wall.

"If you're not going to join us, then you should leave," Greer said. And not in a nice way.

"Yeah," Amanda added. "It won't work with your negative energy over there."

Eve huffed and shot a glaring look at Greer before turning to me with sympathetic eyes. Then she came over and sat down between me and Cheyenne. "I'm only staying for you," she whispered.

Everything in me said this was a bad idea. I honestly couldn't say what worried me more, the thought of stirring up ghosts and demons, or being in a locked room with Greer. I swallowed hard and studied the board in front of me.

The alphabet was broken into two lines: A to M on one and N to Z on another; and beneath that were the numbers zero to nine, laid out in a straight line. Above the alphabet was the word "OUIJA" flanked by "Yes" in the left corner and "No" in the right. And along the bottom: "GOOD BYE".

It seemed simple enough. Harmless, actually.

"Okay." Greer smiled big. I could tell she was used to getting her own way. "Everyone put a finger on the planchette." She must've noticed my blank look, because then she said, "This thing," as she pointed to the heart-shaped piece with a little round window.

Six pointer fingers rested gently on the planchette.

"Are there—oh wait," Greer corrected herself. "I think we have to move it clockwise, three times." After the third repetition, the planchette stopped in the center of the board. She started again, this time with a slightly dramatic voice. "Are there any spirits with us?"

We sat quietly for a moment. Eyes peeled to the board.

Nothing happened.

"This is stupid," Eve snapped, pulling her hand back. "Where did you even get this thing?"

"It's my sister's. I've seen her do this a bunch of times." Greer snarled, "If you don't want to do it, then leave."

Eve pressed her lips together until the color faded and her nostrils flared. She placed her finger back on the planchette and Greer immediately continued.

"It's safe here. We just want to talk."

I could've sworn the planchette vibrated.

Then Greer asked the question again, "Are there any spirits with us?"

The room was quiet and still as we waited for something to happen. My mind, however, was busy with speculation and doubt. *Does this stuff really work?* I peeked up through my lashes. Everyone had their head down, staring at the board. My gaze landed on Greer, and I had to wonder if she was up to something.

Greer looked up, and our eyes met for a fraction of a moment before she looked away. My gaze followed. Did she see something?

I took a long, cleansing breath and lowered my head again.

Time moved at a snail's pace. I could hear the ticking of a clock at least one room away.

Cheyenne flinched. I don't know about the rest of them, but I think my heart literally stopped. She flashed a look over her shoulder, and her hand lifted briefly from the planchette. Did she feel something? Hear something?

"Spirits, are you here?" Greer prodded.

Finally, the planchette moved; it stuttered across

the board and stopped on "Yes."

I looked around, at each of the girls. Only Eve seemed to be as freaked out as I was.

"How many spirits are in the room?"

The board answered, landing on the number "1."

"Ooo," Greer hummed in a whisper, looking around the circle. "Are you a male?"

The planchette slid across the board to "No."

"So, you're a female," Greer stated before her next question. "How did you die?"

The planchette slid from side to side in an arch along the top row of letters.

K - I - L - L - E - D

"You were killed?" Greer asked.

"I know you're moving it," Eve accused, rolling her eyes. She pulled her finger away.

"No. I'm not," Greer answered, hastily. Her wide-eyed look didn't really fool me. I just didn't understand where she was going with this.

"Put your finger back. Don't break the connection," Amanda said.

Before Eve could put her finger back, the planchette jumped to "Yes."

Greer started again, in a calm voice. "Do you know who's responsible for your death?"

The planchette circled the board and went back to "Yes."

"Whoa," Amanda whispered.

My narrowed eyes flashed to Greer. I felt like I couldn't breathe.

"Who are you, spirit?" I noticed Greer and Amanda share a knowing look.

The planchette started to answer. It went to the top

right. M. It moved to the bottom left. O. Then slowly it headed back toward the top right. That's when I noticed the other girls glance up to the top of a dresser where two candles sat on either side of a framed picture. The picture from my sock drawer. The picture of me and my mom.

Chapter 10

I sprang from the floor, flipping the board and sending the planchette flying in the process. Shocked and violated, I swiped the picture frame from the dresser and stormed out of the room.

"Ronnie, wait!" I barely heard Eve's voice over the laughter.

I picked up the pace, running down the hall and around the corner.

"Please, Ronnie! Wait!" She was right on my tail.

I stopped near the stairs and spun to face her. "So, you guys did hear me that day, when I was coming out of Dr. Swan's office?" I accused through clenched teeth and furrowed brow.

"Yes, bu—"

I cut her off with an angry growl and walked away.

"Ronnie, I swear to you, I didn't know they were going to use it against you." This time, she didn't follow.

I threw open the door to my room and slammed it behind me. The rush of air blew Amanda's poster off the wall. It landed curled at my feet, and I gave it a swift kick.

Then, with one sweep of my arm, I knocked everything off the top of Amanda's dresser. Beauty products and gadgets fell to the floor, clinking and clanking as they scattered in front of the door.

A moment later I felt the sting.

"Ow!" I cried, raising the hand down at my side. At some point in all the excitement, I must've clutched the picture of my mom so hard that my thumb cracked the glass.

Steadying the frame with the other hand, I carefully released my grip and set it on my bed. Blood gushed from the pad of my thumb. I grabbed a bunch of tissues from the box on my nightstand and pressed them to the wound.

The pain intensified. I flinched, pulling back.

A small shard of glass was embedded in the skin. "Oh shit, oh shit, oh shit."

Feeling sick, I swallowed hard and worked up the courage to pull the glass out.

I went in slow, steady, and precise, and grabbed it with my fingernails. Then pulled quick and hard, breathing a sigh of relief when the glass was out.

As I held the wad of tissues in place to stop the bleeding, my thumb throbbed in pain. But it was nothing compared to the ache in my chest the moment I looked down at the picture frame.

A web of broken glass and blood distorted my mother's smiling face.

It looked just like my nightmare.

The tears came in a rush. I felt like it was happening all over again.

I couldn't breathe.

My knees felt weak.

"I'm sorry," I cried between sobs as I struggled to catch my breath. "I'm so sorry."

Then an intense need came over me, and I sobered.

"It's okay, it's okay," I told myself while grabbing

the trash can from across the room. "I can fix this. I can fix this. It's going to be okay."

I held the frame over the can, opened the back, and peeled the photo out carefully, letting everything else fall away. My hand shook as I inspected it to be sure there was no damage.

There wasn't.

I collapsed on the bed and stared at the picture of me and her. It wasn't a special occasion or anything. We didn't even look particularly great—my hair was falling out of a ponytail, and Mom's was frizzy. But it was real. And it showed how much we looked alike.

I thought back to the day it was taken. I'd just gotten home from school.

"Hi, Mom. I'm home."

"In here!"

I followed her voice to her bedroom. She worked from home and had set up a small desk in the corner. Walking up from behind, I wrapped my arms around her, rested my chin on top of her head, and watched her fingers dance over the keyboard.

After a minute or two, she stopped typing, pulled the earpiece from her ear, and pressed the power button on her monitor.

"How's my sweet Veronica today?" she asked my reflection in her dark computer screen.

We stayed in that position while I told her all about my day. And at one point, she pulled out her phone and snapped a selfie of our position. She compared me to a hooded cloak by the way I was draped over her. We laughed about that for a long time.

I woke with a start, shivering uncontrollably, huddled in a ball at the foot of my bed. I hadn't meant to fall asleep.

The clock on my nightstand said 10:30.

Cold air swirled around the room, chilling me to the bone.

"What the hell?" I whispered to myself, looking up. The ceiling fan was on full blast.

It shouldn't have been on at all.

Did Amanda turn it on? Was the bitch trying to freeze me out now?

A second rush of panic set in when I realized the picture of me and my mom was missing.

I sprang to my feet and checked the bed, flipping up the pillow and shaking out the covers.

Oh my God, did she take it?

Finally, I spotted it on the floor between my bed and nightstand, thank God.

Amanda wasn't off the hook though. I glanced at the whirling fan again.

Stashing the picture under my pillow, I grabbed my bag of toiletries and headed toward the door. Reaching for the switch, I gave pause.

There were two switches, one for the lights and one for the ceiling fan. Both were in the off position.

That's when I noticed something else. The things from the top of her dresser—the things I'd pushed off—were blocking the door. Amanda couldn't have come into the room without disturbing them.

The hair on the back of my neck bristled as I looked back over the room.

I flicked the switch a couple times and eventually the blades began to slow.

Clearing the path with my foot, I opened the door and scooted out.

Eve was at the sink when I walked into the bathroom.

Tensing, I put my stuff on the counter and ducked into a stall. "Why are you over here, in our bathroom?"

"Hiding out," she said. "I went back and let them have it."

Less than a minute later, I walked up to the sink and reached for the faucet. "A lot of good that'll do."

"Yeah." She shrugged awkwardly and harrumphed. "I don't know why I bother sometimes—" Her eyes suddenly grew wide. "What happened? There's blood all over your hand."

I glanced at it and waved it off. "I cut myself. I'm fine." The soap made my thumb sting, but I tried not to show it.

"I think I have a couple of Band-Aids in here." Eve rifled through her toiletry bag while I finished washing up.

I grabbed a small towel from the stack on the shelf and dried my face and hands.

"Here." Producing a bandage, Eve peeled away the outside wrapper and stepped closer.

I held my hand out.

Eve took a closer look and faked an exaggerated gag. Then she quickly covered up the wound.

As she gently and meticulously smoothed the edges, I took a deep breath and asked the big question on my mind.

"Do you believe in that kind of stuff…ghosts, spirits, Ouija boards?"

As if on cue, the bathroom lights buzzed and flickered.

She glanced up at them, then back at me, her

mouth quirking at the corner. “No.”

As for me…I was undecided.

Chapter 11

The whisper of my name woke me.

The room was deathly dark. I reached for my bedside lamp and turned the switch.

But nothing happened.

I spun the switch in my fingers. *Click. Click.* And still nothing.

That's when I realized that even the glow from our alarm clocks was missing.

Had the power gone out?

Remaining still, I listened intently. But after a couple minutes of silence, I told myself it must've been a dream, so I rolled over and tried to go back to sleep.

Then I heard it again.

"Veronica." The muffled voice echoed strangely, as if spoken into a tin can. "Veronica, can you hear me?"

I scooted up in the bed until my back pressed against the wooden headboard.

"Who's there?" My eyes darted around, straining to see if someone was in the room with me. But it was like trying to watch TV with your eyes closed.

"It's me, Veronica."

Barely above a whisper, my voice squeaked, "Mom?"

After several breathless heartbeats, she spoke again. "I'm here."

"Mom, is that you?" I cried. My pulse raced, and I tried the lamp again. I had to see her. Why wouldn't the light come on? "Is that really you—"

A breathy moan cut me off, filling the room and sending a chill down my spine.

"I'm sorry." My breath hitched in my chest as I forced the words from my lips. "I'm so, so sorry. I wish I could go back and change—"

"You were my everything," she said, cutting me off again.

Then, with a click, the door to my room unlatched. Slowly, it opened a few inches. A sliver of light seeped in from the hallway. Still, I saw no one.

I was afraid to move. Afraid to speak.

"But YOU'RE the reason I'm dead." Her words were like a punch to the gut, knocking the air out of me. "YOU did this to me. You!"

The door slammed shut.

"No, no, no," I cried, sliding lower in my bed, yanking the covers up, and pressing them to my ears to drown out the sound.

"This isn't real. This isn't real." I repeated the mantra over and over.

Until an exhausted, bone-weary sleep claimed me.

When I opened my eyes the next morning, the first thing I noticed was the bright red numbers on the clock on my nightstand. And they weren't blinking.

Old clocks like that usually blink after the power goes out.

Did the power go out though? I seem to remember there being light in the hallway.

My eyes flicked to the lamp on my nightstand. I reached over and tried the switch. A warm, yellowish glow lit my side of the room.

That definitely wasn't working last night.

I sat up and looked around the room, confused. My head ached, and I felt like I'd barely slept a wink. But I was beginning to wonder if it was all a dream. A horrible nightmare.

I looked at the clock again. If that was the right time, I only had fifteen minutes to get to the cafeteria before breakfast was over.

I threw on some clothes and shoes, shouldered my bag, and rushed out the door.

As I rounded the corner and passed the bathroom, I heard voices coming up the stairs.

A quick peek confirmed that it was Greer and Amanda. They hadn't reached the mid-flight landing yet, so I stayed hidden and watched. Listened.

"…And why was Cheyenne invited last night?" Amanda asked. "Since when is she an official member of our group?"

"Why? Do you have a problem with her?" Greer snarled.

"I don't trust her," Amanda said as they reached the landing. "And just because Molly's out, doesn't mean we have room for one more."

"Don't bring up Molly," Greer snapped, stopping in her tracks.

Amanda scowled and looked away.

Who is Molly?

Greer and Amanda crossed the landing and started up the next set of stairs toward the second floor, so I slid back.

"Besides, I wouldn't worry about Cheyenne," Greer said. "She knows I have dirt on her."

"What kind of dirt?"

"I'll tell you later."

"You better." Amanda huffed.

"I will. I promise."

Their voices grew louder as they neared the top. I stayed close to the wall, ready to dart out of sight.

"You deleted the recording, right?" Amanda asked. "You're sure there's no trace of it on your phone?"

Now they really had my interest.

"Of course. I'm not stupid."

"Well…"

"Shut up!" Greer laughed.

"Are you sure your mom isn't going to notice you took her phone?"

"I'm positive. This is an old backup she keeps in a drawer for emergencies."

As they reached the top of the stairs, I ducked into the bathroom. Kept the door cracked and held my breath. *Don't come this way.*

One let out a laugh, and it sounded like they were getting farther away, so I stole another peek. They had turned the other way, toward Greer's room. So, I stayed where I was and continued to listen.

"I can't believe she fell for it," Amanda said, the laughter still in her voice. My pulse started racing as anger stirred the acids in my belly.

"I know," Greer laughed back. Then she mimicked the haunting voice from my room last night. "YOU did this to me!"

Every muscle in my body contracted. Fists at my sides, nails biting into my palms, I struggled to catch my breath as my heart pounded violently in my chest.

I don't remember moving. It happened so fast. But

the next thing I knew, I was face to face with Greer, pinning her against the wall.

"So that was another one of your sick jokes?" I growled.

Greer looked shocked at first, then her eyes narrowed, and a hint of a smile tugged at one corner of her mouth.

That made me even madder. I pressed harder at her shoulders.

"What the hell are you smiling about?" I demanded through clenched teeth.

A glimmer of triumph lit up her eyes. "Because you can't prove I did anything," she whispered with arrogance. "But I can."

Her gaze flashed to a spot over my shoulder, and mine followed. A pair of security cameras hung near the ceiling on the wall across from the stairwell. They seemed to cover most of the upper corridor. I returned my gaze to hers. The look on her face made me want to punch her. Instead, I gave her a small shove and released her as I stepped back. My lips pressed together so hard, they started to go numb. It took every bit of energy I had to keep control.

Then another voice startled me.

"Everything okay here, girls?" It was a voice of authority.

I choked on a gasp and turned. Kerry stood nearby. I held my breath and waited to see what Greer and Amanda would do, because at this very moment, they held all the cards.

"Just a misunderstanding," Greer said.

Kerry glanced from me to Greer, and back again.

My lips curled ever-so-slightly, in agreement.

"Yes. A misunderstanding."

After a moment of pause, Kerry seemed appeased. "Okay then."

Amanda flashed Kerry a smile. "Well, see ya," she chirped and hooked Greer by the arm, leading her away.

"What are your plans for today, Ronnie?" Kerry asked.

I was still trying to catch my breath. "Uh, I'm going on the hike with Ashton's group," I answered, trying to keep my voice from quivering.

"Nice. It's a beautiful day for it."

With a tight-lipped smile, I nodded. "Hey, I've gotta grab some breakfast before the cafeteria closes," I said, hitching a thumb.

"Oh yeah, you better hurry. Have fun on the hike."

My stomach was so upset I didn't even feel like eating at this point. I just wanted to get out of this place.

I hurried down the first set of stairs and turned the corner. The front door lay ahead. I eyed it from the midway landing, hesitating. It taunted me. And for a moment I wondered how hard it would be to just walk out that door and not come back.

Instinctively, my hand went to my bag at my side. With the picture of my mom now hidden with the leaf between the pages of my journal and tucked safely inside, I had all I needed.

I stepped off the landing and slowly descended the second set of stairs, my eyes fixated on that door.

The jingling of keys broke my focus. Down the corridor to the right, the security guard was headed this way, his key ring twirling on his finger.

I came to a stop on the last stair. My jaw clenched

so tight it hurt, I held my breath.

Our eyes met and he greeted me with a nod.

I attempted a smile. But I couldn't help wondering if somehow he knew what I was thinking.

Mrs. Brown's voice popped in my head. *Assume you're always being watched.*

Greer had just made that very point upstairs.

As the security guard passed by, I took a much-needed breath, then stepped off the stairs and went to the right. Maybe sitting amongst the aisles of books in the library would make me feel less like I was on display.

I walked in to find two girls sitting at a table near the front. Brooke and Ashley, they were seniors. I recognized them from my Language Arts class. They both flashed me a friendly smile.

They were the kind of girls I should be aligning myself with. And I had a feeling they'd welcome me to their table if I'd asked.

Maybe another day.

"Hey." I forced a smile, returning the gesture as I walked by.

I went to the end of the farthest aisle—the science and nature section—and lowered myself to the floor. It was the same spot I'd been hiding in when Eve found me on the first night. I liked this spot. I'd used it a couple of times since.

I dug my iPod out of my bag and got my music going. Then I went for my journal, opened it to the first page.

One week down. It's not so bad here.

I remember feeling such hope when I wrote those words. Now they just pissed me off.

The page wrinkled as I flipped it hastily. With pen in hand, my words spilled onto the page like chicken scratch. Barely legible.

I was stupid to think life would get easier.

I think my inner demons are coming for me.

I was beyond starving by the time the cafeteria reopened two hours later.

I went through the line quickly, skipping the tray and grabbing a ham and cheese sandwich, a bag of chips, and a bottle of apple juice. Since the designated meeting spot for the hike was the courtyard at twelve thirty, I decided to sit at a table out there to eat.

By quarter after, students began straggling out. There must have been about twenty gathered by the time two college-aged guys showed up ten minutes later.

The one I assumed was Ashton held up a clipboard and addressed the group. "If your name is already on the list, please check off that you are here. If your name is not on the list, please add it at the bottom."

I worked my way to the front of the line and added my name. When I turned around, Will was right behind me.

"You came," he said, his face brightening.

"Okay, listen up," Ashton shouted above the din. As everyone quieted, he began, "I know most of you have heard this a bunch of times, but we need to go over the rules before we head out. They are easy. There are just three." He threw his hand in the air, holding up one finger. "Don't wander off the main paths." He uncurled a second finger. "Don't get too close to the gorge." Uncurling a third finger, he said, "And for the love of all that is holy, don't try to climb into the gorge." *Okay. We get it. The gorge is off-limits.* "There are a lot of hidden dangers, like crumbling rock, surprisingly deep pockets, and heavy currents. All right, let's stick together," he said with a big arm gesture as he turned and headed out.

The large group followed Ashton through the back gate and to the right. Edging the tree line, we passed the maintenance shed. As we walked, people naturally started breaking into smaller groups.

"See that white house between the trees over there?" Will said, pointing to a small house way off to the right. "That's where Mr. and Mrs. Trumble live."

"Oh. Is that the house you can see on the drive in after the turn off the main road?"

"Yep," he answered. "So, there are three trails up here. Two take you along the gorge rim, so there are some hills to climb. The other one is super flat and easy, Deer Meadow. There's another trail right behind the school, Bear Forest that doesn't go out to the rim either. But it's a nice walk in the woods."

After the short walk we came to a small wooden sign that showed the trails mapped out. Wooden posts marked each of the entrances and indicated destination and distance: *South Rim Trail—1.9 miles; North Rim Trail—1.1 miles; Deer Meadow—.5 miles.*

"We're going to stick to the rim trails today," Ashton said. "I'll take the North, and Jeremy will take the South. I don't want anyone going off alone."

"There's a cool lookout point on the North Rim Trail," Will said. "It's the more difficult one, because it's a steep climb in a few spots. Do you think you're up for it?"

"Sure," I answered and followed his lead. A group

of four fell in step behind us.

The path started out straight and flat, and I quickly found my pace. I just didn't realize that my pace was a bit fast until Will pointed it out.

"Everything okay?" he asked.

"Yeah, why?"

"Because you're practically running."

"What? No, I'm not." I looked to my side and noticed not only was he falling behind, but we were well ahead of the other group. "Sorry."

Will smiled and jogged a few steps to catch up.

I took a deep, refreshing breath and released it slowly as we started again at a slower pace.

"Let me guess…Greer?" He scowled—it's funny how pronouncing that name almost demanded it.

"Ugh," I grunted, kicking a rock off the path. "I hate her. She might actually be the devil incarnate."

"So what did she do now?"

I pressed my lips together and groaned. I wasn't in the mood to get into it right now. I was too busy being mad and focusing on the path ahead as it started to incline. The hard-packed path meandered parallel to the gorge, twisting and turning through the trees. We couldn't always see it, but we knew it was there. At times, we could hear the water rushing below.

After a long stretch of silence, Will said, "I heard that last year, they got a girl kicked out of Evergreen. Supposedly, she was only here a couple weeks."

"What the heck?"

"Yeah. Apparently, the girl knew Greer from her old school although she hardly recognized her. She said Greer used to look a lot different and used to get picked on a lot. But I guess she changed everything about herself when she came here—even her name." Will hesitated, trying to catch his breath as we climbed the steep hill. "Chase said Greer adamantly denied everything, but the girl threatened to provide pictures. Shortly after that, she was gone. Kicked out, I guess."

"Holy crap."

"Yeah. I told you they can't be trusted."

"Do you remember what the girl's name was?"

"Uh, Abby or Ali…something like that," he answered as he came to a stop. "Well, here we are."

I'd been so focused on our conversation that I hadn't noticed the view until he announced it.

From where we stood, we could see waterfalls off to the right. Tall and narrow, the water cascaded into a round plunge pool before spilling over another rocky edge and flowing rapidly at the base of the craggy walls on either side. The valley stretched out to the left, the direction we had come from, and disappeared around a bend in the distance. At its widest, the crevice couldn't have been more than one-hundred feet wide. It was by far deeper. The sun's reach barely dipped beneath the rim of the gorge.

The immense beauty left me speechless. I focused on the sound of the rushing water and took a deep breath, cleansing my lungs and releasing my tension.

"Wanna sit?" Will asked, gesturing to a perfectly placed sitting rock.

I nodded and sat beside him.

Our knees touched, and I looked down, noticing a familiar rectangular shape.

"Is that a phone in your pocket?" I asked.

"No, I'm just happy to see you." Before I could react, he let out a belly laugh. "Sorry, it was too good to pass up."

"It was," I said with a chuckle. "I knew the moment I said it."

Still chuckling, Will slid the phone partially out of his pocket to show me. "Shhh, don't tell anyone."

"Oh my gosh, aren't you afraid you'll get in trouble?"

"Nah. Lots of kids do it."

"Does your dad know you have it here?"

"Yeah. He doesn't care," Will answered. "I only use it on the weekends. There's only like one spot on the property that I even get any bars. But it's definitely nice to have when we go on trips." With that, Will faced the view in front of us again, propping his hands behind himself and leaning back. "So what do you think?"

I gazed out over the beautiful landscape, enjoying the sense of calm it brought. "I could sit here all day."

After several minutes of silence, Will said, "So, are you going to tell me what Greer did?"

My calm was gone in an instant.

My mind going back to that moment, seeing the framed picture of my mother on Greer's dresser, candlelight flickering in the reflection of the glass. Seeing everyone's eyes on me. Hearing Greer's voice, asking who the spirit was, just before the planchette moved to the M.

A mixture of pain and anger began to rise within me, literally. My body shook. My pulse raced. I felt as though my throat was constricting. As I struggled to breathe, my hands began to tighten into fists. The cut on my thumb began to sting and throb, reminding me of how easily I could lose control.

I sprang to my feet and moved closer to the jagged edge. I couldn't handle Will looking at me right now. I didn't want him to see the other side of me. The side that brought me to Evergreen in the first place.

"Hey, are you all right?" Will asked, his hand falling lightly on my shoulder.

His touch felt soft and caring.

And I felt unworthy.

Chapter 12

I knew the evening was going to be hard. When the activities of the day were over, and we were left to our own vices. It would be so much easier if I had my own room to hang out in. But no. I had to share a room with one of the most miserable people on the planet. So the library would have to do. Again.

It was a small library—not even half the size from my old school. But I appreciated it just the same, and I liked the quiet. It reminded me of the old days, when things were simpler, when I enjoyed school, and my mom was still alive.

I walked up and down the aisles, straightening and tidying as I went. I was so bored that in one whole aisle, I pulled every book to the edge of the shelf so that all the spines lined up evenly. I eventually got bored with that too, so I went to my usual spot and plunked down on the floor.

With my iPod fully charged, I was prepared for the long evening ahead.

It was between songs that I thought I heard something. I paused the music and pulled the buds from my ears. There it was again. Like a book sliding on a shelf. I waited quietly, wondering who was in the library with me. A shadow moved in the next aisle. I could see it between the books on the shelves, hear the movement getting closer. I wasn't alone.

I got to my feet and peered around the corner. I didn't see anyone. So, I checked the next aisle—the one where I'd arranged all the books evenly in line along the edge. Again, it was empty. But I knew someone had been there, because every other book in that aisle was pushed in, resembling the teeth of a comb.

"Hello? Who's there?"

My heart pounded like crazy.

I hurried through the library, glancing down each aisle as I went.

Nothing.

I rushed to the door and looked in both directions, hoping to catch the culprit sneaking off.

The corridor was empty.

But I refused to fall for another one of their pranks.

"Nice try," I called out, in case they were still nearby watching. "You don't scare me."

I turned and stepped back into the library.

The lamp on the main desk flickered, and a chill ran through me. But I held my head high and went back to where I'd been sitting. Even though there was a part of me that wasn't sure if it was them or not, I didn't want them to think they'd chased me away. I couldn't let them think they were getting to me.

At 9:55 I finally gave in and went upstairs to bed.

I heard Amanda's voice on the other side of the door around quarter after ten.

"Yeah, Ker, I'm heading to bed now." I heard her hand on the doorknob.

Kerry was making rounds.

I heard the mention of my name and then Amanda say, "She's already asleep."

That really pissed me off. Amanda didn't have a

clue whether or not I was in the room, or if I was asleep. What was the point of her lying?

I heard more mumbled conversation and then Kerry saying good night from a distance.

"Night, Kerry," Amanda called out, and the doorknob turned.

I pretended to be sleeping but peeked through the lashes of one eye, but the door never opened.

I gave up watching the door around midnight, and still Amanda hadn't returned. I was beginning to see how manipulative those girls really were. And that was worrying.

It felt like I had just dozed off when…

Bang!

"If anything is missing, you're dead!"

Slam!

My eyes sprang open. Amanda's light was on, and she was standing at her dresser.

"What the hell?" I grumbled, blinking away the sleep and checking the time. "It's two o'clock in the morning. What is your problem?"

Her shrill voice began again. "You're my problem! Stay out of my stuff!"

Oh my God, this again. "I didn't touch your stuff."

"Then who opened my drawers?"

"How should I know?" I rolled away from her, pulling the blanket up to my neck and snuggling in to get warm.

"And why is it so cold in here?" she said.

"Would you shut up. I'm sleeping." Amanda huffed loudly, and under my breath, I added, "You should try it. Maybe then you wouldn't be such a bitch."

She continued opening and closing drawers. Not quietly, I might add. I knew the picture of my mom was safe for now, and that's all I cared about, so I went back to sleep.

The next time I opened my eyes, it was just before seven. Normally, I'd resist waking up so early, but not today. I figured now was a good time for paybacks.

"Hmm. What to wear?" I mumbled to myself, as I opened my shirt drawer. I closed it and opened the next one down. "Wonder what the weather's going to be like today?"

I bumped the drawer closed with my hip, went to the window, and threw back the curtains. Sunlight poured in. Oops. Right in Amanda's face. She rolled over and yanked the blanket over her head. I grinned ear to ear, then went back to my dresser and gathered a bra and underwear from the top drawer. *Slam.* Got a shirt from the second drawer. *Slam.* And pulled a pair of jeans from the third drawer. *Slam.*

Amanda growled and jerked under the covers.

I smiled again, then shoved my feet into my slides, grabbed my toiletry bag, and headed down the hall to the bathroom.

A few minutes later, dressed and ready for the day, I headed back to my room to swap out my toiletry bag for my canvas hobo.

I could hear Amanda's grating voice before I even opened the door.

"Oh. My. God. Could you not?"

I know I'll probably regret this, but... "Who are you talking to?"

Amanda bolted upright in bed, throwing the covers aside.

"You!" Her hair hung in front of her face. "Stop it with the fucking drawers!" she griped, flinging her body back down and pulling the covers over her head.

"I just walked in…" My voice trailed off as the hair on my arms stood on end. All the drawers in the room—twelve to be exact—were open to one degree or another and everything on the top of our dressers was knocked over.

The room felt cold and stale.

It took me almost a full minute to move from the spot by the door. Something weird was definitely going on at Evergreen.

Chapter 13

The dining hall was practically empty when I sat down at quarter after seven. I had about a half hour before the breakfast rush, but I planned to be gone before then.

I pulled my iPod from my bag and put in my earbuds. I needed to drown everything else out right now, including my thoughts, lest my imagination get the better of me. With a French toast stick in one hand, I scrolled down to my "Ultimate" playlist and turned up the volume. Heavy bass helped clear my head.

I was just about to leave when I saw Cheyenne go into the cafeteria. I pulled my buds from my ears, grabbed my tray, and stood. After hearing Greer and Amanda talk about her yesterday, I kind of wanted to talk to her. I almost had this fantasy of bringing Cheyenne and Eve to my side, leveling the playing field a bit.

I timed it perfectly, managing to cross paths with her on her way into the dining hall with her tray.

"Hi, Cheyenne," I said as I moved toward her.

"Hey," she answered, nervously flicking her gaze away.

I stopped in front of her. She looked uncomfortable, so I tried to sound casual and friendly. "Hey, um, can I talk to—" *Crap. Here come the rest of them.* I let out a sigh. "Never mind," I said and walked away.

I approached the kitchen window to return my tray, my head spinning with frustration.

"Everything okay, dear?"

"What?" I raised my gaze. A woman wearing a hairnet and white apron, with the name Nancy clipped to the front, held her hand out. "Yeah, sorry, I guess I'm still half asleep," I answered, passing her my tray.

She smiled. "Gotta love Mondays, huh," she quipped and went about her work.

"I feel like the past year has been a Monday," I grumbled to myself as I turned away.

I managed to avoid direct contact with the girls the rest of the morning, including Eve, which was odd. I figured she'd been directed to stay away from me. I kind of missed her. She wouldn't even look at me in Bio.

Will and I sat together, but Mr. Erickson kept us busy with a five-page test on heredity. Luckily, we were allowed to use our textbooks. Mr. Erickson said finding the topic in-question and relaying the answer was just as—if not more—important than memorizing the answers; it teaches us research skills. Skills, he said, that we could use for the rest of our lives. Much unlike, he joked, knowing who the "father of modern genetics" was. It was Gregor Mendel, by the way.

I liked Mr. Erickson. He was practical.

He stood near his desk and collected our papers as we crowded the aisles and funneled past. "Thank you," he said as he took each one.

Will was in front of me in line. He handed his test over and proceeded.

I was next. I held my papers out. Mr. Erickson

started to take them but stopped, handing them back. "You forgot your name."

Shoot. I stepped to the side and scribbled my name at the top. Mr. Erickson barely missed a beat, reaching over another student and taking my paper once again. "Thank you."

I spotted Will ahead, three kids between us. I scooted around them, in hopes of catching up. But as the hallway crowded with students, the space between me and Will grew. Amongst the crowd were Sam and Amanda. Amanda was shuffling some papers when a couple of boys began fooling around. One boy bumped her, and the papers went flying.

"Sorry," he laughed and bent to pick them up.

She smacked his shoulder. "Don't touch my stuff!" she barked.

The boy straightened with his hands raised in defense and backed away. "Okay, geez."

I peered through the crowd again, looking for Will. When I spotted him, he was alone, standing off to the side.

Our eyes met, and he fell into step beside me.

"There you are," he said with a smile. "How did you get so far behind?"

"I forgot to put my name on my paper," I answered. "So, how do you think you did on the test?"

"I thought I was doing okay until that last section. I'm not good at writing out definitions like that. If it was multiple choice, no problem. How about you?"

"Pretty good, I think."

We entered the cafeteria, and Will grabbed two trays from the stack. He passed one back to me as we stepped forward and set our trays on the metal rack. As we slid them down the line, Will glanced back at me. "You're sitting with us again, right?"

Before I could answer, Sean budged ahead of Will and stole his tray.

"Jerk." Will laughed and went to get another.

I absolutely wanted to sit with them again—no offense to Taylor—so after going through the line, I stepped to the side and waited for Will to get his food. Then, with our trays in hand, we headed toward his table.

I know Amanda saw us, and I'm sure she didn't waste any time blabbing to Greer. But I didn't care. Their disgusting prank wasn't going to change my mind about being friends with Will. If anything, it drove me closer to him.

After having Bio, lunch, and gym together, Will and I were going to have to part ways for sixth period as he had Language Arts next, and I had World History.

We lingered toward the back of the crowd, leaving the gymnasium. Even though I tried not to let the girls continue to rent space in my head, I couldn't help but find myself keeping tabs on them. I figured you should always know where your enemies were.

Ahead of us, Amanda ducked into Mr. Santori's room, and Eve continued on, stopping in front of Mrs. Oliviera's. She and Greer were in Will's Language Arts class. Across the hall, Greer and Sam exited the Art room and split up. Sam was in my history class with Mr. Thomas at the far end. And so was Cheyenne, but I didn't see her anywhere.

Greer and Eve got one look at me approaching with Will, and quickly headed into the classroom.

Will rolled his eyes and chuckled.

"See ya later," he said as he veered off and followed them in.

"Have fun." I simpered, continuing down the long hall.

Pssst.

Slowing, my eyes scanned from side to side.

Pssst.

I stopped and looked around. *Was someone trying to get my attention?*

Besides a few students down the way, there was no one around.

But there wasn't even anyone nearby. And the few students who were chatting down the way seemed oblivious to my presence.

"Over here."

I followed the hushed voice to a nearby door marked "Maintenance Closet" that was ajar.

"Hello?" I whispered. "Who's there?"

"It's Cheyenne, come here."

I checked the hallway again, to be sure no one was watching, then slid inside and closed the door. Darkness hugged me, and the smell of Pine-Sol tickled my nose. With a click, a bare bulb lit up the room. I squinted at the sudden brightness.

A pull string swayed above Cheyenne. "I could tell you wanted to talk."

"Yeah," I answered hesitantly as I took in the small room around me.

Shelving full of paper products and cleaning supplies covered the back wall. Behind Cheyenne was a rolling mop bucket sitting in a drainage tray on the floor. The faucet over the bucket dripped to the count of four Mississippis.

"So, I heard you were new here too..." I straightened a stack of tissue boxes on the shelf as I scrambled for words. "And I kind of got the impression that you weren't as tight with the rest of them, so I kind of thought..."

"They can't know I talked to you," Cheyenne said. I saw the worry in her eyes.

"I swear, whatever you tell me stays between us."

Her shoulders fell as if relieved. "I just go along with them so I'm not a target." She dropped her gaze and nervously flicked one thumbnail with the other. "And I'm really sorry about the other night. I didn't know what they were going to do, and that was really messed up." Her brow dipped, and her narrowed eyes met mine. "Everything is a frickin' game with them."

"Yeah, I kinda got that impression—"

"No," she snapped. "You don't understand. When they go after someone, it's not for a laugh or to embarrass the person. Their goal is to break them. And they do whatever they have to, to protect the group. It's like they've made some kind of blood sister pact or something. They all wear those silver heart bracelets with their initials, which by the way is an acronym for GAMES. They think they're so clever," she added under her breath. "Look, I know I shouldn't be telling you any of this, but I thought you should be warned since you are their prime target right now."

My lips parted, but I didn't know what to say. That was a lot of information to unpack.

GAMES. Greer, Amanda, Eve, and Sam. Who's the M? Could it be the Molly they mentioned?

Then Cheyenne began again. "Sam says someone came into our room last night. She said when she woke up, all of her drawers were open, and some things had been moved—"

"That's weird," I interrupted. "The same thing happened to us this morning." *Could this be another strange occurrence I can add to my growing list of things that can't be explained?*

"That is weird." Her brow wrinkled. She shook it off and went on, "Well, I wouldn't be surprised if she tries to point a finger at you. I heard them talking. I think they might be planning something. So, watch your back."

"Okay. Thanks."

Cheyenne shifted toward the door, put her hand on the knob. "We better get to class before Sam gets suspicious."

"Cheyenne, wait." I hesitated a moment, looking her straight in the eye. "You need to be careful too. I've heard things, and…I don't know if you should trust Greer and Amanda either."

She pursed her lips and nodded, obviously not surprised by what I'd said.

I pulled the string, turning off the light. Cheyenne cracked the door and peeked out.

She turned back. "Wait at least a minute after I leave," she said, before slipping out and pulling the door shut behind her.

I stood in the dark for well over a minute, listening to the faucet drip while I tried to process what had just happened. While I believed Cheyenne and I had made a real connection, I had to wonder how long it would be before they turned her.

Opening the door slowly, I peered out. The coast was clear, so I hurried off to class.

****

I was relieved when the final bell rang as I'd had to pee for the last twenty minutes. But Mr. Thomas was on a roll, and I didn't want to interrupt.

Quickly, I made my way down the long hall toward the bathrooms in the main corridor. All three stalls were full when I walked in, but it didn't take long for one to come available.

By the time I came out of the stall, the bathroom had emptied. I washed and dried my hands, threw the paper towels in the trash, and reached for the door. It opened before my hand made contact.

Startled, I took a step back.

And in walked Greer, Sam and Amanda on her heels.

"Just who we were looking for," Greer said.

This can't be good. "And why is that?"

She folded her arms across her chest, and I made note of the silver heart bracelet Cheyenne had mentioned. I hadn't really paid much attention before. I also noted the "G" etched on one side.

Greer cocked her head. "You wouldn't happen to know who was poking around in Sam's room, would you?" And there it was. Just like Cheyenne said.

"What are you talking about?" I asked, gruffly. Then I eyed Sam with disregard. "And why can't she speak for herself?"

"Just answer the question," Sam said.

I sighed and answered, "I haven't been in your room. But whoever it was, is probably the same person who went through our room this morning while I was in the bathroom, and she was sleeping…" My voice trailed off as I gestured toward Amanda, and a thought occurred to me. My eyes narrowed. "Or maybe Amanda wasn't sleeping?"

She snarled. "What are you talking about?"

I continued to address Greer and Sam. "She was alone in our room, and she had opportunity. Maybe Amanda is messin' with all of us." Of course, I didn't actually believe what I was saying.

The other girls turned their attention toward Amanda, who clearly didn't like the implication.

"You're not going to believe *her* over me, are you?" Amanda spat.

I walked away before any of them could respond.

Whoa, that felt good. After spending the first week walking on eggshells, I was done. I now had a pretty good idea how things worked around here, and if I wanted to survive, I was going to have to play the game.

Chapter 14

After talking to Cheyenne yesterday, I was looking forward to talking to Will. Something she'd said had been eating away at me, and I was hoping he'd have the answer.

I looked for him at breakfast, but he had a habit of coming late.

So I waited until lunch.

"Hey, can I ask you something?" I said as we approached the noisy table. I wanted his attention first.

"Yeah, sure. What's up?" Will set his tray down and slid into his seat. I sat to his right.

"Who's Molly?" I asked.

"Molly," he repeated with pinched brow. "Why? Where did you hear about her?"

"I heard Greer and Amanda say something about 'Molly being out,' and I just wondered who she was."

"She used to be Amanda's roommate, but she took off a few weeks ago. I'm sure they did something to drive her away." He picked up his burger and took a bite. Chewing, he added, "She may have been a part of their little group, but she wasn't really like them."

"What do you mean, she took off?"

"She ran away," he said. "Left all her stuff behind and booked. That's one of the reasons she was here—she kind of used to do that a lot. Well, that, and drinking and smoking pot." He snickered. "Her parents said she was too disruptive to the family. But damn, she has seven younger sisters and brothers. That would make me want to run away too."

Disruptive. That sounded familiar. "So, I take it you two were friends?"

"Yeah. I've known Molly a long time—since elementary school, actually." He shrugged and looked away. "We used to hang out."

I'm pretty sure that meant they dated. Jealousy nipped at my insides, but I tried not to show it. Will and I were just friends.

"Wait, wait, I've got a good one!" Damien held his arms forward and wide, getting the table's attention. When all eyes turned to him, he said, "DC…or Marvel. Which franchise do you think is superior?"

The boys went wild, calling out their favorites.

"Marvel," Will and I answered at the same time. We looked at each other and laughed.

And with that, we were done talking about Molly.

****

I loved sitting with Will and his friends at lunch. They were so fun to be around, and they made me feel included.

I was still riding that high as I made my way to art class. But it didn't last long.

I heard her before I saw her.

Greer.

She was sitting at the front of the classroom, carrying on in a way that demanded attention.

What was she even doing here? She didn't normally share this period with us.

What's she up to now?

"Ronnie!" Eve waved from a table toward the

opposite corner. "I saved you a seat."

I guess she's talking to me again...

Funny how she usually sat with Amanda in this class, but now that Greer was here, Eve had been given the boot. There was an obvious pecking order with that group. And it was apparent that Eve was near the bottom—maybe only slightly above Cheyenne.

Miss Whipple gave the instructions for our assignment. We were to create a mixed media theme board—similar to an inspiration board. It was to have a quote of some kind, and a theme. It could be a lyric from a song, or a line from a poem, whatever. Just something that spoke to us. And we needed to decorate the rest of the board using two or more medias: pencil, pen, paint, magazine clippings, anything we desired. She wanted the entire board covered, and we had three days to work on it.

The example she showed was one another student had done. The quote was "Music heals the soul." It had music notes and a guitar, and an ethereal theme to it, decorated with a mixture of colored pencil drawings and clippings from magazines.

Some kids seemed to know what they wanted to do, without much thought. They were grabbing paper and supplies and getting started.

But I couldn't think of a thing. I liked the idea of using words from a song. Although at the moment I couldn't think of a single song, let alone any of the words.

While my mind was busy thinking, I grabbed a poster board from the stack and a nicely sharpened pencil.

Greer's voice caught my attention from across the

room, and I tensed. She had this way of using a phony, overly sweet voice when she dealt with people of authority. It was sickening. Greer was explaining her idea for the project to Miss Whipple—something about best friends. Amanda, who sat next to her, was going to do the same thing. *I think I'm going to throw up.*

I examined Greer, taking in her perfect hair and skin, watching the way she held herself with confidence, and the way she smiled even while she spoke. I knew it was all an act. She was as fake as they come.

Sure, I got it. Some people transform themselves, become the person they want to be. But usually that meant becoming a better person through some sort of personal growth. That wasn't the case with Greer. There was no growth, only ambition and desire to play God with other people's lives.

But I know the truth about you, Greer. Or whatever your real name is. And it's time for someone to knock you down a peg or two.

Suddenly, a song popped into my head, and I had my theme for my art project. The song was called "Take the Mask Off." It was about exposing someone for pretending to be something they're not.

Funny thing was, I knew the concept would go right over Greer's head.

I deposited the supplies at my table and went to the bookshelves that ran the length of the outer wall. Just three feet high, the shelves filled the space beneath the large windows. There were bins full of old magazines, everything from *Popular Mechanics* to *Horse and Hound*, and *Vogue*.

I had a vague idea of how I wanted my project to

look, so I grabbed a stack from a bin of fashion magazines and a few with farm animals on the front. Then I spread them out on the counter above the shelves and pulled one of the stools over. We had three days to work on the project. I wasn't in a hurry. In fact, it was nice sitting in the sun by the windows.

I started flipping through the pages and realized this might be harder than I thought, but I bookmarked a few possibilities.

After a while, my mind began to wander, and I picked up the pace. Flip. Flip. I caught movement in my peripheral. A few students were setting up along the same counter by the windows, looking at magazines. Then my eyes shifted upward, gazing out the window for one brief moment as I brought my attention back to the page in front of me.

Wait. What?

My gaze flashed back to the second-floor window across the courtyard. It stood out because it was the only one that didn't appear as a large, off-white rectangle, like the others. This one was partially obstructed by a dark figure. Which was odd because no one should be up in the dorms this time of day.

Could that be the person responsible for the recent break-ins?

From the shape and build, I guessed it to be a woman or a girl. But because of the glare on the glass, it was impossible to make out a face. And while I couldn't tell for sure, I felt like she was staring at me.

"How are you doing over here, Ronnie?" Miss Whipple asked, suddenly at my side.

I startled. "I'm fine."

"Did you come up with an idea, yet?"

"Um, yeah, I think so," I answered, stealing a glance at the second-floor window again. But when my eyes fell upon her, she disappeared. Not like, she walked away or slid between the curtains. But more like…she vanished right before my eyes.

The hair on my arms stood up. *What the…*

I returned my attention to Miss Whipple. "Can I go to the bathroom?"

"You've got five minutes," she said.

I grabbed my bag and left the art room, heading down the hall toward the main corridor. Lucky for me, no one was in sight, so I slipped past the restrooms and up the grand staircase, taking two steps at a time.

After a quick look to the right, I rushed around the corner to the left. The long hall lay before me. Empty. My heart pounded with anticipation. I hoped to catch the culprit and put this mystery to rest.

It was the fourth window from the interior corner of the building. I figured each room had one window, so I counted the rooms as I made my way down the hall.

One. Two. Three. Four.

Room 225.

Colorful artwork decorated the door. This was Eve and Greer's room.

The door was slightly ajar. I hesitated, trying to catch my breath.

My hand shook as I gingerly pushed the door open. "Hello? Is anyone in here?"

The room looked as though it had been ransacked. Items of clothing hung from open drawers, and things normally displayed on dresser tops were strewn about, as if knocked over in a rush.

This had to be the right place. So I went inside.

As I feared, my voyeur was gone. My body ached with disappointment.

I went to the window and peeked through the split in the curtains. From this position I had a perfect view into the art room. I could see the kids sitting near the window—as I had been a few minutes before. Beyond them, I could see Eve working on her project. As well as Greer and Amanda.

"Who were you watching?" I whispered curiously.

Suddenly, a chill—like no other—ran through me. I rubbed at the goose bumps on my arms and backed away from the window.

I had to get out of here. I needed to get back to class before I was missed.

Pulling the door shut behind me, I hurried back down the hall. Only when I caught a glimpse of a security camera hanging near the ceiling, did I remember they were there. I suddenly felt sick.

How is this going to look?

I had no way to explain why I was up here—let alone, in their room—or that I wasn't the one who went through their stuff. I considered going back and cleaning up, but I thought the least amount of time I spent in there, the better.

I rushed down the stairs to the main floor, ducked into the girls' bathroom, and quickly closed the door behind me.

With no windows, the room was pitch black.

I groped the wall for the switch, and when the room finally lit up, I released the breath I'd been holding.

My breaths came hard and quick as I moved away

from the door. I didn't expect anyone to be hiding out in the dark room, but I still checked the stalls. Going down the line, I pushed each of the doors to the open position. I felt better knowing I was completely alone. I had to pull myself together before anyone saw me.

I went to the center sink and set down my bag.

Above me, the fluorescent lights flickered.

Not now. Please, not now. I sighed. This was not helping my current state.

After a few seconds the flickering stopped. The tension in my shoulders eased, and I bent over the sink, using my arms to keep me upright as I hung my head and tried to steady my breathing. In through the nose and out the mouth. Again. In and out.

I lifted my chin and caught a glimpse of myself in the mirror. I looked horrible. Sweat beaded on my forehead, and my cheeks were pink and blotchy. Yet the chill seemed to follow me.

I reached over and turned the knob on the right, letting the water run as I breathed slowly for a third time.

In, two, three. And out, two, three, four.

My breath floated away, like steamy plumes of fog.

My brow narrowed. *What's happening?*

The lights flickered again. Only this time it went on longer and was accompanied by a loud buzzing. I swallowed hard and glanced around the room, my mind going to that place again. I felt like I wasn't alone.

"Is someone here?" My voice shook.

Suddenly, the water blasted out of the faucet.

Startled, I grabbed both knobs and cranked. They just spun. Noisily, the water continued to rush, splashing beyond the basin.

I took a few steps back. My eyes wandered the room, trying to see every corner at once.

My heart pounded painfully in my chest. "Are you the one I saw in the window? Are you following me?"

A musty stench passed by my nose, and seconds later white frost began to form along the bottom of the mirror. Like icy flowers, the frost grew, working its way up, until the entire mirror was covered. The muscles in my legs twitched. Clearly, my body was telling me it was ready to run. But I was determined to find answers. Even though I feared the truth might break me.

"Mom?" I whispered. "Is that you?"

I sensed movement behind me and spun around. One of the stall doors was slowly closing. My body trembled. I couldn't move.

A sob hitched in my chest. "Why are you doing this?"

As if in response to my question, the stall door slammed shut.

With a sharp inhale, I jumped.

Then one by one all three of the stall doors began swinging. Back and forth. Over and over. Banging open and slamming shut. And with the buzzing lights and hissing water, the hysteria of the room reached a crescendo.

"Stop! Stop it!" I cried, slapping my hands over my ears as I fell to the ground.

Chapter 15

Warm hands gripped my shoulders and shook me.

My eyes sprang open, and I lowered my hands from my ears.

Dr. Swan knelt in front of me, concern weighing heavily on her soft features. "What's wrong, Ronnie?"

"Is she gone?" My voice was barely a whisper.

"Is *who* gone? There's no one here, honey."

From my position on the girls' room floor, I raised my gaze. Tears dripped from my nose and chin, and the bitter taste of bile stung the back of my throat.

The room was still and quiet. It was over. Not a single sign of what had happened remained. I pulled in a ragged breath and released it. Even my foggy breath was gone.

"But…" My wide eyes met hers again. "But you heard it, right? You had to have heard the banging."

I could tell by her blank stare that she had no idea what I was talking about.

I knew it wasn't in my head.

I jumped to my feet and went to one of the stall doors, pushing it open. It hit the wall with a thud and bounced back, barely making a sound as it slowed to a close. It was so much louder moments ago.

My hands went to the sides of my head, and I grabbed fistfuls of hair. It was real. I knew it.

I inhaled a quick breath, and my eyes darted to the

sinks. My legs took me there. I cranked both knobs on one of the faucets, and the water came on. Then I cranked the knobs the other way, and the water turned off.

"I don't know how she was doing it." I looked up to my reflection in the mirror.

"Doing what? Tell me what happened so I can help."

I spun slowly, as I ran off the list, pointing at the haunted objects. "The faucets, they were blasting and wouldn't turn off…and, and…the doors were banging and slamming…and the lights…they were buzzing and flickering. She was everywhere."

"Who was? Did one of the girls hurt you?" After a beat of silence, she put one arm around my shoulder. "Come on. Let's go to my office."

Dr. Swan guided me down the corridor to her office and deposited me on the couch. While she moved about the room, I stared at the painting on the wall. The feeling of doom surrounded my thoughts.

The cushion on the couch shifted, rocking me slightly to the side, then a warm hand landed on my back.

Dr. Swan sat beside me. She held a cup out, interrupting my line of sight. I let my lids close over my dry, stinging eyes.

"Take a sip," she said when my eyes blinked open.

While barely half full, the small plastic cup felt heavy in my hands. I took a few sips and lowered it.

"Would you like me to get you more?" she asked, taking it from my hand.

After another slow blink of my eyes, I shook my head, and she placed it on the side table.

Her hand rubbed a small circle on my back, reminding me it was there. She leaned forward and eyed me from the side. “Tell me what you’re thinking.”

At the moment, I was thinking about the painting on the wall. I used to think it was colorful and pretty. Leaves of orange, red, and brown filled the trees surrounding a small cabin and reflecting off the glassy water of the nearby lake.

But looking at the painting now, I saw the truth. The truth of what was to come. Death. Skeleton-bare trees and leaves decomposing on the ground. No color or life to the water. And a cabin, neglected and cold.

“Ronnie,” Dr. Swan interrupted my thoughts. “I need you to tell me what happened back there? And if someone hurt you, I need you to give me a name.”

Opening my mouth to speak felt like a chore, and I didn’t have the strength, so the words fell from my barely parted lips. “She’s punishing me.”

“*Who’s* punishing you?”

I struggled to pull my focus from the painting and meet her gaze. “My mother.”

Dr. Swan’s features remained stoic, but color drained from her face. She was clearly not prepared for the answer I gave. She did her best to hide it though. And after a beat or two, her professional mind kicked into action.

“Why do you think it was your mother doing those things?” she said pragmatically as she rose and moved toward her desk.

With my elbows resting on my knees, I lowered my head and pressed at my temples. “Just a feeling.”

I wasn’t going to tell her about the Ouija board.

“Now, I’m not dismissing the fact that something

scared you," she preempted. She'd retrieved a notepad from her desk and now moved to the red chair across from me. "But I think we should consider other explanations. I mean, the things you described—leaky faucets, old light fixtures, and uh...unbalanced doors...couldn't these things just be characteristics of a hundred-year-old building?"

"It wasn't," I mumbled.

"Tell you what, I'll ask maintenance to check it out and make sure everything is working properly."

I shrugged. "It doesn't matter."

Dr. Swan's eyes lowered. A slight "hmm" rumbled in her throat. Then her eyes met mine. "I think we need to talk about the accident."

I swallowed hard.

Panic must've shown on my face.

"I know it's difficult, but I truly believe that talking about it will help you," Dr. Swan prodded. She made a quick note on the page and lifted her gaze to meet mine.

She was in full session mode—ready to get down to business.

I shifted my eyes away.

As much as I didn't want to, I knew I couldn't fight it anymore. If I ever wanted to get out of this school, I was going to have to deal with this.

"How did the day start for you?" she gently pushed. "Do you remember?"

I remembered the day perfectly. In fact, I couldn't stop remembering that day. It played over and over in my head. And I wanted nothing more than to go back and do everything differently.

"It's okay," she said. "Take your time."

I took a deep breath and cleared my throat.

"It was an average summer day." I spoke as if on autopilot. Not thinking. Just spilling. "It was a Saturday, so my dad was home too, working in the yard. Mom was doing things around the house and trying to keep Tori entertained, because none of her friends were available for a playdate." I paused, pulling a pillow onto my lap and petting the tassel. "Then around dinnertime, my friend Katie called and invited me to spend the night at her house."

"Did you go over to Katie's often?"

"Yeah, she was one of my best friends," I answered. "She said her parents were out of town that night, but her older sister, Justine, would be there. And my parents were fine with that."

"How old was Justine?"

"Seventeen," I answered.

Dr. Swan made a couple of notes. "You and Katie were fifteen?"

"Yeah."

She nodded. "Okay, go on."

I twirled the tassel around with my finger. "When I first got to Katie's, the three of us hung out for a while and had some pizza. Then Justine went to her room, and Katie and I made popcorn and started a movie. We were more than halfway through *The Conjuring* when Justine barged into the family room, insisting we go to a party with her. Katie was pissed that she interrupted our movie, so she said no and told her to get out. But Justine begged. She said she wouldn't have asked if it wasn't super important. She laid it on thick too. 'I *have* to go, and I don't want to show up alone. Come on, Katie, you know I'd do it for you.' "

"Did she say why it was so important?" Dr. Swan

asked.

"Apparently, one of her friends had texted that she was at a party with her boyfriend, and Brandon—the guy Justine had a crush on—was there. And when Justine went on social media to see if anyone was posting from the party, she saw that another girl who Justine referred to as 'that-backstabbing-bitch-Ramsey' had posted a pic with her arm around Brandon."

Dr. Swan nodded. "Ah, I see."

"Yeah." I nodded in return, my mouth pulling to one side. "I mean, I totally got why she wanted to go, but why did *we* have to go with her?" I said with a sigh. "It was ten thirty at night, and we were settled in, doing our own thing.

"Then Katie gave me this look. And I just knew that if we didn't go, Justine was going to blame me. So, I agreed."

I thought for a moment before continuing, my gaze wandering the room as I spoke. "So, yeah. Without a whole lot of thought, I got in the car and headed to a party. It wasn't until we were driving out on some back road that I thought to ask where this party was.

"Justine wasn't even sure. She handed a piece of paper with an address to Katie. I glanced at it from the back seat. It had a bunch of directions on it, with 1721 N. Smithville Rd written in bold print on the bottom. Katie asked her whose house it was, and Justine didn't know. Other than it was some guy's uncle's farm. Who, by the way, was out of town." I cleared my throat and swallowed hard. "While Katie helped navigate, I started to have a bad feeling. I mean, we were on some winding country road in the boondocks, and my cell phone was already down to two bars."

I stopped and looked Dr. Swan in the eye. Anger tainted my voice. I asked her point-blank, "Why didn't I say no? Why didn't I call my parents—at least ask if it was okay to go to that party?" I pursed my lips and shook my head. I didn't expect anything from Dr. Swan. These weren't her questions to answer. "Of course, I knew they'd say no. That's probably why I didn't call them. I didn't want to complicate things. I thought it wouldn't be a big deal. I expected a smallish party where Justine would flirt for a little while and we'd be back home in no time. Then I could still spend the night with my friend, and we could finish our movie."

I sighed. "But oh my gosh, there had to be close to a hundred people. And they weren't from our school. I'm pretty sure they were college kids. Katie and I stayed in the field near the bonfire, and Justine disappeared to find her friend. After an hour of dodging drunken advances, we'd had enough. Katie and I went looking for Justine. A bunch of people were hanging out in the barn. That's where the beer was. And the stalls, uh, they were, um"—I looked down at my twirling thumbs—"being used for hookups."

Dr. Swan's mouth formed the word "oh" but nothing came out.

"Yeah." I blushed. "Well, we eventually found Justine. She was making out with Brandon—the reason we had to go to the party in the first place. And man, was she pissed when we interrupted and told her we wanted to leave. That's when we also realized that she was drunk. So now what were we supposed to do? She couldn't drive. And we didn't have our licenses."

"So what did you do?"

"The only thing we could do…called my mom." I sighed, shaking my head. "God, it was awful. I mean, calling my mom at one o'clock in the morning from some stranger's house in the middle of nowhere, saying I was at a party and I needed a ride because everyone else was drunk. That was so not me. And to make matters worse, my phone only had one bar, so the connection wasn't great. I could actually hear her pretty good, but she said my voice kept cutting out." I paused a moment, feeling pressure and tingling in the bridge of my nose. I took a deep breath as my sight blurred with tears. "She sounded so worried. I tried to tell her we were totally fine, that we just needed a ride home…but I don't think she heard me.

"After that, Katie and I went out to wait by the road so we could watch for my mom, and about a half an hour later she called my cell phone. She said she was at twenty-one North Smithville Road and asked where I was. I could barely get a word in. She sounded so upset. 'Where are you, Veronica? I'm at the door, but the house is dark. Are you okay? Is Katie still with you?' "

I wiped the tears away with my hands, and Dr. Swan held out a box of tissues. I took one and blew my nose.

"I told her that Katie was with me and that we were safe. She was just at the wrong house. We were at seventeen-twenty-one North Smithville Road, not twenty-one." My chest quivered as I tried to take a breath. I continued, though my voice was shaky. "She was just so frantic, and I couldn't get her to calm down."

My eyes fell shut as it all played back in my head. The clicking of the car door opening. And the dinging of the chimes before it slammed shut again. And of course…my mom's voice. The harder I tried to push it away, the louder it got.

Finally, it spilled from my lips without intention.

"Click. Ding. Ding. Ding. Slam. 'I'm coming, Veronica. Don't worry, baby. I'm coming—' " My eyes popped open. "CRASH!"

Dr. Swan startled and stared at me with wide eyes.

"My mom was backing out of the driveway at twenty-one North Smithville Road in her little Elantra when she was hit by a pickup truck. The guy had just left the party. He was drunk and going way too fast." I wiped more tears and blew my nose. "The truck hit the driver's-side door. My mom was killed instantly. The driver of the truck died in surgery a couple of hours later."

Dr. Swan dabbed her eyes with a tissue. She seemed embarrassed as she turned her head away. "Please excuse me." She sniffled and cleared her throat. "I apologize. This isn't very professional of me."

It might not have been professional, but I think we connected on a different level at that moment.

Chapter 16

With my head hung, my hands rested on the tile wall in front of me, keeping me upright as the hot water pelted my body. If only it was possible to wash away my sins. I raised my chin, letting the water hit my face. It made it hard to breathe, but I didn't care.

This had been one of the hardest and most tiring days of my life—reliving *that* day, speaking those words for the first time. I'd never told anyone about the phone call before. About hearing the last moment of my mother's life.

Wiping the water from my eyes, I reached for the dial.

Click. Knock.

It sounded like someone else was in the room, just outside my shower stall. I really didn't want to deal with anyone right now, so I left the water running. I would stay where I was until the coast was clear.

I heard them moving about the room—doors opening and closing, faucets running—but strangely, saw no shadow through the foggy glass door.

"Hello?" I called out, cringing. "Is someone there?"

No one answered. I wished I could say I was relieved. My stomach twisted, and my body shook in fear as I shuffled toward the back of the long narrow shower stall.

The overhead lights flickered twice, then began to dim.

"Not again," I cried softly to myself.

She's here. I could feel it. Even the air felt heavy.

I kept my eyes on the glass door. Scared it would start banging, like the bathroom stall doors had earlier.

I waited.

Was this the calm before the storm?

The inhale before the scream?

But then, just like that, she was gone. I knew by the sudden shift in the energy of the room. And the way the overhead lights returned to normal.

I wasn't sure why until a moment later when I heard the voices. It seemed my visitor had been chased away by two chatty girls.

I had to get out of there.

Turning off the water and grabbing my towel, I dried and dressed quickly.

My shorts and tank clung to my still damp skin as I gathered my things and darted out in such a rush that the girls, who I didn't know well, seemed confused.

"Everything okay?" one asked as the door closed behind me.

"Uh huh," I grunted.

I didn't stop until I got to my dorm room door.

My room was dark and quiet when I returned. Almost too quiet. I felt like my senses had been through the wringer, leaving every nerve in my body raw. Exposed. And on high alert.

I made my way in the dark, unloading my shower supplies on top of my dresser and pulling my wet hair into a bun on top of my head. The back of my tank was soaked, chilling me to the bone.

I grabbed my iPod I'd left charging on my nightstand and quickly climbed in bed, pulling the covers over my head. My entire childhood my covers protected me from monsters, so it made sense they'd protect me from whatever was lurking now. At least that was my hope, anyway.

Next, I put in my earbuds and turned on a bedtime playlist. I didn't want to hear anything other than my music.

Even though it was barely nine o'clock, I just wanted sleep to take me.

I wanted this day to be over.

But with visions of my mom haunting my dreams…even the night was exhausting.

****

Tired and sluggish, I dragged myself to breakfast Wednesday morning.

Eve was waiting for me in the cafeteria, leaning against the back wall.

"Hey, what happened to you yesterday?" she asked as she sprang forward. "You never came back to class. I didn't even see you at dinner."

"I didn't feel well," I answered quietly as I took a tray from the stack. "Dr. Swan let me rest in her office for a while."

"Oh." Eve grabbed a tray and slid in behind me. "Nothing contagious, I hope."

"No. You don't have to worry. I'm not going to get you sick."

Eve stopped at the hot breakfast station, while I continued down the line. I was in the mood for cold cereal this morning.

Suddenly, Greer stepped in front of me. The usual

glare on her face, she slapped her hand down on the metal tray slide.

"Line starts back there." I tipped my chin to the end of the line.

With her posse close behind, Greer looked me up and down. "We're not here for the food. I just thought you'd want to know that I told Trumble, and she's going to Mrs. Brown."

"What are you talking about?"

"I'm talking about you trashing all our rooms—"

"Oh my God, this again," I huffed, rolling my eyes as she continued.

"—taking our things and unplugging our clocks. Thanks to you, Eve and I overslept, and I didn't have time to wash my hair this morning." That explained the top knot. Normally, she wore her hair down, in long, perfect waves.

"You ruined two of the pictures I had taped to my mirror when you ripped them down!" Sam added hastily.

"I've never even been in *your* room. And I've never touched any of your stuff," I answered, glancing from Sam to Greer and then to Amanda. Then, addressing them all, I lowered my voice, "What's happening around here…it's happening to all of us. And it's your fault…for playing around with that Ouija board!"

"What's that supposed to mean?" Greer smirked.

Shit. My stomach knotted. *Why did I say that?*

"Nothing." I took a step to the side.

Greer mirrored my movement. She cocked her head, giving me a look of disgust. "Look," she groaned. "It was just a joke. Everyone knows those things aren't real." With a wave of her hand, she gestured to her friend. "It was Amanda moving the planchette around the board."

"Uhh, no, it wasn't." Amanda flashed Greer a skeptical look.

"Yeah," Greer argued, narrowing her eyes. "I came up with the idea and asked the questions, and *you* moved the planchette."

Amanda grinned. "Nice try. I'm not falling for it."

"For what?"

"*You* were the one moving the thing around."

"No, I wasn't," Greer spat. "I swear, I wasn't."

"If you weren't, then who was?" Cheyenne asked timidly, her eyes growing wide.

All eyes turned to Sam. Her face scrunched. "Don't look at me. This was Greer's thing," she said, shifting the blame back.

"Ugh, whatever," Greer said, rolling her eyes. "Maybe it was Eve. The point is, it's over. So, drop it already."

"Yeah, drop it," Amanda chimed. Her and Sam's expressions were identical. I had to wonder if either of them had an original thought. There was still hope for Cheyenne though. She chewed on her bottom lip and kept her eyes to the floor.

I looked over my shoulder, wondering where Eve was for all of this. Conveniently, she had disappeared.

For a moment I almost fell for it. *Was Eve the one moving the planchette?*

I shook it off. I didn't believe that for a second.

"Whatever, I'm so done here," I said as I tried to squeeze by Greer again.

And once more, she blocked my move. This time

getting right in my face. "That's right, you're done here. Your days are numbered, Verr-onica," she said, exaggerating the pronunciation of my name.

Without another word, I snubbed my nose and shouldered my way through her barricade. I wouldn't give her the satisfaction of seeing me crumble. I tucked *those* feelings away, deep inside.

Holding my head high, I crossed the dining room to an empty table.

When I leave, it'll be on my own terms. I set my breakfast tray down with a bit of force and plopped into the chair. *Ugh, she makes me so mad! One of these days she's gonna get what's coming to her.*

A loud crash and subsequent cry suddenly got my attention.

"What the heck, Greer!" Amanda cried.

Both Amanda and Greer stood in the middle of the dining hall. While Amanda still held her breakfast tray, Greer's tray lay at their feet. Oatmeal, orange juice, and what I guessed was hot chocolate had covered them both and dripped from their hair.

"I didn't do it on purpose," Greer barked. "Someone bumped my tray!"

"Who?" Amanda scowled, dramatically looking around. "I was the only one anywhere near you, and I sure didn't do it."

I stared, mouth gaping, completely dumbfounded.

I wanted to laugh.

I *needed* to look away.

But I just couldn't. I couldn't stop thinking that somehow my thoughts had been heard.

And answered.

Later, as I headed to first period, Eve magically

appeared by my side.

"Tennis starts tomorrow. We should sign up," she said casually.

I stopped and threw her a look. *Did she really not see what had happened back there?*

My brow tensed. "Where were you?"

Eve stared back at me, blankly. "When?"

"When Greer was ripping me a new one," I answered in haste. "One second you were right behind me, and the next second you were gone."

"I'm sorry, I…" Worry weighed heavily in her features. "Are you mad at me?"

"No. But I could've used your help," I huffed. "I thought we were friends." I didn't like having this conversation in the middle of a busy hallway.

"We *are* friends." Her gaze flashed to the floor and back. "But Greer is my friend too, and my roommate. I can't go against her."

"Because of the pact?" I said quietly as a group of kids walked around us to get to their class.

Her eyes narrowed. "What?"

"Never mind," I said, shaking my head. Then, with a heavy sigh, I dropped my shoulders. "Look, I just don't know how you and I can be friends when your loyalty is to her. And she's making it her job to make my life miserable. Does she even approve?"

She gave a timid shrug. "Maybe she'll come around." The tone of her voice wasn't very convincing. But I had to give her extra credit for positivity. Eve was so different from those other girls. She was nice and easy going. And for that reason, that's probably how she got caught up in their drama.

I cocked my head and looked at her through my

lashes. "Seriously, do you honestly believe she'll come around?"

Eve pursed her lips. Then she grabbed my arm and pulled me to the side. "Ok, to prove I'm not exclusively loyal to her…I'll share something with you." She craned her neck to see if anyone was watching, leaned in, and lowered her voice to a whisper. "She doesn't want people to know this, but the reason she got kicked out of her last school is because"—she looked around again—"she stole a pig fetus from the science lab and switched out a girl's packed lunch."

My mouth gaped, and my eyes grew wide. I didn't even know what to say to something like that.

"The girl was vegan," Eve continued. "And when she opened her salad container, the pig was spread-eagle with its abdomen sliced open and its guts pulled halfway out. The girl started throwing up all over the place. She was completely traumatized."

And now, so was I.

Holy shit. Who does something like that? That's…diabolical.

"Pretty sick, right? I can understand why she doesn't want it to get around."

"The secret is safe with me," I answered. *Mostly because I could never bring myself to repeat such a thing.*

I suddenly realized the hallway had nearly cleared out, meaning the bell was about to ring.

"We better get to class," I said, taking a step. I didn't have far to go as Mr. Santori's room was the first one in that wing.

"So," Eve said, grabbing my attention again, "do you want to sign up for tennis with me?"

"Yeah, sure, whatever," I answered, looking back at her.

She had a big smile on her face, and I realized how lucky I was to have Eve in my corner. Anyone else would've given up on me by now. Heck. Everyone else had. But Eve was persistent. She continued to chisel at the wall I'd built around myself.

I lightened up and smiled back. "It'll be fun."

"Cool! I'll put your name down." And with that, Eve was off to class.

I took a refreshing breath, releasing the last of my tension. With Eve's idealistic attitude, and now having something to look forward to, I might be able to overcome everything that had happened over the last twenty-four hours.

****

It was a beautiful spring day, so Mr. Thomas held gym class outside. I liked gym days. It meant I got to spend three periods in a row with Will. And I really liked Will.

About half the class went to the side field and played kickball, while the rest of us chose to walk the grounds. Since the driveway was a large loop, it was an easy path to follow. Will showed me that if you add in the extra loop around the back of the school—and do it two times—it was supposedly a mile.

I much preferred this mile walk to when we had to do four laps around the track at school. It was so boring. But since this path twisted and turned, in and out of the woods and around buildings, passing the game of kickball, it didn't seem as long.

Will and I talked nonstop—the conversation was all over the place. He was just so easy to talk to, and he had a story for everything.

For example, I mentioned that I used to like to ride my bike and this place would be perfect because it was so flat. That's when Will told me about the time a kid in his neighborhood stole his bike. It happened just last year.

"Oh no. Did he give it back?" I asked.

"Nope," Will answered. "And I even went to his house to try to steal it back, but the jerk had it locked up."

"Did you call the police and report it?"

"No. I didn't have any proof." Will paused a moment and smiled. "It's all good though."

"What did you do?" I grinned skeptically.

"Well, I figured he owed me so…I kinda stole their grill."

"What?" I laughed.

"Yeah," Will snorted. "His dad came to our house the next day accusing me of stealing his grill."

"Oh my God. What did you say?"

"I asked him if he had proof that the grill on our back patio was his."

I gasped. "You didn't?"

"I did," Will replied proudly. "And then he said, 'knock it off and just give me my grill back.' I told him I would as soon as his idiot son gave me back my bike."

"Well, did he?"

Will grinned from ear to ear. "I got my bike. Mr. Ostrander got his grill. And TJ got grounded for two weeks."

"Ha!" I laughed. "That's hilarious."

As we passed the tennis courts and edged along the tree line behind the school, something in the woods caught my attention, although I couldn't say exactly what it was. It wasn't anything I saw, or a sound, necessarily. It was more of a feeling. Like something was there, just beyond our view.

The feeling was more intense on our second lap around.

I slowed, staring off into the woods.

"What's up? Did you see something?"

"I'm not sure," I answered as I veered off the path.

Leaves and twigs crunched beneath my feet as I left the grass and wound between trees and saplings. I heard Will's footsteps crunching behind me.

"Uh, Ronnie, we're not really supposed to wander into the woods," he said.

I stopped and turned. I couldn't have been more than thirty feet in.

He stood halfway between. "At least use one of the trails. There might be poison ivy out here. We just passed the Bear Forest Trail right over there."

My gaze moved to where he pointed. From where I stood, I could make out the sharp lines of the signpost at the entrance. Sunbeams broke through the wide opening and sprinkled the trail as it carved through the forest and curved in this direction. It looked as though if I kept walking straight in, I would cross its path.

The sound of Mr. Thomas's whistle could be heard in the distance. I met Will's gaze.

"Time to go in," he said.

With one last look over my shoulder, I agreed. "Fine. But don't you feel it? Something's out here."

"I don't feel anything. Except maybe a little thirsty," Will joked.

Chapter 17

The last bell of the day rang, and the halls of Evergreen came alive. Most students had jobs or activities to get to, while others hung around socializing, before eventually dispersing to their dorms. I headed to Dr. Swan's office. After what happened yesterday, she wanted to meet again today. Which unfortunately meant I would miss yard duty with Will.

Straight ahead, at the end of the corridor, sat Mrs. Trumble's office. Her shadow appeared in the frosted glass of the door, just before it opened.

Standing in the doorway, she searched the crowd.

Then her gaze landed on me, and my shoulders tensed.

She dipped her chin and glared over the top of her glasses. Her finger curled.

Damn.

At first glance Mrs. Trumble might seem like your average grandmother, but she wasn't like any grandmother I knew. This woman didn't shuffle—she trudged. She didn't smell like apple pie. She smelled like sauerkraut. She was a sturdy woman, who probably looked older than she was.

I brushed past her. She closed the door behind us and gestured for me to sit.

She rested against the edge of her desk. "Greer tells me you made a mess of her room yesterday."

"It's not true," I answered lazily, shaking my head.

"Are you saying that she made it up?"

"No, I'm just saying that I didn't do it."

"We know you went upstairs during fifth period," she said. My breath caught in my throat. I pressed my lips tighter. *I have the right to remain silent.* "However," she continued with a voice of accusation and one brow arched. "By some stroke of luck there seems to have been a glitch in the recording on the second floor, so we're not sure where you went, or what you were doing up there."

I tried not to show my relief. "If you had just asked, I would've told you what I was doing upstairs." I kept my voice steady and did what I did best, lied. "On the way to the bathroom, I realized I had started my period, so I went up to my room because I needed a tampon."

Her eyes narrowed. "We supply feminine products in the girls' restrooms."

I flashed an innocent look. "Oh, I guess I never noticed. I guess I'll know for next time."

She let out a sigh that grumbled deep in her throat. Then she rose and circled her desk. "The girls say this isn't the first time something like this has happened," she continued without pause. "Sam complained that her and Cheyenne's stuff had been disturbed the day before—even your roommate, Amanda, lodged a complaint."

"Did Amanda happen to mention that someone got into my stuff too?" After a beat of silence, I scoffed, "I thought as much."

She had nothing to say to that either.

"I'll be talking to Mrs. Brown further about this

matter. But consider this your first warning," she said with a wave, dismissing me.

I shot out of the chair and got out of there as quickly as I could. Once around the corner and out of sight, I stopped to breathe. My pulse was racing. I leaned my back against the wall, just outside Dr. Swan's office, and I closed my eyes. *That was close.*

"There you are." Dr. Swan's voice startled me. My eyes popped open, and I straightened. She smiled. "I thought maybe you forgot about our appointment."

"Nope," I answered genially and scooted inside. "Sorry I'm late."

"That's all right—it's only a couple of minutes." Dr. Swan closed the door behind us. "So…yesterday was tough," she began as we settled into our seats. "How are you feeling about everything today?"

I wasn't entirely sure how to answer that. I mean, for the most part, I was feeling better. But that didn't change the fact that I had this eerie feeling that karma was coming for me. And if I didn't do something, my classmates were about to be collateral damage.

Dr. Swan and I talked a lot longer than usual. And if she hadn't had another appointment, I would've been there longer.

I only had about five minutes before dinner, so I found a free chair in the main corridor and sat down. I made myself comfortable, pulling my feet up, sitting cross legged, and taking out my book. I had finished *The Alchemist* a few days ago, and even though I still had to write a report on it, I was looking forward to starting a new book. I'd opted for a contemporary this time, something by Sarah Dessen about friendships and romance.

I opened the book and flipped to the first page.

Chapter one

My name is—

Familiar voices on the stairs pulled my attention away.

"What's wrong with my shirt?"

"Nothing, Cheyenne. I said it's cute," Greer replied. "I bet my little sister would love it."

I heard the mocking tone in Greer's voice. Saw the hurt feelings on Cheyenne's face as the group stepped off the stairs and rounded the corner. Sam and Amanda were chuckling until they saw me, then their smiles faded. As did Greer's. I knew what they were thinking. *Oh, it's her.*

They did their best to ignore me as they passed.

Not Eve, though. She acknowledged me with a small wave and a "hey."

Cheyenne kept her eyes glued to the framed portraits on the wall opposite. Like, suddenly she found them extremely interesting. I'm sure partly because the girls had embarrassed her, but mostly because she knew she couldn't be seen consorting with the enemy.

Suddenly, something strange caught my eye. A sixth shadow reflecting in the glass of one of the portraits.

What was that?

After a moment of doubt and wonder, I shoved my book in my bag and followed. I had to know if I really saw what I think I saw…or if my mind was playing tricks on me.

I focused on the next portrait ahead. Watched the glass as they passed, clearly making out each of their reflections. Greer's top knot. Sam's ponytail. Amanda's waves. Cheyenne's braids. And Eve's shoulder-length cut and glasses. But then, just as I expected, following a few steps behind the rest of the group was a dark figure. From the shape and build, I could tell it was the same dark figure I'd seen in the window from the art room.

A panicked quiver began in the center of my chest.

As the group continued, their reflections moved between the glass panes, and I hoped to get a better look. To put a face to this entity lurking in the shadows of Evergreen. To confirm, once and for all, that it was my mother standing before me. But alas, there were no identifiable features to be had. It seemed that she too was just a shadow.

"What do you want?" I murmured to myself as I watched the glass.

The shadow figure stopped. Shocked, I did the same. Then she turned and faced her reflection. I could see now that her hair looked to be slick to her head and draped over her shoulders.

I stole a glance at the group of girls. They had to be a good twenty feet away now.

I faced the reflection again. "Why are you following them?" I whispered.

"What?" Amanda barked, startling me. They all stopped abruptly and spun around. "Do you have something to say to us?"

Crap! "No," I answered with wide eyes and an unassuming tone.

"Then who are you talking to, because I can hear you mumbling back there?"

Greer moved through the group, coming front and center. "She's probably talking to one of her friends that we can't see." Sam and Amanda joined Greer in a laugh.

Where did that come from?

"Where are they?" Greer reached out, slowly moving her arm back and forth as she scanned the area to my right. Then her gaze swept to my left, and she switched arms. "Or maybe they're over here?"

A sudden rush of ice-cold air passed through my body, hitting me so hard it took my breath away. My eyes flashed to the glass-covered portraits on the wall. The shadow figure was gone.

I turned my gaze to Greer again, and I saw it in her eyes. She felt something too. But she was trying to play it cool.

She fidgeted with the chain of her necklace. "Come on, girls, let's get out of here before she gets her freak on one of us."

I said nothing as they walked away. Because no matter what Greer said about me, I knew she was scared, and it was only a matter of time before she realized I was telling the truth.

At least a minute passed before I could move from where I stood. I was still in shock over what I saw in the glass. And that feeling that she'd passed right through me.

I shivered again.

The corridor sprang to life as students seeped from their dorms and after-school activities and funneled toward the cafeteria. I had to get away from the crowd.

Working against the flow, I made my way to the girls' bathroom to splash some water on my face and take a few minutes to catch my breath.

By the time I got to the cafeteria, the line had mostly cleared. The spaghetti and meatballs were gone, so my only choice was tuna casserole or a cold sandwich. I grabbed a plate of the casserole, a dinner roll, and a drink. Then picked up my tray and headed into the dining hall.

Immediately, the din quieted, and all eyes turned on me. The feeling of déjà vu hit me like a brick. It felt like my first day all over again.

After a moment of hesitation, I made my way through the room. The path before me widened as if some invisible plow cleared the way. Gawking eyes stared as I passed, igniting whispers and giggles in my wake. Some more obvious than others.

I cast a glance toward Will's table, hoping to find a friendly face, but his chair was empty. Of his friends, only Sean and Chase were looking my way. And neither were smiling. I saw compassion in their eyes.

I approached my usual table with Taylor, who, as always, had her face buried in a book. Feeling I'd reached a place of respite, I set down my tray, slumped into the chair, and sucked in a much-needed breath.

Without so much as a glance my way, Taylor picked up her things and left.

A loud burst of laughter erupted a few tables away.

My head snapped in that direction, eyes falling on Greer's table.

Greer's voice rose above them all. "Even Taylor won't sit with her," she cackled.

I felt a spark deep in my chest. The rage awakening, traveling through every nerve in my body like an electric current. The feeling was familiar, but at the same time, foreign. Like an old friend who'd drifted apart. But I knew one thing for certain, once the circuit was complete, the *other* Ronnie would be in control.

It was the *other* Ronnie who put me in this school. In fight or flight, *she* always chose fight.

I have to get out of here.

I stuffed my bottle of juice and dinner roll in my bag and jumped to my feet, wishing I could quietly slip away unnoticed. But no, my table was at the back wall, opposite the doors. Greer sat between me and my exit. She'd get to watch with full satisfaction as I fled.

The quickest way out was along the outer wall, which would take me within feet of her. It sucked, but it was my best option. As I passed, I threw a glare her way, pursing my lips and biting my tongue. *Someday you'll get what's coming to you—*

I'd barely finished my thought when…

Snap!

Then in quick succession came a buzzing and sparks, followed by a rattle. Just before the enormous chandelier fell from the ceiling, crashing down on Greer's table. All five of them ran screaming as gasps broke out around the room. Students jumped to their feet, some distancing themselves from the crash zone while others edged closer for inspection.

That's when I learned there was a third option: fight, flight…or freeze.

The next thing I knew, Joe was hovering over me, arms wide, making himself even bigger than usual. His mouth formed words that my ears couldn't hear.

Why couldn't I hear him? Why couldn't I blink, or turn away?

These were all thoughts that slowly moved through my brain while chaos erupted around me.

Finally, it was Dr. Swan's voice that broke through.

"Come with me," she said, throwing her arm around my shoulders and maneuvering me toward the door.

At the threshold, I stopped and looked back at the scene.

Joe worked to clear the surrounding area. "Be careful of the broken glass. Watch where you step."

"Leave your trays!" a kitchen lady advised. "We don't want to take any chances of someone swallowing a piece of glass." She helped Joe direct the students from the nearest tables, ushering them toward another lady in a white apron, standing near the center of the room.

That woman, in turn, kept the students moving toward the kitchen. "Go see Kathy, and she'll get you a new plate of food."

Mrs. Brown handled the rest of the room, pacing the aisle. "Everyone, please stay in your seats and finish your dinner while we take care of things."

Dr. Swan's hand pressed against my back, but I didn't budge.

"Where are they?" I asked, scanning the room again.

"Who?"

"Greer and her friends. They were sitting at that table," I answered, looking at their table again. It looked like a warzone: food scattered and spilled, mixed with broken dishes and crystal shards, and overturned chairs—all evidence of a quick getaway.

"They went with Mrs. Trumble to her office."

"Are they okay?" I hated that I cared. But I couldn't help thinking it was all my fault.

Chapter 18

As I lay in bed, staring up at the ceiling, my thoughts continued to race. All this time I'd been mad at *them* for everything that had been happening. For what they did. But how could I blame them when it's *my* mother doing these things? It was because of me she was angry, and now it seemed she was taking it out on everyone who was in the room that night.

I couldn't get the vision of her shadowy figure out of my head. The thought of my mother roaming aimlessly in the spirit world tore at my heart.

A shiver ran up and down my spine. I could still feel her presence.

I pulled the covers tight to my chin, but it did nothing to chase the chill away. A chill that was bone deep.

I had to find a way to talk to my mother. To tell her I was sorry and ask for her forgiveness. I didn't know if it would help, but I had to try something. What happened in the dining hall was proof she was more than capable of doing harm. She needed to be stopped.

I wiped at my watery eyes and rolled to my side, hoping sleep would claim me soon. That's when my thoughts turned to Will. I wished he'd been at dinner tonight. Maybe I wouldn't have felt so completely on my own.

****

It was sometime after one a.m. that I finally fell asleep, only to be woken an hour later to the sound of someone pacing the room. Moonlight shone in through a crack in the curtains. I could see fairly well. Enough to be sure that no one was in fact pacing my room. I lifted to my elbow and peered toward Amanda's bed. I needed someone else to witness this.

Her bed was empty.

Once again, I was alone.

I didn't get much sleep after that. It was in those early morning hours that I decided I needed to confide in someone about what had been happening around here. But who? Eve? Will? I'd already told Dr. Swan that I thought my mother was haunting me, and as expected, she didn't believe me. I was afraid if I said too much, she'd have me committed to an institution.

I know I'm not crazy.

I was actually grateful when the alarm on my clock went off at six thirty. I needed to get out of this room.

I showered and dressed quickly, then made my way downstairs and grabbed breakfast from the cafeteria.

As I entered the dining hall, the yellow caution tape caught my eye. While the destruction of last night's accident had been cleaned up—the broken table and chandelier removed—the area had been blocked off. Probably due to the gaping hole in the ceiling.

The atmosphere in the dining hall during breakfast hour was always more laid back compared to lunch and dinner. Students tended to straggle in, eat, and be on their way with minimal socialization. The average teen tended not to be a morning person.

"Good morning, Ronnie." Eve wasn't your average teen.

"Morning."

She pulled out the chair to my left and sat on the edge, facing me. "Crazy what happened last night, right?"

"Yeah," I answered, feeling my brow rise toward my hairline. *And you don't know the half of it.*

"Everybody's talking about it—it was so scary. I mean, one of us could've died, ya know?" Eve still looked truly scared. "How does something like that even happen?"

I swallowed hard, then turned in my seat. Our knees bumping, I leaned in close. "I think what's happening around here is because of the Ouija board."

"The Ouija board?" she repeated skeptically. "Are you serious?"

"Yes," I answered with determination.

"No." She flashed an uncomfortable smile. "You don't really believe in that stuff, do you?"

I pursed my lips and shrugged. "I didn't used to."

"Wow." Eve looked away and huffed. "I didn't believe Greer."

"What are you talking about?"

"Greer told me you were blaming her and the Ouija board for what's been happening around here, and I didn't believe her. But she's right. It's just a board game, Ronnie. Like Candy Land or Monopoly." Eve shook her head and scoffed, "Do you think *those* games are real—that you could end up stuck in Molasses Swamp or go to jail without passing Go?"

I turned my head to the side and snickered, rolling my eyes. "It's not the same thing."

"Listen, I'm still pissed about the whole Ouija board thing too. What they did really crossed a line. But think about what you're implying here," she said. "I mean, using a slab of wood to contact the dead…talk to spirits…that's insane."

"It is insane," I answered, staring off. "Although…" I started, with apprehension.

"Although, what?" Eve barked.

"Have you ever lost someone close to you?" I didn't wait for an answer. "Because I have, and I would give anything to talk to her again."

Eve grabbed my arm, concern filling her eyes. "But you know you can't really do that, right?"

I'm not so sure about that.

Eve must've picked up on my hesitation. She dropped her hand from my arm. "Ronnie, that stuff isn't real. It was just a game!" she said sternly, as she rose to her feet and looked down on me.

I struggled to keep my voice even. "But haven't you noticed that ever since that night there have been weird things going on around here?"

Her eyes widened. "What are you saying?"

"We're being haunted, Eve," I blurted. "They opened a door to the other side, and something came through."

And with that, Eve turned and stalked off.

****

Will never did show up for breakfast.

In third period Biology, I waited for him to come through the door. The seats around me filled as the minutes ticked by. He wasn't normally late for this class. My eyes moved to the clock, watching the second hand lurch closer to the twelve.

Three…two…one.

The bell rang.

“Okay class, quiet down. Let’s get started,” Mr. Erickson said as he got up from his desk. He moved toward the whiteboard and picked up a marker. “Yesterday we started talking about genetic engineering. Can anyone tell me one way…” His voice trailed off. I had other things on my mind.

Will’s roommate, Chase, sat at the table in front of me. I leaned forward and tapped his shoulder. Keeping my voice low, I said, “Hey, do you know where Will is?”

“Detention,” Chase whispered.

My brow wrinkled. “What! Why?”

The room quieted. I lifted my gaze toward the front of the room. Mr. Erickson’s eyes were on me.

“Sorry,” I blurted, sitting back in my seat.

Mr. Erickson turned toward the board again and began writing. Chase took the opportunity to push back in his chair, lifting the front legs off the ground and balancing there. I leaned toward him again, and he whispered over his shoulder. “Ask her.” He tipped his chin toward Eve, sitting across the aisle. “She was there.”

Eve was busy taking notes. She glanced up, meeting my stare. Her eyes widened blankly. She mouthed, “What?”

I shook my head and faced forward, picking up my pen as Mr. Erickson gave the room a cursory glance. And while I copied the notes from the board, my mind was elsewhere.

Why didn’t Eve tell me Will was in detention?

What could’ve happened to put him there?

After what seemed like the longest class on earth, the bell finally rang. Everyone started rising from their seats and gathering their things.

I shoved my notebook into my bag and got to my feet, meeting up with Eve in the aisle.

"You knew something happened with Will and you didn't tell me?" I know my tone was accusatory, but I didn't care. "What happened? Why is he in detention?"

"Well, I don't know exactly—"

"Chase said you were there."

"I was in the same room, but I wasn't a part of it," she answered as we made our way out of the classroom. "All I know is that Will and Adam started arguing, and then he yelled something at Greer, threw a chair, and stormed out of the room."

I stepped in front of her, looked into her eyes, and asked again. "And you have no idea what Will was mad about?"

I could tell by her hesitation that she knew more than she'd let on before. So, I cocked my head and held my stare.

After a couple of beats, she sighed. "Will overheard Adam repeating a rumor."

"What rumor?"

"About you," Eve answered with an apologetic look. "Greer was trying to make you look bad."

"Of course, she was," I said, rolling my eyes. "What was she saying?"

Eve looked around to be sure we were alone. "That you're a freak who claims to see ghosts and that she thinks you're dangerous, and that we should all keep our distance or else…"

My brow shot up. "Or else what?"

Eve pursed her lips. Her eyes flashed to the floor and back. "Or else we might end up like your mother."

That felt like a punch to the gut, knocking the wind out of me. Then a thought crossed my mind.

"Wait." My eyes narrowed. "When did it happen?"

"Yesterday. Last period. Before you and I talked," she answered in a rush. "And I swear I would never repeat what you said to me. I promise, Ronnie."

I felt the anger rising inside me until it came out as a growl. "Ugh, I can't stand her! Why does she have it out for me?"

"I told you," Eve said with a hint of frustration, "because she likes Will."

"But *he* doesn't like *her*," I argued, growling again as I spun around and started toward the cafeteria.

Eve appeared by my side again. "I'm sorry I didn't tell you about Will or the rumor. I just thought the whole thing was so stupid, and I didn't want to upset you."

While the sentiment was nice, I felt like it was an excuse.

As I picked up my pace, Eve fell behind.

I entered the cafeteria and blew past the line, reaching between bodies and blindly grabbing a cold, wrapped sandwich. I snatched a bag of chips and a water and ducked back out the door I'd come in. I was in no mood to deal with anyone right now.

I didn't mean to take my frustration out on Eve and walk away from her like that, but I was just so upset about Will. *What if he gets himself kicked out of Evergreen?*

Suddenly, it was like I was back at day one, roaming the empty halls. The feeling of loneliness surrounded me like storm clouds.

Dr. Swan's office door opened. "Oh, hi, Ronnie,"

she began as she stepped out. Her brow furrowed. "Is everything all right?"

Funny how that question seemed to unlock the tears. Hastily, I wiped them away.

"Yeah, I'm fine." I forced a tight-lipped smile.

She didn't look convinced. Noting the lunch in my hands, she asked, "Where are you headed?"

"I don't know, probably the library," I said with a shrug.

"Come on." Hitching her chin, she put her arm over my shoulders and directed me inside. "Let's chat while you eat your lunch."

Had it been anyone else, this simple act would've made things worse. But Dr. Swan had a way of comforting me.

"I was just about to grab my lunch from the kitchen," she said as she dragged a wooden chair to the front of her desk and gestured. "Have a seat, and I'll be right back."

I sat down, unwrapped my sandwich, and took a bite. My eyes gazed curiously over her desk. It was very tidy. Even the notes and scribbles on the large desk calendar were neatly organized. In the corner opposite her laptop was a framed picture of her and a guy. They were wearing helmets and life jackets and sitting in kayaks.

I'd finished half my sandwich by the time she returned, a plastic container in hand. A savory aroma followed her in.

She circled to her desk chair and set the container down. "Leftovers," she replied with a grin as she popped the lid.

"Is that your boyfriend?" I nudged my sandwich

toward the frame on her desk.

"It is. His name is Evan," Dr. Swan answered. Her eyes went to the picture, and she smiled. "That was my first time going extreme kayaking. He's big into that kind of stuff—basically anything involving danger." She laughed and shook her head. "Not me. But I'm trying to be braver."

"Did you like it?" I asked between bites. "The kayaking, I mean."

"Yeah, it was pretty fun. Have you ever been?"

"No."

"So, what's up?" she asked. "What had you so upset?"

I swallowed and heaved a sigh. "I don't know. I guess that…back home…if I was alone, it was because I wanted to be, and if I wanted company, I knew where to find it. But here…it's different." I took a deep breath and blew it out slowly. "And the one person I've come to rely on got himself thrown in detention," I said bitterly.

"Aaah, Will Tucker," Dr. Swan said with a nod. "I didn't realize you two were close."

I shrugged, looking toward the floor. "Yeah, I guess."

Dr. Swan sighed, pursing her lips. "Are there any girls you've been hanging around with? I thought I've seen you with Eve a couple of times. She's a good role model."

"Yeah, she's fine, but I don't like the rest of the group she hangs out with," I answered. One side of my nose twitched. "What's wrong with Will?"

"Well, he is in detention for throwing a chair," she answered with a reluctant expression. "He just has some behavior issues. He can be quick-tempered, and I worry the two of you together could be like fire and gasoline."

And just like that, I felt the threat of tears once again, fearing they would try to separate us.

"I'm sorry, Ronnie, I didn't mean to upset you," Dr. Swan said. "I'm glad he's been a good friend. Just promise me you'll make good choices and you'll be careful."

I chomped down on my lip to keep it steady and nodded. The last thing I wanted to do was argue with her; she was my safety net. But I didn't want to stay and talk any longer either.

I gathered my trash with both hands, rolling it into a ball and edging forward in my seat.

"I can take that for you." Dr. Swan extended her hand, and I passed it to her. The look on her face oozed sincerity. "Are we okay?"

"Yeah, we're good," I answered as I got to my feet. I shoved the chips in my bag and grabbed the bottle of water. "I think I need some time alone now, to do some thinking."

****

We still had about fifteen minutes of lunch period left, so there was no movement in the main corridor. The library was equally barren—just the way I liked it.

I went to my usual spot, slipped my bag off my shoulder, and lowered myself to the floor. Pulling my knees in close, I propped my arms on them and rested my head.

I didn't even want my music right now. I just wanted a few minutes of quiet.

And a few minutes was all I got.

Buzz. Buzz.

I lifted my head.

I had a strange feeling that I wasn't alone.

"Is someone here?"

The lights overhead dimmed briefly, buzzing again.

I tensed. *Was this my chance to talk to her?*

I didn't know what to say.

So I started rambling.

"Mom, is that you? I'm sorry for what happened—you have to know that. I would do anything to go back in time and change the course of that night. Anything." Tears pricked my eyes as I continued. "I miss you so much, and I want you to be at peace, but I don't know what it is that you want. You have to tell me. You have to give me a sign."

Bump! Bump!

Heart pounding, I got to my feet. I shouldered my bag and walked toward the front of the science and nature aisle. My eyes scanned the main room—from side to side, across the tables and chairs, and to the entrance.

No one was there.

Nothing looked out of place.

But then I heard it again along with another familiar sound. Just like a few nights ago. It was the sound of books sliding and moving on the metal shelves.

She's here.

I continued walking along the front, peeking down each aisle as I went.

"Where are you?" I asked. "What are you trying to tell me?"

A loud *thump* came from behind, and I rushed back to the last aisle.

A hardcover book lay face down in the middle of the floor.

It wasn't there a moment ago.

I stepped toward it, my hand shaking as I bent to pick it up.

I turned the book over. The author's name, Peg Kehret, was at the top in big red letters. And the title read: *I'm Not Who You Think I Am.*

I felt like I couldn't breathe.

Oh my God. I asked for a sign, and I got one.

Although *this* wasn't the sign I was looking for.

Suddenly, I was more afraid. If this spirit wasn't my mother…then who was it, and why was it here?

I dropped the book and spun toward the door, looking over my shoulder as I rushed out of the library. I felt the same quiver in my chest as when I was younger and would race up the basement stairs. I was always scared something was going to get me.

Coming to a stop in the middle of the corridor, I turned back and stared.

My mind raced. I had such mixed emotions.

While I was relieved it wasn't my mother, back from the dead to punish me, I couldn't help the feeling that I was losing her all over again.

Chapter 19

When I walked into art class, Eve was back at her place next to Amanda at the front of the room. She wouldn't even look my way. I feared I might have completely alienated her at this point.

Maybe she's afraid of me? I wouldn't blame her. I know what I said sounded crazy. And I wish with all my heart what I said wasn't true. But it was. Evergreen was undeniably haunted.

Even Amanda ignored me, and she usually didn't give up an opportunity to throw me a dirty look.

When class was over, I grabbed Eve before she left the room. I needed to know where I stood with her.

"Hey, are we still on for tennis this afternoon?"

"Yeah, sure," she answered with less enthusiasm than I was used to from her. "I have to change. Wanna meet by the first-floor bathrooms at four?"

"Sounds good," I replied with a smile, relieved she was still going to give me a chance.

****

At the end of the school day, I headed upstairs to change for tennis. Sam and Cheyenne were ahead of me. I heard bits of their conversation. They'd signed up for tennis too.

I sighed inwardly. *Of course.*

But I wasn't going to let them deter me. Sam and Cheyenne were the least of my worries. It was Greer and Amanda who seemed to be the biggest troublemakers. Besides, I was looking forward to getting outside and curious if I'd feel the woods calling to me again.

With a sudden yelp, Sam lurched forward on the stairs. Her books went flying. Her knees slammed the corner of the tread, and she caught herself with her hands.

I gathered Sam's things while Cheyenne helped her up.

Steady on her feet, Sam spun toward me. "Did you push me?"

"What?" My brow furrowed as I looked up at her from six or seven steps down. "I wasn't anywhere near you."

"She wasn't, Sam," Cheyenne added.

I went up the steps, closing the space between us, and offered Sam her things.

She swiped them out of my hands. "Well, it sure felt like someone pushed me."

I gave a half shrug. "I don't know what to say, but it sure wasn't me."

Sam harrumphed, giving me the side eye before turning back to Cheyenne.

Although, I bet I know who it was. I let my eyes wander.

Cheyenne convinced Sam to let it go, and they continued up the stairs.

We turned our separate ways at the midway landing, and I picked up the pace in hopes of getting in and out of my dorm room without running into Amanda.

Once in the room, I moved quickly, dropping my

bag on my bed and kicking off my black ankle boots before going to my dresser and pulling a pair of shorts from the third drawer. I changed out of my jeans and tossed them on the bed for later, along with my black crew socks.

Then I grabbed a pair of athletic socks from the top drawer, closed it, and slipped them on.

Opening the door to my closet, I snatched my sneakers from the floor and turned, bumping my arm on the open drawer.

“Ow!” I groaned, more out of surprise than pain. Weird. I could’ve sworn I’d closed it.

With one hand I gave it a shove, and it closed with a bang.

I sat down on the side of my bed, facing the door as I put my socks and sneakers on. A slight chill reminded me to grab a hoodie. So, as I slipped my bag over my shoulder, I turned back toward the closet.

And I stopped dead in my tracks.

The top drawer to my dresser was open. Again.

Apprehensively, I approached. I put one hand in the center of the draw and pushed. But the drawer wouldn’t budge. I let out a grumble and tried again with both hands. And it still wouldn’t move.

I’d never had a problem with these drawers before. Why now?

“Ugh, come on!” I wiggled the drawer up and down as I pushed. Everything inside bounced and shifted. Then I saw it. A flash of silver.

What the heck is that?

I reached in and pulled out a large-link silver bracelet. The bracelet had a heart charm and the letter G etched on it.

My throat constricted. "Oh my God!" The words tumbled from my lips with breathy horror.

This was a setup.

A knock at the door startled me. My head snapped toward it. Amanda wouldn't bother knocking. So, who was it?

"Just a second, I'm changing," I replied, reaching for a pocket. But my gym shorts didn't have any, so I stuffed the bracelet down my T-shirt and into my bra. I gave the drawer one last push, finally managing to get it to close.

With quick thinking, I tossed my bag back onto the bed, sat on the edge and slid my sneakers off.

"Come in," I said with one shoe in my hand.

The door opened.

Mrs. Brown stepped into the room. Behind her, standing in the hallway, were Greer and Mrs. Trumble. Greer normally stood tall, shoulders back, confident. Now she stood hunched with her arms crossed, hugging herself, while Mrs. Trumble held her with one arm and squeezed her close. Greer's body language said *victim*, but the look in her eye said *gotcha.*

We'll see about that, I mused.

"Good afternoon, Miss Campbell," the head mistress said in her usual always-means-business voice. "Sorry to bother you. This should only take a few minutes."

"What should only take a few minutes?" I asked, feigning surprise. Although the moment I saw that bracelet, I knew something like this would be coming. I continued the charade. "I don't want to be late for tennis," I said, propping my shoeless foot over the opposite knee and tugging my sneaker on for the second time in two minutes.

"Miss Hendriks, here," Mrs. Brown said, gesturing to Greer, "says her bracelet is missing and she has reason to believe it is in your possession."

My nose scrunched. I couldn't help it. "Why would she think I have her bracelet?" I snapped as I got to my feet. "Does she have some kind of evidence? Because this is ridiculous. She's had it out for me since the day I arrived." I looked past the head mistress, meeting Greer in the eye. "I don't have your stupid bracelet."

"Well, Miss Campbell, then you won't mind if we have a look around then, will you?" Mrs. Brown said.

I pursed my lips and waved my arm. "Have at it. But I can tell you right now that you aren't going to find it because I didn't take it."

With that, Mrs. Trumble stepped into the room. Greer began to follow, but I put my foot down.

"I don't want her in my room," I griped. "How do I know she's not going to try to plant something in here?"

Mrs. Brown eyed Greer and Greer fought back.

"Ugh," she groaned. "I can help. You don't know what you're looking for."

"I think they know what a bracelet looks like," I sneered, crossing my arms in front of my chest.

Mrs. Brown put a hand up, essentially holding Greer back, while Mrs. Trumble checked my side of the room, lifting and moving and opening things. I held a straight face when she searched the very drawer I'd found the bracelet in. Too bad Greer couldn't have done the same. She looked confused.

After a few minutes, Mrs. Brown put an end to it. Curling her fingers and addressing Mrs. Trumble,

"Thank you for your help, Shirley. I think we're done here."

"But what about my bracelet?" Greer asked in a rush. Seemingly desperate, she pointed toward my bed and insisted, "Check her bag!"

Mrs. Trumble stood in the center of the room and waited for direction from the head mistress.

Maybe I was feeling cocky. Or maybe I just wanted to make Greer look like a fool in front of Mrs. Brown.

"Here you go!" I snatched my bag and turned it upside down, dumping its contents all over the bed. I knew I had nothing to hide. "Are you happy? I don't have your bracelet!"

"Thank you, Miss Campbell, you've been more than accommodating. Sorry to have bothered you. You're free to go," Mrs. Brown said.

"Thanks," I replied as I scooped up my things, slid my bag over my shoulder, and grabbed a hoodie.

"Miss Hendriks, this is the second time you've made accusations against Miss Campbell," Mrs. Brown spoke extra sternly. "I think you owe her an apology. And next time…you better have proof before you go crying to Mrs. Trumble. Do I make myself clear?"

Whoa. This was both uncomfortable and very exciting to witness.

"Yes, Head Mistress," Greer answered with furrowed brow, before passing me a sidelong glance.

The air was thick with tension.

Mrs. Brown put one hand on her hip and with raised brow stared Greer down.

Finally, Greer met my gaze. Her nostrils flared, and the muscles in her face twitched. "I'm sorry…Veronica." She spoke through tight, hardened lips. It looked like it was physically painful for her to say those words.

I gave a nod, accepting her apology, then started for the door. "Hope you find your bracelet," I said, feeling like the smug one now.

Greer didn't budge from the doorway.

"This isn't over," she whispered as I squeezed past her.

"I think it is," I replied softly. I took a few steps down the hallway, then turned, continuing backward. "Oh, one more thing. It's Ronnie, and don't forget it." I smiled.

I rushed down the main stairs and found Eve pacing near the girls' restroom.

"There you are. I really have to pee," she said as she pushed through the swinging door.

I followed her into the bathroom and stayed by the sink while she went into a stall.

"I'm sorry I was late."

"That's okay. I just didn't want you to think I left without you," she answered from behind the stall door.

I looked around, assessing the room. I had to get rid of this bracelet.

There wasn't a lot to work with in this space.

The trash can under the sink, overflowing with paper towels, gave me an idea.

I grabbed one off the top.

"Yeah, I was late because the head mistress showed up at my door," I said as I carefully scooped the bracelet out of my bra and wadded it in the used paper towel. I continued talking to cover up any sounds while I worked to get rid of the evidence. "Greer accused me of taking her bracelet, so they came to search my room. Of course, they didn't find it because she's a liar, and now she's extra pissed because Mrs. Brown made her apologize."

"Oh wow. I bet that didn't go over well." It sounded like Eve was finishing up in the stall.

"It sure didn't." I moved away from the sinks and checked my work.

Perfect. I'd stashed the wrapped bracelet with the others on the floor between the trash can and the wall. It would look like it fell off when she washed her hands. At least that's what the staff would think when they found it. Greer would know better, but she couldn't say any different without making herself look guilty. Either way, I'd be off the hook.

The toilet flushed, and the stall door opened.

Eve went to the sink and washed her hands.

I offered her a stack of paper towels and smiled. "Ready?"

As we left the girls' restroom, I felt a weight lifted. I'd done it. I'd pulled it off.

Thinking back to finding the bracelet in my drawer, it seemed like I had help. Like maybe *somebody* wanted me to find it. And *somebody* wouldn't let me close the drawer until I had.

****

Nine kids showed up for the first day of tennis: seven girls and two boys. There were three courts.

Everyone got a chance to work one on one with Mr. Thomas on the first court. The rest of the students used the other two—either taking turns sitting out or all playing doubles. To be honest, none of us were particularly good, so we got tired pretty fast.

At one point, Eve and I teamed up against Sam and Cheyenne. I was surprised at how well it went. Not the game, but our interaction. Sam never even mentioned what happened on the stairs. I bet I had Cheyenne to thank for that. And I was surprised how different Sam was away from Greer and Amanda. She was even kind of funny.

As I watched her run around the court, laughing and making jokes with Cheyenne, I wondered if this could be the turning point in our relationship. Then Sam's bracelet caught my eye, reminding me of her allegiance, and not to get my hopes up.

After chasing yet another ball to the far corner of the court, I yanked at the neck of my T-shirt. I was sweating my butt off. I tossed the ball to Eve. It was her turn to serve.

"Aren't you hot?" I asked. She wore a long-sleeve shirt. Everyone else was in a T-shirt and shorts.

"No, I'm fine," Eve answered. Come to think of it, she always wore long sleeves. Maybe that's why I'd never noticed her wearing one of those bracelets Will told me about.

Now I would pay more attention. I was curious.

Eve raised the ball high into the air, preparing her serve. Her wrist peeked out, stretching beyond her sleeve. There definitely wasn't a bracelet on her left arm.

The ball sailed over the center net and bounced once.

Sam yelled, "Got it!" as she ran forward to meet it. He hit it with a little too much power and not a whole lot of technique. The ball made a swift and direct line right toward Eve's face.

"Watch out!"

The ball had barely made contact when we each voiced our shock.

"Oh my God! Are you all right?"

"Are you hurt?"

Bent at the waist, with her face buried in her hands, Eve responded with a moan.

Her glasses lay a good eight to ten feet away. I ran over and grabbed them. One of the lenses was shattered, and the frames were cracked at the bridge of the nose.

Mr. Thomas came running. The three of us backed off so he could talk to Eve.

"Can you tell me what hurts?" He put a hand on her back.

"My nose," she answered, still hiding her face.

"Can you show me? Is it bleeding?"

She groaned, moving her hands away slightly. "I'm not bleeding, but it really hurts."

"Okay, let's get you inside to see Mrs. Trumble—"

"I'll take her," Sam said eagerly.

"Thank you," he said, letting Sam replace him at Eve's side. Then, addressing everyone, he said, "I think we're going to pack it up and call it a day. It looks like it might start raining. So, if everyone can start gathering the equipment and help me bring it in, please."

Before Sam carted Eve off, I approached with her glasses. "Here, Eve. Sorry, they're pretty smashed up."

Eve raised her chin. "Oh, thanks, Ronnie."

Her eyes and nose were already beginning to swell. "Sure."

"Does it look bad?" she asked as she reached out. I might have been more transparent than I intended.

"Uh," I stuttered a moment while we held the glasses between us. I placed my other hand on her forearm, patted it, and lied. "No, I think after a little ice, you'll be fine."

"You think so?"

"Yes. Absolutely." I patted her arm again.

Suddenly, something clicked in my brain, and my gaze flashed down to my hand on her arm. Her right arm. There was no bracelet there either. Curious.

After Eve and Sam left, I joined the group in gathering the equipment. We had most everything picked up in just a few minutes.

As the first raindrops fell, several of the kids took off toward the gymnasium door.

"Did anyone get the balls that went over the fence?" Mr. Thomas asked.

"Probably not," answered one of the boys. "I'll get the ones on this side." He gestured behind him, to the area between the courts and the school.

"Great," Mr. Thomas said. "Grab 'em and get inside."

"I'll get the ones on the other side," I offered as I retrieved my belongings from the bench.

The rain began to pick up. I threw on my hoodie and slipped my bag over my shoulder.

"Thanks, Campbell," replied Mr. Thomas as he hoisted the bag of rackets over his shoulder and lifted the metal ball baskets. "Hurry up and meet us inside."

I exited the gate on the end and ran around the tall fence. The grassy area between the courts and the woods was maybe seventy-five feet, and I spotted three bright green tennis balls. Of course, they were all spread out.

With two in hand, I took off for the last. It was way out. Almost to the edge of the woods, and within feet of the Bear Forest Trail entrance.

Shaking my head, I wondered who the heck hit it out so far. But then something else distracted me.

That strange pull again. Something drawing me toward the woods. And the closer I got to the tree line, the more I felt it.

I tried to ignore it.

The rain was coming down in buckets. I had to ignore it.

So, I plucked the ball from the ground and turned toward the school.

But I couldn't bring myself to walk away. Even though my clothes were soaked through, and mud and water sloshed in my sneakers.

Without another thought, I shoved the balls in my bag, spun on my heel, and headed down the trail.

Chapter 20

The presence in the woods grew stronger with each step. As did a strange, high-pitched ringing in my ears. I plugged them with my fingers and gave them a wiggle. It did nothing to quiet the noise.

I knew it was *her.* And *she* wanted my attention.

As I turned my head, the noise seemed to get louder or softer, depending on the direction. So, I followed it like a game of Hot and Cold.

She led me off the trail, over fallen limbs, and through the underbrush. I stepped lightly through the bright green vegetation that poked up through the thick leaves and muck covering the forest floor. It was still early in the season—the new growth hadn't yet taken over.

I almost didn't notice it at first; it was covered in a green film. Luckily, I saw it before I stepped on it.

I bent and picked it up.

The ringing stopped.

I held in my hand a large-link silver bracelet with a heart charm. It had obviously been out here for some time, judging by the thick tarnish. I swiped my thumb over the face of the heart. It was tough to see, but it looked like two rounded humps, maybe from the initial E done in cursive.

This must be Eve's bracelet. She must have lost it out here.

Now it made sense—why I never noticed her wearing it. Although, I found it interesting that *this* was what the spirit had led me to.

Raising my gaze, I scanned the area around me. Nothing else stood out. So, I tucked the bracelet into an inner pocket in my bag and started making my way back to the trail.

I thought it would be cool to surprise Eve with her bracelet. First, I'd try to clean it up. I'd seen my mom use toothpaste to clean a silver ring once, so I'd give it a shot.

As I stepped out into the open, I realized how much I'd been protected from the downpour even though the canopy was still sparse with spring growth. I pulled my hoodie back over my head and took off running.

The gymnasium door opened.

"What are you doing out there, Campbell?" Mr. Thomas called out as I crossed the grassy area between us. He handed me a towel as I slowed to cross the threshold. "Good Lord, you've been out there a long time. I was ready to send out a search party."

"Sorry. I waited in the woods for a bit, hoping the rain would let up." I wiped my face with the towel, threw it over my shoulder, then reached in my bag and pulled out three green tennis balls. "Here you go."

"Thanks," he replied as he took them. "And good thinking. Now watch yourself. The floor is slippery when it's wet."

My sneakers squeaked on the high-gloss wood floor as I crossed the gymnasium to the main corridor. I was cold and wet and needed a hot shower before dinner.

When I opened my dorm room door, I came face-to-face with Amanda. She was on her way out.

We did the polite thing and ignored each other's existence. And as I stepped inside, she slithered past me and disappeared down the long hall.

I grabbed a clean set of clothes and my shower supplies and headed down to the bathroom. The showers were usually free this time of the day, so I knew I wouldn't have to wait.

Today was no different.

I went all the way to the back stall, stepped inside, and closed the frosted glass door behind me. The stalls were long and narrow, leaving plenty of room to dress in privacy. I set my stuff on the small bench at the front and hung my bag and towel on the hooks above.

The warm water felt good. I didn't want to get out. I closed my eyes and let it run over my face.

Then I heard it. Just like last time, it started with a knock.

But I had to be sure.

I crept toward the front of the stall, attempting to sneak a peek through the glass door.

"Hello?" My voice sounded odd to my own ears. Distant.

The sound of my own heartbeat drowned out the beating sound of the water raining down from the shower. But soon the ringing in my ears overtook both. And the lights began to dim as if the electricity couldn't keep up with a heavy draw.

I could feel it. She was back.

I grabbed my towel from the hook and covered myself.

I needed answers.

Taking a deep breath of courage, I asked, "Who's

there?"

No answer.

"What do you want from me?"

Squeeeaaaaak.

I stumbled back as a line appeared on the glass, as if drawn by a finger in the steam.

Down. Down. Across. Letters appeared, slow and stuttered.

HELP.

My mouth gaped open, letting the last of my oxygen escape as I stared in disbelief.

"H-how am I supposed to h-help you?" My words stuttered.

Breathlessly, I waited for a response.

"Hello?" I opened the stall door. "Are you still here?"

My gaze roamed the room.

Then a shadow moving across the mirrors over the sinks caught my eye. She was headed toward the door. But I couldn't follow her. I wasn't dressed.

I rushed out. "Please, don't leave."

It worked. She stopped and turned her face toward the mirror. I moved closer, so I too was standing in front of the mirror.

I felt as if our gazes met in the reflection, even though hers looked dark and hollow and one eye was partially hidden by her wet hair that clung to her face and scalp and draped her shoulders. Her hair might have been light brown or dirty blonde—it was hard to tell. She had a turned-up nose and a small mouth with full, pouty lips.

"Who are you?"

At that, she turned around as if to face me, and her

reflection in the mirror revealed that the back of her head was stained with blood.

My hand clamped over my mouth, locking in the scream that wanted out.

My stomach turned. And before I knew it, she was gone.

But our brief encounter left a mark on me.

I felt her pain.

I knew this wouldn't end until I helped her.

And one way or another, that's what I was going to do.

****

After dinner, I spent some time in the library, looking for books on the paranormal.

There were none. Not in the nonfiction section, anyway.

I thought about searching online for help on how to deal with this kind of thing. But since the school monitored our internet use, I decided against it.

I had one more idea.

What if I got ahold of the Ouija board...

No. Even the thought of it scared me.

It was close to nine o'clock by the time I headed upstairs. As I reached the second floor, a startling scream echoed from the north wing.

Two girls ran out of the common room and headed in that direction, while a few others watched from the doorway.

Frozen, I stood at the top of the stairs and observed.

Several girls, including Cheyenne, congregated outside the north wing bathroom.

Brandi ran out of her dorm room. "What's going

on?" she asked, rushing toward the girls.

Several answered at once, making it hard to understand what they were saying.

Cheyenne looked my way and caught me watching. After a quick glance back at the growing crowd, she headed toward me.

"What happened?" I asked. "Who was that screaming?"

Cheyenne kept her voice low. "It was Greer. I guess she was taking a shower and her hair started coming out by the handful."

My brow pinched. "Oh my God."

"Yeah. She's really freaking out." Cheyenne had a scared look on her face.

"Do you think someone did this to her?" I asked.

Cheyenne shook her head and shrugged. "I have no idea."

The bathroom door opened, and out walked Sam. She shook her head and grimaced. A moment later, Greer followed, a towel wrapped around her head and Brandi's arm wrapped around her shoulders. With Amanda on their heels, she cleared the threshold and took up Greer's other side, wrapping her arm around her friend and shielding her from onlookers.

Brandi held a protective arm out. "Let us through."

The crowd parted, and Brandi led Greer toward her own room.

The bathroom door opened again, and another girl rushed out, a shower caddy in her hand. "I've got your stuff, Greer," she announced.

"Thank you," Brandi answered with a look over her shoulder. "I'd like to have a look at it to be sure no one tampered with anything."

"Why would someone do this to me?" Greer cried dramatically.

A chill ran up my spine. I had a feeling my visitor from earlier had something to do with this.

And that *this* was just the beginning.

****

As I lay in bed that night, all I could think about was that poor girl.

Who was she? What happened to her?

And more importantly, *how was I going to help her?*

My entire knowledge base of ghosts and hauntings came from television and movies—probably not the most reliable.

Either way, I couldn't get her face out of my head. It was worse when I closed my eyes.

And then the strange dreams started.

I roamed the empty halls of Evergreen.

Where had everyone gone?

Everywhere I went—every door I opened—not one soul.

The only sound, a far-off tick-tick-tick, echoed from somewhere deep inside the school.

In the common room, a Monopoly board filled the center of a table. Stacks of pretend money and property cards lay arranged in front of each of the four chairs, and four small metal tokens were spread out across the board. The thimble sat in jail. Snacks and drinks also lay nearby. Amongst them was a half-eaten apple. It hadn't started to turn brown yet. The room looked as though everyone had just gotten up and walked away.

As I made my way down the stairs, the ticking got louder.

On the first floor, I found more of the same. Desolate rooms and offices left in various states of use.

I stood in the doorway of a classroom and looked in. The hands on the clock, hanging above the teacher's desk, pointed to 4:13. But the second hand was stuck, stuttering between the five and the six with each loud tick.

I went to the next room. The clock on the wall said 4:13, and the second hand couldn't move past the six.

Each room I went to, the clocks ticked loudly, but time stood still.

It was starting to scare me.

"Is anyone here?" I shouted at the top of my lungs. But it was as if my words had taken the long way. By the time they reached my own ears, they were barely above a whisper.

At the end of the corridor, I spun around and called out again, "Hello!"

Nothing.

But something caught my eye.

Wet footprints dotted the floor for as far as I could see. They were pointed in my direction. My gaze followed the path right to where I stood.

I stared down at my own feet; water puddled around them.

Confused, I studied my own body, eyes panning up. My legs looked too pale, slightly gray, and I was wearing a dress. I couldn't remember the last time I'd worn a dress. The fabric clung to my body, wet and dripping.

Slowly, I lifted my chin and caught a reflection in a pane of glass. I recognized her. But she wasn't me. Although every move I made, she did the same.

Suddenly, I couldn't breathe.

I began to choke and gasp for air. Never taking my eyes off the reflection, I watched in horror as water dribbled from her mouth and down her chin.

I woke with a start, gasping and choking. Clutching my chest, I rolled onto one elbow, and water spewed from my mouth and nose. My body trembled. Tears ran down my cheeks.

A groan and movement in the next bed startled me.

"Quiet, I'm trying to sleep," Amanda complained as she rolled over and pulled the covers over her head. "And turn the damn fan off. It's freezing in here."

I couldn't move. Fear had taken over.

I don't know what that was, but it wasn't a dream.

I think the ghost was trying to tell me something.

Chapter 21

The dream—if you could call it that—stayed with me throughout the next morning. As I moved from class to class, I couldn't help but picture the empty hallways and classrooms with the broken clocks, stuck at 4:13.

I was quite certain the ghost girl reaching out to me had drowned.

I'd felt the struggle myself.

What if I hadn't woken up when I did? A chill ran down my spine.

I walked into the science room, and as I took a seat at a table in the back, I caught a glimpse of Will coming through the door. I looked away before our eyes met.

I thought I'd be happy to see him, but something rumbled deep inside me, and I had no control. I was mad at him.

"Hey," he greeted as he approached the table and sat in the chair beside me.

I kept my eyes forward. "What's wrong with you? Are you trying to get yourself kicked out of Evergreen?"

"I was pissed off," Will barked.

My head jerked. I cut him a look. "You could've hurt someone!"

"I just wanted them to shut up." Will turned in his seat, glaring back. "You mean to tell me that you've never gotten so mad that you wanted to throw things?"

The image of Tori, covered in coffee and blood, popped in my head again. I had a feeling that vision would haunt me for the rest of my life.

I swallowed hard and faced forward again.

Anger turning to dismay, my voice softened. “Yes, but—”

“But what?” he asked with agitation.

“Ugh,” I sighed. “I don’t know. You just seem like you’ve got it together. I guess it surprised me that’s all. I didn’t expect you to do something as stupid as throwing a chair in a classroom—in front of a teacher no less.”

His eyes narrowed in hurt and disgust. “Are you saying I’m stupid?”

“No. I said what you *did* was stupid,” I answered hastily, pulling my gaze from him. He was infuriating. *Maybe he is the gasoline to my fire.* “And you don’t have to fight my battles for me,” I grumbled.

“That’s not what I—” He shook his head. Placing his elbows on the table, he pressed his mouth against his fisted hands and spoke into them with a breathy sigh. “Forget it.”

“No, I don’t want to forget it,” I argued. Something quivered deep in my chest, and I braved the gasoline once again. “I was really scared you were going to get kicked out of Evergreen. I want to know why you would risk everything because of Greer?”

“It wasn’t because of Greer. It was because of you!”

“What do you mean it was because of me?” I snapped curiously.

“Not here.” Will heaved a sigh, jumped up from his seat, and grabbed me by the wrist. “Come with me,” he ordered.

"Where are we going?" My feet moved fast to keep up as he dragged me behind.

"Somewhere we can talk in private."

We moved swiftly out of the room and down the hall. "We only have four minutes until the bell rings," I complained.

He ducked into the entryway to the gymnasium, stopping at the locked doors. Then swung me around, back to the wall, and released his grasp. The space—maybe three feet deep—hid us well.

I started talking before he could get a word out. "I'm sorry I complained to you about Greer. I wasn't saying I needed help with her. I was only venting—"

Will raised his hands, fingers tensed and splayed. "Oh my God, would you shut up."

My mouth snapped closed. I let him speak now.

"That's not what I meant," he spat. "I wasn't saying this was your fault."

"Oh," I answered, my tenacity along with my posture deflating.

Frustration eased from his expression, slowly turning to a smile. His eyes stared deep into mine, as though he was searching for an answer there. When he spoke again, his voice was much softer.

"I got involved because I like you. I was trying to protect you."

I think my heart stopped. I wasn't sure how to respond. Or if I even could. Because at the moment, I couldn't breathe.

Will's face turned red. He stuffed his hands in his pockets, straightening his arms and hunching his shoulders. It was clear his confidence was wavering.

"You get what I'm saying, right?"

"Umm." I licked my lips, then pressed them closed. My face felt hot. "I think so," I answered, smiling nervously.

Will leaned closer, raised one arm, and rested his hand on the wall above my shoulder. He stood so close that I could feel the warmth of his breath on my face. "I *really*…like you, Ronnie."

Is he going to kiss me?

My mind raced, thinking back to my very first kiss. It happened at a party last fall, with a boy named Garrett, when we were chosen for a round of Seven Minutes in Heaven.

It was a real let down.

The kiss was awful. Wet. Too much tongue. I've kissed a few boys since then, but mainly out of sheer boredom. Sadly, I've never felt a thing.

But now, as Will inched closer, my body began to tremble with nerves. The moment seemed to last forever—the anticipation brutal. Exciting.

Finally, he surrendered a smile. "You're such a brat," he joked, placing his other hand on my hip and touching his lips to mine.

The kiss was short and sweet—by far the best I'd ever had.

Because it was Will.

The bell rang, yanking us from the moment. He took a step back, cheeks flushed. Mine felt warm and red too.

"Oops, we missed last bell," he said with an awkward grin.

"Yeah." I pulled my bottom lip between my teeth and gazed up at him.

Will took my hand as we turned to head back to class.

It seemed we weren't the only ones who were late for class.

Greer watched from the corner.

Will and I stopped in our tracks. I didn't know about him, but I felt uneasy. It was something in her eyes—or maybe it was that something was missing. Like her unabashed confidence, or her normal look of contempt?

While she looked cute with the decorative scarf covering her head, I knew she wasn't wearing it by choice. And what was Greer without her long, bleached locks? Judging by her silent stare, I'd say *vulnerable.*

Something wavered in my belly. Was I feeling sorry for her?

"Let's go, people. Time to get to class." Joe was headed our way.

Without a word, Greer disappeared down the hall. She was out of sight by the time Will and I turned the corner, hurrying back to class.

All eyes were on us as we made our way to our table in the back. I didn't need a mirror to know my face was beet red.

And to make matters worse, Mr. Erickson had to make a comment. "Glad you two could join us." To which, everyone responded with snickers.

Everyone except Eve. She acted more interested in the textbook in front of her. She looked so different without her glasses. Or maybe it was the reddish-purple bruises under her eyes.

I had to admit I felt like, somehow, I'd let her down. From day one, she'd been trying to keep Will and me apart—supposedly for my own good. But here I was, running right into his arms.

Mr. Erickson began today's lesson, calling our attention to the board. But I couldn't think about nucleotides right now.

I felt myself blush again. *Will kissed me.* And at the moment, I didn't care about anything else. I didn't want to *think* about anything else. Not Eve or Greer, or any of those girls. Because I didn't want anything to bring down this feeling. Feelings I'd never felt before. An excitement different from any other. It was like Christmas morning and a fantasy theme park all wrapped up in one. And I couldn't wait to see what was next.

After an excruciating hour, the bell finally rang.

Will and I stayed close, exiting the room together. Once in the main corridor, he nudged me with his elbow.

"Sooo…you can see ghosts now, huh?" He flashed a silly grin, and I chuckled. Leave it to Will to make a joke.

I wasn't ready to tell him the truth, so I played along, shrugging with a closed-lip smile.

"If it came from Greer, then it must be true."

He laughed. "Good point. Well, I'm sorry I wasn't there for you. Chase told me it was quite a scene."

"Yeah."

"He said that chandelier falling on Greer's table was like, literally the best thing though," Will joked. "Chase said he never believed in karma before, but he does now."

I attempted a smile, but something he said distracted me. Here I'd been thinking I was the target, and the others were just in the way, but maybe I was wrong. Maybe I wasn't the target after all. And if this spirit haunting us wasn't my mother, then who was it, and who was it after?

Up ahead, I saw Dr. Swan standing in her doorway, watching over the crowd.

As I got closer, her gaze met mine, and she waved me over.

"Dr. Swan wants to see me. I'll catch up with you in a bit," I said to Will and stepped out of the flow of traffic.

"Do you have a minute?" she asked.

"Sure."

"I'm glad I caught you now," she said as I followed her inside.

I was nervous this was about me and Will. She'd surely seen us walking together.

"I won't be around this weekend." Going straight to her desk, she picked up a pad and pen and started jotting something down. "I'm going out of town for a wedding, so I wanted to give you my extension. You can call it from any phone in the building if you need me while I'm gone. I'll be forwarding all calls to my cell phone." She ripped the page from the pad and handed it to me.

I breathed a silent sigh of relief.

"Okay, thanks." I folded it and put it in my bag.

She cocked her head. "Are you getting enough sleep?"

I shook my head. "I haven't been sleeping well."

"If that continues, we can talk about some options, so let me know." She clapped her hands together. "Well, if there's nothing else…I'll let you get to class."

"Okay. Have fun at the wedding." I started for the door.

"Oh, one more thing," Dr. Swan blurted as I reached for the knob. I stopped and turned. "I wanted to let you know that you can call your dad on Sunday if you'd like." She smiled. "Can you believe it's been two weeks already?"

My chest tightened. It seemed like so much longer.

I flashed an apprehensive smile.

"No, I can't believe it," I said and slipped out the door.

Chapter 22

I had World History the last period of the day. It was a class I shared with Sam and Cheyenne. When the final bell rang, the room quickly cleared. A couple of boys and I remained, taking our time. I'd felt sluggish all day.

I was almost to the door when Mr. Thomas stopped me. He was toward the back of the room, straightening desks.

"It looks like Cheyenne left her sweatshirt," he said, bringing it forward. "Could you make sure she gets it? I wouldn't want her to go the weekend without."

I took the sweatshirt and went directly up to her room.

I didn't come to the north wing often; it was Greer's territory. And seeing as her room was directly across the hall, I knocked softly.

Cheyenne opened the door. She seemed surprised to see *me* standing there. "Hey, what's up?"

"You forgot this in Mr. Thomas's room," I said, handing her the sweatshirt.

"Oh, thanks." She took a step back, opening the door wider. "Wanna come in? Sam's not here—I'm just hanging out."

"Um, okay." I stepped inside, and Cheyenne closed the door.

Their room was cute. Decorative pillows and throws adorned both beds, along with faux fur area rugs, and an oversized bean bag chair in the corner. And with the splashes of turquoise and fuchsia, the pea green walls were hardly noticeable.

It looked comfortable and lived in. Basically, the complete opposite of our dorm room—which looked more like a morgue. Now that I thought of it, I seemed to recall Eve and Greer's room being nicely decorated as well. It must be nice to be friends with your roommate and want to spend time in your own room.

"So…" Cheyenne began awkwardly. "How's it going?"

I shrugged, pulling my mouth to one side. "It's going." Neither of us were good at small talk.

Cheyenne plopped down on her bed, one leg bent and the other hanging off the side. She pressed her lips together and lowered her eyes as she picked at her peeling nail polish. "Can I ask you something honestly?"

"Yeah, sure," I answered and sat at the foot of her bed, mirroring her position.

"What have you…*seen*?" she asked, arching her brow and putting extra emphasis on the last word.

I was pretty sure I knew what she was getting at. But I wasn't sure why.

After a moment of hesitation, she elaborated. "Because weird things have been happening and…" She paused with a sigh. Then shook her head. "I don't know really. But things haven't felt the same since *that night*, and I don't know how to explain it."

I pursed my lips and exhaled. "You don't know how relieved I am to hear that someone else sees it too."

Cheyenne's eyes widened. "I mean, I thought I was going crazy. I swear every morning when I wake up, things have been moved around. Little things. Like, a pillow on the floor across the room or stuff on our dressers getting rearranged. Or Sam's pictures hanging on her mirror," she added hastily. "Every morning, at least one of them is on the floor."

"What does Sam say about it?" I asked.

"Well, the first time it happened, she was sure it was you messing with us," Cheyenne answered. "Now she blows it off—has an excuse for everything. Like, she just needs to get more tape to hang her pictures or that she probably forgot to shut a drawer or that she had used something else and not put it back in the same place." Her tone sharpened. "I'm sorry, but you don't need a piece of tape to keep your picture from falling off the mirror and landing six feet away. You need a goddamn exorcist."

I chuckled, partly at Cheyenne's extreme idea for a fix, but also because the thought made me uncomfortable. It was a little too real. But it also brought up the idea again.

"Do you know what happened with the Ouija board? Like, where it is now?" I asked.

"I'm not sure. All I know is that Greer brought it from home that same day. She showed us right before she sent Sam to get you and Eve. She had it hidden in a Risk game box so she wouldn't get caught bringing it into the school." Cheyenne fussed with her braids, bringing them forward over her shoulder. "The next day, I overheard Sam telling Greer that she better get rid of it before Brandi or Trumble found it. Sam was worried we'd all get in trouble. She said she'd be pissed if anyone got kicked out because of it." She shook her head. "Anyway, I haven't seen it since that night."

"Although Greer hasn't left the school since then, has she?" I didn't wait for an answer. "So, it's probably still here somewhere."

"Yeah, probably. But…" Cheyenne cocked her head, lowered her brow. "You're not thinking about using it again, are you?"

"No," I lied, glancing toward the door. Truth was, I still hadn't ruled it out. Even though I knew getting ahold of that thing was a terrible idea. I thought I could use it to figure out who the spirit haunting us was, or what it wanted, or maybe just send it back.

Cheyenne was quiet a moment, watching me. Reading me. I felt it out of the corner of my eye.

"You've seen a lot more than the rest of us, haven't you?" Concern filled her voice. Apparently, my poker face wasn't as good as it used to be. "You're…actually scared."

I briefly met her gaze. I didn't like this feeling of vulnerability.

I heaved a sigh as I stood and paced casually, looking everywhere but at Cheyenne. "If only I could figure out how to help—" I stopped short as something caught my eye.

In two steps I rushed to the dresser with the pictures tacked around the outer edge of the mirror—the pictures Cheyenne had been talking about. I yanked one down. It was a group photo.

"What are you doing?" Cheyenne asked, suddenly by my side.

"This picture…" I couldn't put my words together.

I couldn't take my eyes off it. Greer, Eve, Sam, and Amanda posing in front of the tiger exhibit at the local zoo. But there was a fifth girl in the picture. "Who is that?" I asked, pointing to the girl with the turned-up nose.

"That's Molly," Cheyenne answered. "I never met her. She left just before I came to this school. Why?"

"That's her." I stared in shock. Now it all made sense. The board wasn't spelling out *mom*. It was spelling *Molly*!

"What are you talking about? That's who?"

I lifted my eyes to meet Cheyenne's, my entire body breaking out in goose bumps.

"Molly didn't just run away…she's dead."

"No. No, no, no," Cheyenne repeated, shaking her head. Her eyes were the size of saucers. "You don't mean—"

I nodded. "Most of the time she's only been a shadow—a silhouette. But last night…I saw her face in the mirror after my shower. Right after she asked me for help."

"Holy shit. I don't want to hear any more." Cheyenne closed her eyes and covered her ears. She rocked back and forth.

"Okay, okay." I patted Cheyenne's shoulder. She lowered her hands and looked up at me with dread in her eyes.

"I'm sorry, Ronnie. I thought I could handle it, but…I just can't," she said, shaking her head. "Not right now."

I completely understood. It's one thing to look at something out of place and wonder how it got there. It's entirely different to learn that the *how* has a face. An identity. And it—strike that—*she* was reaching out from the other side. Communicating.

I turned back to the dresser and raised the photograph in my hand, giving it one last look before returning it. They were all flashing the "I love you" sign. Molly's head was cocked to one side. She gave a tight-lipped grin, showing a bit of attitude.

I gazed into her eyes. *What happened to you?*

It was strange how deeply I felt the loss of a girl I'd never met.

I stuck the picture back on Sam's mirror and turned. "Maybe you shouldn't say anything about this."

"I agree," Cheyenne replied. "This is huge."

"Yeah, I need to see if I can find some sort of proof, before we alert anyone." My head was suddenly swimming. I started for the door. "I've gotta go. Take care, okay. And let me know if anything else happens."

I left Cheyenne's room and took off for my own. I felt a weight on my shoulders. This *was* huge. There were so many questions that needed answers.

Did she really run away, or was it assumed?

How did she die?

Was it an accident, or did someone kill her?

And even more worrying...where is her body?

By the time I got to my room, I felt nauseous. At least Amanda wasn't around. I needed to lie down for a little while. I hung my bag on the doorknob of my closet and slipped off my shoes.

Thunk.

My bag lay in a pile on the floor.

I picked it up and hung it on the knob again, taking care to be sure it WAS secure this time before walking away.

Turning toward my bed, I heard it again.

Thunk.

I spun around and stared down my bag and some of its contents sprawled across the floor.

"What the heck?" I whispered to myself as I bent. I was starting to have that feeling again. Like I wasn't entirely alone.

My eyes roamed the room as I gathered my belongings: my iPod, a couple of pens, a lip balm. As my fingers grazed the last object, darkness blurred the edges of my vision. I stumbled to my knees and steadied myself on all fours as a memory flickered across my mind.

Everything around me was dull and gray. From the bare, leafless trees to the hard-packed dirt beneath my feet. The only sound, my own breath rasping in my ears as I moved at a brisk pace. My chest felt heavy.

I came to a stop and swiped tears from my eyes with the back of my hand.

Then I looked down at a silver bracelet on my wrist.

Anger filled me.

I yanked it off and threw it deep into the woods and took off down the path again.

I startled back to the here and now.

My fingers curled around the silver bracelet I'd found in the woods, and I realized what I'd just witnessed was not my own memory. It was a clue from Molly.

With the bracelet in hand, I grabbed my toiletry bag and headed for the bathroom.

Under the running water, I worked all the loose crud and dirt free. It wasn't enough to make out the initial etched on the heart. So, I coated it in a thick layer of toothpaste.

The bathroom door opened, startling me. A girl from down the hall walked in and went to a stall.

I grabbed a washcloth from the shelf and covered the bracelet. It needed a few minutes to sit anyway.

I was brushing my hair when the girl came out of the stall.

"Hey," she greeted as she stepped up to the sink next to me.

"Hey," I returned.

My shoulders relaxed, and I breathed a sigh of relief when I was alone again.

Hunched over the basin, I used the washcloth to rub and polish the heart charm. The toothpaste looked like it was actually working. And after a few short minutes, I had my answer.

It was so unexpected it took my breath away.

I stared down at the M etched into the silver while my heart pounded, and I pondered the significance.

A shadow in my peripheral captured my attention, and my gaze flashed to the mirror in front of me.

Molly stood over my right shoulder.

My gaze met hers in the reflection, and for one long moment, we just…were. Two broken schoolgirls sharing sadness and longing without speaking a word.

Finally, she reached up and put her hand on my shoulder. Though the touch felt cold, a warm rush ran through my body. Overwhelmed with the feeling of love and understanding, my eyes fell shut.

And when I opened them, she was gone.

I stood there for several minutes, staring at my own reflection in the mirror as I processed what had just happened.

Then, like a shot of adrenaline to the system, I moved into action. Concealing the bracelet in the washcloth, I rushed back to my room. I tossed my toiletry bag on my dresser and scooped my bag off the floor, tucking the folded washcloth in a zipped pocket for safety.

Shouldering my bag, I left my room and made my way down to the main corridor.

The weather was nice. I thought I remembered hearing the boys talking about going outside to play basketball after school.

Joe, the daytime security guard, was sitting at his station behind the glass.

He looked up from the screens. "Where ya headed?"

"Basketball courts," I answered nonchalantly.

He made a note on his clipboard and waved me on.

As I walked across the grass, I could see four boys on the court and three more sitting on the nearby bench. I couldn't make out the faces until I got closer. Jeremy, one of the boys' dorm leaders, was teamed up with Sean, playing against Damian and Robert. Will, Chase, and Drew watched from the sideline.

Chase saw me first and elbowed Will to get his attention.

Will saw me and smiled. He jumped to his feet and came over to greet me. "Hey, what's up? Did you come to watch?"

I couldn't help but smile back. I loved the warm greeting. "Um, actually." I hesitated. "I was wondering if I could talk to you alone?"

"Uh, sure." He looked over his shoulder and waved

to Chase. "I'll be right back."

Chase gave him a thumbs-up.

Will led me toward a couple of trees at least fifty feet away. With plenty of distance and a bit of cover, Will finally said, "It sounds serious. Is everything all right?"

I wasn't sure how to answer that. Everything wasn't exactly all right. I had to take a second to choose my words carefully.

"You know you can tell me anything," he coaxed gently, putting his hand on my arm.

"I know," I answered. "But what I really need is to *ask* you something." His brow cinched. "And you can't ask why," I added.

"Okay." He flashed a skeptical sideways glance.

"What do you know about Molly's disappearance?"

"I don't understand." He was visibly taken aback.

"It's important." I stared into his eyes. "Was she upset about something? Did she let on that she wanted to leave?"

"Umm," he hummed, pressing his lips together. He gave a half shrug and let his eyes wander as he considered my question. "I mean, she and her crew were going at it the last few days, but I don't know. She didn't say anything to me about wanting to leave. I thought she was pretty happy here."

"Do you know what they were fighting about?"

"No," he answered definitively. "I asked her several times, but she wouldn't tell me."

"Had they fought like that before?"

"Not that I saw."

"So what was going on the day she disappeared?" I

asked again.

"I don't understand why all the questions about Molly."

"I told you that you couldn't ask why."

"Okay," he said with a sigh. Will ran a hand through his hair. "Uhhh, it was a Saturday…and she'd gone home for one of her sister's birthday party. She came back late in the afternoon and as far as I know, she was gone again before dinner."

"Did she leave a note or tell anyone she was leaving?"

"Not that I know of—"

"Will!" someone called out.

Will peered around the tree.

Chase was walking our way, the basketball propped between his hip and arm. "Dude, we're up!"

"Okay, I'll be right there," Will answered, holding up a finger. Then to me, he said, "I've gotta go. Talk more at dinner?"

"Sure," I replied, and he took off.

I watched as Will half-jogged across the grassy field, meeting up with Chase and playfully stealing the ball away. The two continued to laugh and wrestle for the ball as they made their way back to the others.

I loved Will's light-hearted nature. Even with this heaviness hanging over me, he made me smile. If only he knew.

I lowered myself to the base of the tree, where I had full view of the court. I didn't really care about the game itself; I just didn't want to be alone right now, and I enjoyed watching Will with his friends. I envied their friendship. It always seemed so much easier for guys.

My mind wandered to the girls.

Will said they had been fighting.

Could they have been trying to run her out of the school? I wouldn't put it past Greer. She'd threatened me on more than one occasion. Could it have gotten violent?

Of course, there was always the possibility that it didn't have anything to do them.

Will said she had just gotten back from a family visit.

Did something happen at home to upset her enough to do something drastic? Could she have done something to hurt herself? Or maybe she was truly trying to run away and there was an accident.

Whatever the case, I felt she had to be close.

Chapter 23

Dinner with Will didn't offer any new information regarding Molly. He had already told me what he'd remembered, and the dining hall wasn't the place to push any further. So, I decided to let it go for now and enjoy my time with Will and his friends.

I didn't talk much. It was more fun listening to their banter.

Slowly, the crowd around us thinned, until only Will and I remained. I felt like we could talk forever. We had already discussed our favorite music, TV shows, and places to eat. And we'd realized both our birthdays were in November; his was the third and mine was the twenty-first, so for eighteen whole days, he was a year older than me.

"What's your biggest pet peeve?" I asked.

"Umm, when someone tells me to calm down," he answered. "I will literally lose it."

"Yeah, same here. Another thing I absolutely hate is when someone says something rude or insulting and then says, 'no offense' or 'I'm just being honest.' It's like, no, you're just being mean."

"Ugh, I hate people like that."

I noticed a lady from the kitchen was gathering tablecloths and straightening chairs. I felt weird sitting there while she worked around us.

"Maybe we should help her."

Will's lip curled. "Seriously?"

I cocked my head.

His shoulders fell. "Fine."

We started on the opposite side of the room. We might not have been as proficient as she was, but I could tell by her smile that she appreciated our help.

"Where do you want these?" I asked as I approached with a load of dirty tablecloths.

"You can add them to pile," she replied, pointing. "Thank you so much. You kids have been a great help."

I threw them on top of her pile. "Anything else you need help with?"

"Not that I can think of. Thanks for asking though."

Will and I made our way out of the dining hall. As we passed through the double doors, the backs of our hands brushed.

I didn't make an effort to pull away.

Neither did Will.

After a couple of steps, he reached out with his pinky and hooked mine. It sent a hot rush up my arm and directly to my face. I felt it in my cheeks as I tried not to smile too hard.

"Sooo, are you going to tell me why all the questions about Molly?"

I kept my eyes to the floor in front of me.

"There's really not much I can say…" That was the truth. I'd given it a lot of thought. I'd even considered going to one of the security guards or calling the police myself. But how would that go?

Hey, I have reason to believe that this girl I've never even met is dead. I don't have a body, a weapon, or motive. Just the word of her ghost. Oh, and a bracelet I found in the woods.

We came to a set of chairs, and Will stopped, gesturing for us to sit. And since I wasn't ready to be alone yet tonight, I did. Even though I knew I'd have to offer up a little more information in an attempt to appease his curiosity.

"I can't really explain, but…" I sighed, meeting his gaze. "I just have a strange feeling that something happened to her. That maybe she didn't run away like everyone thinks."

Will's eyes narrowed. "What do you mean 'something happened to her'? Do you think she's in danger or something?" he asked frantically.

"I don't know," I answered hastily, my chest tightening. *How can I be jealous of a dead girl?* I shook it off. There were more important things to focus on. Now was not the time to be selfish. "But I think whatever happened might have been impulsive. Like, I don't think she'd necessarily been planning on leaving." I reached in and unzipped the compartment in my bag. "Also, I found this," I said, pulling out the washcloth and inconspicuously revealing what was inside.

Will leaned in, inspecting the charm. The lines in his face drew heavy. "Where did you find that?"

"In the woods off the Bear Forest Trail." I covered it back up and returned it to my bag. "I had to clean it up some in order to read the initial."

After a second, Will relaxed, sitting back in his seat. He waved his hands in disregard, and his mouth pulled to one side. "Well, like I said, they had been fighting. So, I'm not surprised she tossed it. She was pretty pissed at them."

"But what if they did something to her?"

"Like what?" Will pulled his head back, tucking his chin. "What are you trying to say?"

"Greer has threatened *me* before," I answered sharply.

"But with physical harm?" he asked, shaking his head. "I don't think that's her style."

"I don't know what they're capable of." I heaved a sigh and let my eyes fall shut. Then, in a calmer voice, I said, "Look, all I'm saying is that I think there's a chance someone knows more than they've let on." I shifted to rise out of the chair.

Will put his hand out. "Don't go, yet. I'm sorry."

I rested on the front edge of the chair. "There's nothing to be sorry for." My lips pulled into a tight, straight line. "I know I sound crazy. I probably shouldn't have said anything."

Will reached for my hand. "You don't sound crazy. If anything, it's sweet that you're concerned."

"Gag," I joked.

Will smiled, his nose scrunched. "Too sappy?"

"Just a little." We both laughed. I was relieved that the heaviness of that conversation didn't completely ruin the night.

I settled back in the chair.

We hung out there for over an hour, chatting and watching people come and go. I couldn't believe it. For the first time I felt comfortable in my surroundings. Ghost notwithstanding.

I guess, up until now, I always felt like I was supposed to be confined to the dorms if I wasn't in class or some other scheduled activity. Every time I hid out in the library, I worried I'd get in trouble.

But we even saw Kerry come in and wave to us before going up to the dorms.

It was awesome.

Around nine p.m. the nighttime security guard arrived to relieve Joe. They stood in the doorway of the small room. After a few minutes of friendly exchanges, Joe handed over the clipboard and began running through a list with the other guy.

Distracted, I listened in.

"We've got a couple lights out. One in the boys' wing and the other down near the classrooms," he said, gesturing with a wave in that direction. "I reported them to maintenance. They're also going to check the lock on the emergency exit in the dining hall. It doesn't seem to be latching properly, so I had to disable the alarm. It kept going off."

Will and I flashed a glance to each other, raising our brows. I wondered if we should be listening.

"Those cameras still glitching?" the night guard asked.

"Yeah at least once or twice a day, one camera at a time will go out for a bit and then come back on," Joe answered, and they redirected their attention to the monitors. From where I sat, I had a view of the upper half of the screens through the security glass. Other than the light they threw off, I couldn't see much of what was on them. I was too far away.

"Strange," the other man groaned.

Joe nodded. "Yeah. It doesn't look like anyone is tampering with them—just some sort of short or something. Probably have to call the IT guy to come out and look at it if it keeps happening. But for now, just log it when it happens," he said and walked out of the office.

"You got it," the night guard answered as he pulled out the chair. "Have a good weekend!"

"You too." Joe turned toward Will and me and waved. "See ya Monday!"

"See ya!" Will replied.

I smiled and waved back.

"He's so nice."

"Joe?" Will glanced back to Joe as he disappeared around the corner. "Yeah, he's pretty cool. As long as you're straight with him."

"Oh yeah?" I smiled. "Have you ever been on his wrong side?"

Will shrugged. "Maybe," he answered with a devious smile and a glint in his eye. Damn, he was cute. I looked away, chuckling at his boyish charm.

That's when the shadow caught my eye. It moved across the window of the security office.

On the other side of the window, the guard looked up from his paperwork. Although it seemed it wasn't the shadow that had drawn his attention, but something on one of the screens in front of him. Or should I say the lack of something on the screen. One of the cameras had gone dark.

He tapped the screen with his finger.

"Damn thing starting already," he mumbled, shaking his head.

He rose from his seat and stepped out of the office. From where he stood, he scanned up the corridor and down, his eyes moving right past us. Then he looked back at the monitor. It flickered with squiggly lines for a second before returning to normal.

He heaved a loud sigh and went back to his seat.

The hair on the arms stood on end. *She's here.*

I didn't want her anywhere near Will.

"Well, I think I'll head up to my room now," I said as I got to my feet.

"Okay." Will stood. "It's been nice, uh, hanging out and stuff." He moved awkwardly. Like he wasn't sure if he was supposed to walk me to the stairs or something.

I brushed the hair from my face and smiled. "It was nice. I hope we can do it again soon."

Will glanced toward the office, checking on the guard, who was busy writing in the log. Then he turned back to me, leaned in, and planted his lips on mine. His lips were soft and warm, and gone much too quickly.

"Good night," he whispered in a breathy tone as he pulled away.

"Good night." I smiled, caught up in the moment until…

The pendant light over Will's shoulder began to sway, hurtling me back to reality. *Molly.*

A lump the size of my fist lodged in my throat as I stared into Will's eyes. What if our kiss made her mad? I didn't want her to hurt him. I had to draw her away.

"See ya tomorrow." I spun around and headed toward the main stairs.

When I got to the midway landing, I stopped and pulled out the bracelet again. "If you ever want this back, you better follow me," I said, just above a whisper, for only Molly to hear.

Creak.

My head snapped back toward the first-floor landing.

Then again. *Creak.*

My heart pounded hard in my chest. It was working.

I felt Molly's presence right behind me, heard the creaking of the floorboards as she followed me to my room.

Her presence felt stronger than it had in the past.

As I reached out to open the door, I heard voices on the other side. I was surprised to find Amanda and Sam hanging out in our room. They were lying side-by-side on her bed, looking at a magazine. With their heads toward the foot of the bed, they rested on their elbows, feet swaying in the air behind them.

They both looked up briefly, then went back to what they were doing. I breathed a little easier. Only a little though. I still had Molly to deal with. And I was concerned she'd cause a scene.

I clutched the bracelet tighter, hiding my hand, as I turned my back on the girls and carefully closed the door. Nervously, I crossed to my closet and kicked off my black ankle boots.

Then, with a quick look over my shoulder to be sure they weren't watching, I tucked the bracelet in the pocket of my jacket hanging amongst some other things—for now, it seemed safer than my bag. While they were preoccupied, I changed from jeans to shorts, grabbed my iPod from my bag, then hung the bag on a hook in the closet and closed the door.

As I turned toward my bed, I noticed a slight movement of the ceiling fan. My eyes flashed to the switches on the wall by the door. Both were down, in the off position. My body tensed, and my gaze moved back to the fan, which now spun as if it were on high.

"What's up with that stupid thing?" Amanda

complained, sitting up and eyeing the fan from her bed directly below.

Sam sat up and rubbed her bare arms. “Turn it off.”

“It is off,” I answered and rushed to the switch anyway, flicking it up and down several times.

But it only spun faster. Well beyond the highest speed possible, it whirred like an airplane propeller.

My eyes shifted to the girls and back. It spun so fast the entire fixture wobbled, and I feared it might come loose.

“Watch out,” I shouted over the whirring and knocking.

Sam and Amanda sprang off the bed and pressed themselves against the wall.

Pieces of plaster fell from the ceiling. I jumped onto Amanda’s bed and grabbed the swaying pull chain, pulling it once and hopping to the floor.

Finally, it began to slow. The room to quiet.

“Holy crap!” Sam muttered in astonishment.

I moved back to my side of the room and plopped down on my bed, back resting against the headboard. As I unwound the cord of my earbuds from my iPod, my gaze met Amanda’s. From her shifty eyes to her awkward body language, I could tell she wanted to say something.

But she didn’t. And that was okay because I could tell her attitude toward me was changing. Same with Sam. I’d gotten the impression over the last couple of days that she’d gone from intense hatred to a mild indifference toward me.

“Um, I think I’m going to head back to my room now,” Sam said, grabbing the magazine off the bed.

“I’ll come with you,” Amanda replied.

Alone in my room, I covered my face with my hands. I felt tears bubbling to the surface. This was all too much. I couldn't take it anymore. How was I supposed to make friends with the living when I was busy dealing with the dead?

I had to end this.

I lowered my hands and scanned the room. Jaw clenched, my chest heaving as I inhaled. "Either tell me what you want or leave me alone," I cried.

My heartbeat echoed in my ears.

"I want to go home." I heard the whisper close to my ear. Felt her frosty breath.

Sitting stock-still, I looked out of the corner of my eye. I could feel her lingering close.

"O-k-kay," I stuttered.

Then she whispered again. "Help me. I'm just so cold."

My breath hitched. "Where are you?"

I waited several minutes, but she never answered. She was gone. I was sure of it.

I leapt off the bed, slipped into my slides, and ran out the door.

As I rounded the corner at the end of the hall, I saw Eve step out of the common room. *Just who I was looking for.*

I picked up my pace and called out her name, "Eve."

She stopped and turned my way, waiting in place until I caught up.

"I was hoping to find you," I said, taking a breath after my short jaunt. Her bruises were looking shinier and more colorful today.

She must have known what I was thinking, because

she said, “Looks worse than it feels.”

“Oh, well, that’s good I guess.” My brow rose to a pinch at the center.

“What’s up?” she prodded.

Standing at the threshold of the common room, I glanced inside and didn’t see anyone. So, I went for it. “I need to talk to you about Molly.”

With furrowed brow, Eve gave me an uncertain look. “Why? What about her?”

“What do you remember about the day she disappeared? Did she say anything to you about being upset or wanting to leave?”

“Um.” Eve shook her head, pulling it back. I’d clearly caught her off guard.

“Do you know where she was last seen?” I added, hoping she knew something. Anything.

She eyed me quietly. Hesitantly. “I don’t understand. Why all the questions?” Eve’s gaze left mine, drifting to the side and her chin following with a look over her shoulder.

“Because I don’t think she ran away,” I answered. “I think she’s—”

Greer appeared behind Eve in the doorway of the common room.

“You think she’s what?” She didn’t wait for an answer, her lip curled. She leveled her stare. “What would *you* know about Molly? You never even met her.”

I released a long tense breath.

“Forget it,” I grumbled, turning back toward my room.

Greer always had to have the last word. “If you know what’s good for you, you’ll keep your nose out of everyone else's business."

Back in my room, I paced the floor.

Ugh! I'm so stupid. Eve was trying to hint that we weren't alone. But I wasn't paying attention, and now Greer overheard me...

"You know it would be really helpful if you could just tell me what happened or who's responsible," I said into the space above me in hopes she was listening.

Hearing a faint knock, I stopped in my tracks and scanned the room.

Then I noticed a note on the floor. It had been slipped under the door.

I picked it up and unfolded it.

Every letter, written all in caps, had been scribbled and traced several times, making the author's penmanship indiscernible.

MAYBE HER BOYFRIEND KNOWS.

WILL TUCKER WAS THE LAST TO SEE HER.

I grabbed the knob, threw the door open, and rushed out into the hall. But whoever had delivered the note was long gone.

Was it Eve—did she know something?

Or had someone else heard me asking questions?

An uncontrollable shudder swept over me, leaving goose bumps in its wake, and I looked down at the handwritten note again.

The implications were damning. Not only did it seem like someone knew something, but they were pointing the finger at Will.

I suddenly felt so betrayed.

I figured Will and Molly were kind of dating, but seeing the word "boyfriend" bothered me more than I expected. And why didn't he tell me he was the last person to see her?

Did he have something to hide?

A few tears broke loose, sliding down my cheek.

So stupid. I wiped the tears away in haste. *Maybe Dr. Swan was right about Will. She told me to be careful. Maybe I don't know him as well as I thought.*

But could he really be capable of violence?

I didn't want to believe it.

I crawled under the covers and let sleep take me.

Molly haunted my dreams.

Everywhere I went, she was there. No matter if my dreams took me to familiar or fantastical places, Molly watched me. She always looked the same and never said a word. Just stood lifeless and soaked. Eyes hollow. Water dribbling from her mouth.

An endless amount of water.

Chapter 24

The next morning, I got dressed and grabbed breakfast on my way out to meet Chief. I was apprehensive about seeing Will, so I had my fingers crossed that I wouldn't have to work closely with him today. At least not until I had time to figure out the truth.

And wouldn't you know, Chief paired me up with Will and Damian.

A massive, heaping pile of mulch had been delivered, and Chief wanted it all moved and spread today. He broke us into groups and put us each in charge of an area to be done. Basically, the mulch was going everywhere. He wanted it in the areas along the buildings where there were flowers and bushes, a little bit in the courtyard, and bordering the fencing around the tennis courts.

We started out with Will on the wheelbarrow. He'd get the mulch and dump it where we needed it, and Damian and I would spread it out with our rakes. We didn't talk much, but I didn't think either of us were big on unnecessary chitchat.

Then, about halfway through, Will and Damian switched places.

"Are you going tonight?" Will asked.

"Where?"

"The movies. It's movie night."

"Haven't been here long enough."

"Oh, I forgot about probation." Will took a break from working. Holding the rake upright, he rested his other arm on its top. "A month, right?"

"Yep." I continued raking.

"I can't believe Mrs. Brown didn't say I couldn't go because of detention. I think she forgot. But I'm not going to remind her."

"Uh-huh."

Damian approached with another load, and I was grateful for the distraction.

"Maybe dump that one over there," I said, pointing toward the other end of that particular area. "Then we can rake it all inward and meet in the center." I honestly didn't care where he dumped it as long as I could put a little space between me and Will.

I followed Damian and began spreading the mulch as he dumped it. After he walked away to get the next load, Will dropped his rake and came closer.

"Okay, so what's going on?" he asked. "It kinda seems like you've gone back to avoiding me. What happened?"

I kept my head down and raked harder.

"Seriously. What's wrong, Ronnie?" He sounded confused and slightly irritated.

I released a raspy breath and straightened. "You really want to know?" I snapped.

"That's why I asked," he bit back.

"I'm upset that you didn't tell me the truth about the day Molly disappeared."

Will's brow cinched. He leaned his rake against the building. "What are you talking about? I told you everything I knew."

"You didn't tell me that you were the last one to see her."

Will put his hands on his hips and cut me a look. "How would I know if I was the last one to see her? Besides, what difference would it make? She didn't tell me she was leaving." He ran his hand through his hair and shook his head. "Why are you so obsessed with Molly?"

My brow shot up. "Why aren't you more concerned about what happened to your girlfriend?" I tossed my rake to the ground.

"Whoa. Whoa. Whoa." Will waved his hand like he was trying to shut down my argument. "I never said I wasn't concerned. And I never said she was my girlfriend."

"Are you saying she wasn't your girlfriend?"

"She wasn't," Will protested. "Molly was into girls."

Well, *that* shut me up.

"It wasn't something that she shared with many people, but it's true." Will relaxed his shoulders. "We may have led people to think we were dating, but we were just friends. Like I said, I've known her forever." He paused, sighing. "And if you had asked, I would've told you."

I wasn't sure if I was buying his story. "Why did you want people to think you were dating?"

"It was Molly's idea. She wasn't ready to come out and she said if her friends thought we were a couple, they would stop trying to set her up with different guys all the time," Will said. "Molly also said boyfriends were off-limits, so I'd be safe from them. I didn't understand what that meant at first, but I quickly caught on and…anyway, it worked." Palms up, Will shrugged. Then his mouth pulled to the side in a grimace. "That is, until Molly ran away, and Greer decided I was fair game."

"Except that she didn't run away," I replied.

Will rolled his eyes and sighed. "How do you know she didn't run away this time? That's what Molly did!"

I clenched my teeth so hard my jaw was beginning to ache. "Because she's dead!"

Will's eyes grew wide. He opened his mouth to speak. Closed it again and shook his head. "What?"

He looked truly distraught.

Two thoughts ran through my head.

Can I believe him?

Can I trust him?

I took a chance.

Smoothing the edge from my voice, I offered my condolences. "I'm sorry to have to tell you, but it's the truth. I've…seen her ghost."

Will exhaled with a noisy whoosh, running his hand through his hair then leaving it to rest on top of his head as he turned away.

I waited, giving him time to absorb what I was saying.

He turned back, his eyes meeting mine just before I saw the revelation register in his expression.

"Wait," he said, holding up his index finger. With a crease in his brow, he cocked his head. "So, the rumor…it was true?"

"That I can see ghosts?" I said, quirking my mouth. "Kind of. But this is my first and only ghost sighting, sooo," I added, raising my hands, palm side up.

"But how? When?" His mouth opened again, but nothing came out.

"Remember when I was so upset with Greer last week, but I wouldn't tell you why?"

His stare grew more intense. "Yeah."

"That night, Eve and I were in the common room watching TV when Sam came in. She said Greer had something to show us. Of course, I was skeptical of anything having to do with Greer, but like an idiot, I went anyway. I thought maybe she'd had a change of heart. She hadn't. It was a setup." I hesitated, clearing my throat before going on. "When I walked into the room, there were candles and a Ouija board laid out. Greer said they were just going to have a little fun…but what I didn't know was that they'd stolen a picture of my mom."

"What the…" Will groaned.

"Yeah. Their idea of fun was to pretend to make contact with my dead mother in a séance."

Will shook his head in disbelief. "Talk about twisted."

I pressed my lips together and gave a slight nod. "I didn't realize until recently that the spirit they'd let in wasn't my mother—that it was Molly."

"So you've honestly seen things? And you think it's because of the Ouija board prank?" His voice and the look on his face oozed skepticism and doubt.

"Yes!"

His manner softened. "I mean, I'm not saying I don't believe you…it's just…" Draping both arms over his head, his mouth gaped as he heaved a sigh. "That stuff is real?"

I saw the trepidation in his eyes.

"I'm afraid so, because that's when it all started," I said. "And she seemed to have latched on to the six of us who were in the room that night."

"All what started?" he asked.

"Strange sounds, doors opening and closing, lights and other things turning on and off. Probably a bunch of other things too."

"Like what?"

"The chandelier. Greer's hair falling out. Something causing her to drop her tray, covering her in oatmeal. Something causing Sam to trip on the stairs…"

Will's nose wrinkled. His eyes narrowed.

"What?" I asked.

"Those last few things you mentioned sound an awful lot like some of the stupid crap the girls would do to mess with other people."

"Really?" I found that a little eerie. It were as if Molly were doing to them, what they had done to others.

Will nodded. "What do Greer and the others say about all of this?"

"Nothing. They don't believe me. I don't know if they just aren't seeing it or what. But whenever possible they blame me for what's happening." I shook my head, then corrected. "Well, except for Cheyenne."

Will reached for his rake and started moving it back and forth. "Damian's coming," he whispered.

I picked up my rake and started looking busy. As he approached, I directed him again. "How about right there," I said, pointing about four feet away. "Then I think two more loads and we'll be done here."

"I think you're right," Will said.

Damian dumped the wheelbarrow and took a moment to rest, wiping his brow with his forearm.

I wanted to finish our conversation, but Damian lingered.

"So, what are you guys talking about?" he asked.

My eyes met Will's, then he turned to Damian. "We were talking about who's going to movie night tonight." Will waved his hand at Damian. "I know you're going. You never miss an opportunity to leave the school."

"True dat," Damian replied with a smile. "Hey, I heard you mention Cheyenne's name—is she going?"

Will tossed me a goofy look. "Damian kind of has a thing for Cheyenne?"

"Really?" I smiled. "I'm sorry but I don't know if she's going. She might be like me and hasn't been here long enough."

"Oh yeah." His lip curled. "That's such a stupid rule." With that, Damian grabbed the handles on the wheelbarrow and sulked off.

Will waited until Damian was around the corner and well out of earshot before he said, "Okay, so what does Cheyenne say about all of this?"

"Not a whole lot. It was only yesterday that she confided in me. She'd left her sweatshirt in class, so I took it to her dorm—she's roommates with Sam, but Sam wasn't there, so she asked me to come in to talk. That's when she told me that she believed me because she'd experienced strange things too. That's also when I saw a group picture taped to Sam's mirror." I paused, reliving that moment. "I asked Cheyenne if she knew who that fifth girl was," I said, my eyes shifting to the ground. "I recognized her, but I knew I'd never met her…and suddenly it all made sense."

Narrowing my eyes, I looked up at Will. "I wonder if she is connecting most with me because I'm sleeping in her old bed?"

Will's brow rose. "Maybe."

We worked in silence for a few minutes. Finally, he asked, "So, now what?"

"Now I'm going to find her."

That obviously shook him up. "What?" he snapped, face contorted.

"Yes," I replied, very matter-of-fact. "She *wants* to go home. She *deserves* to be put to rest, Will."

"But how are you supposed to find her?"

"She's helping me—giving me clues. I really need to get out into the woods again. I think she's out there, or maybe even in the gorge."

Chapter 25

The weather changed shortly after lunch. It looked like it was going to be one of those all-day rains where everyone was stuck inside, bored and grouchy. At least most of the others had movie night to look forward to.

Kerry threw an impromptu craft party in the common room, and Cheyenne was the only one from that group to show up. Eve had gone home for the day, to get another pair of glasses. The other girls were doing their hair and nails for the big night off campus.

Cheyenne wasn't able to go yet either. Although, she only missed the probation period by two days.

Kerry had brought some pictures for us to choose from and let everyone do their own thing. There were eleven of us today—the biggest group yet. Some girls painted, some used color pencils, and others, like me, did a pencil drawing.

Cheyenne and I sat together. She kept her voice low. "Anything *interesting* happen lately?" I knew what she meant.

"I think I'm getting closer." I glanced around. No one seemed to be paying attention to us. "You wanna go on a hike with me tomorrow?"

"A hike?" Her eyes grew wide. "Why, what do you think you're going to find?"

I don't know why I asked her to go with me when I knew she couldn't handle it.

"I'm just looking for clues," I answered, hoping to put her mind at ease. I decided that was all I was going to say about the subject. I had a new one in mind. "So, what do you think of Damian?"

"He's cute," Cheyenne answered. Then looked up at me. "Why?"

Keeping my lips sealed, I grinned.

Cheyenne's cheeks flushed. She put down her pencil and turned her body to me. "Tell me what you know."

I laughed and went on to tell her about the exchange between me and Will and Damian.

It was obvious by her smile and the way she gazed off that her feelings were mutual.

"Are you gonna go for it?" I asked.

Cheyenne pressed her lips together, though she was still smiling. She shrugged. "Maybe."

"You should!" I said. "He's super nice and a lot of fun. That whole group of friends is."

"So, what's the story with you and Will?" she asked. "Are you together?"

I nodded. If she'd asked me yesterday, I would've been more sure of myself. But there was a tiny part of me—a part so small it could fit in my pinky toe—that wondered if he was telling me the truth. That stupid note. I didn't even know who wrote it, but it had me questioning someone I really cared for, and I thought I knew.

****

The bus left right after dinner, and the school got extremely quiet. With only three girls and two boys left behind, all the dorm leaders went on the bus trip. Mrs. Trumble and the security guard were here if we needed them.

The bus wasn't due back until around ten thirty. Eve was due back some time this evening as well.

I hung out in the common room with Cheyenne and that other girl, Ashley. We watched a movie on TV. Something with the guy from that movie with the maze. It was good, but I found myself dozing off toward the end because I was so tired.

My eyes opened as the credits started to roll.

"This was fun, but I'm so tired." I yawned and hoisted myself up.

"Yeah, I had fun tonight," Cheyenne said.

"Me too," Ashley agreed.

"Good night, guys," I said.

"Night," the girls returned in unison.

I stopped in the bathroom on my way to my room.

As tired as I was, I felt like I had the remnants of a smile on my face. For the first time in a long time, I felt content. Hanging out on the couch in the common room, watching a movie, felt so normal. Even home hadn't felt normal for a very long time.

I finished in the stall and went to the center sink. The lights flickered once.

My body tensed, and I closed my eyes, praying I was alone. I hadn't slept well all week. I just wanted to go to bed.

The temperature in the room dropped.

Frost began to creep up the mirror.

"Please, not tonight," I whispered.

I turned on the water and reached for the soap dispenser that hung to the right of the sink. Each basin had one. With my hand still inches away from the lever, the liquid began to flow. I looked to the right and the left. All three dispensers were emptying onto the counter. Three lines of pink liquid raced toward the edge of the counter.

"Stop it!" I ordered in a hushed tone.

I washed my hands quickly. Then, careful to avoid the soap now pooling on the floor, I turned toward the door. Suddenly, the paper towel dispenser exploded, sending the folded sheets everywhere.

"Why are you doing this?" I asked.

"Help me," she answered. The voice seemed to echo all around me.

I didn't know where to look.

"I told you that I'd help you, but I don't know what you want from me."

She'd gone silent.

I looked around the room. She'd made a mess. And I didn't want to get blamed for it, so I scooped up the paper towels and left them in a pile in the corner of the counter. As for the soap, I wasn't sure what to do. I had to leave it and hope it went down as a malfunction.

It was 10:17 when I got back to my room, and I planned to be fast asleep before the bus returned.

The lamp on my nightstand lit the way as I crossed the room and readied for bed, kicking off my slides and slipping out of my sweatpants. I pulled on my shorts and tied my hair in a bun on top of my head.

Then a foreboding feeling came over me.

It was too quiet.

After the scene Molly had caused in the bathroom, something didn't seem right. It didn't seem likely that she would go away so easily.

I stilled and listened to the room, my eyes darting side to side.

The hair on the back of my neck stood on end.

I wasn't alone. I could feel her lingering.

But why so quiet?

Seconds passed as I considered the options. I could stand here and wait for something to happen, or I could use this time to get some sleep.

Choosing sleep, I climbed in bed. No sooner had my body touched the mattress when I felt something cold and damp. I jumped up and threw the covers back.

In the dim light and shadows, I wasn't sure what I was looking at.

I ran across the room and switched on the overhead lights.

My heart dropped to my stomach.

In my bed was a muddy, wet imprint of a body. Dead leaves dotted the surface, and the stench of rot began to fill the room.

I couldn't breathe.

My body shuddered violently, and I swatted and brushed at my arms and legs. I had just lain in that.

Ew! Ew! Ew! I wanted to cry.

But then the overhead light went out.

I spun around and grabbed the doorknob.

It wouldn't turn.

With panic taking over, I rattled the knob and yanked the door. But it was as if it was locked from the outside.

"Is anyone out there?" I cried. "Help! I can't get the door open—"

Boom! Boom! A loud knock sounded from behind, and I whipped my head around, hand still firmly gripping the knob.

Boom! Boom! It struck again, like the pounding of

a fist. My body jerked with each vibration.

It was coming from inside my closet.

As I stared, I thought I saw something strange. It didn't seem real. I wiped my eyes with the heel of my palms. Blinked. And looked again.

The wood surface of the door was pulsating. As if it were breathing. Right in the center. Expanding out, like oxygen filling the lungs, and then contracting.

Meanwhile, I held my breath.

Then it occurred to me, her bracelet was in there.

"Molly?" I began with a pause as the pulsating stopped at the sound of my voice. "What are you trying to tell me?"

From behind the closet door, I heard the hiss and hush of a whisper. Though nothing discernible.

I stepped closer, listening. *Pss. Pss. Pss.*

Hand trembling, I reached for the knob and opened the closet door slowly, just a few inches.

The whispering stopped abruptly.

I pulled my hand away and took a step back, swallowing hard. I took a deep breath, considering my words. "You've been trying to get my attention all night. You've got it," I said. "So tell me what you want?"

My heart beat faster.

She answered with one word. Barely audible. "Come."

Come? Did I hear her right? I bent my neck forward and peered into the small, dark opening.

"Come," she said again just before the door flew open with a rush so forceful, loose tendrils blew in front of my face. I followed the misty burst of energy with my eyes as it traveled once around the room and then left through the closed window, the curtains flapping in the breeze.

I ran over to the window and pulled back the curtain.

The night was so very dark, and the rain hadn't let up. My gaze dropped to the courtyard below, spotting Molly. She stood under a lamppost near the back gate. A pale, transparent figure with hollow eyes looking up at me. She almost seemed brighter than the light around her, as if she, herself, illuminated.

She wanted me to follow her.

Chapter 26

A part of me knew it was a bad idea to go out into the night. Still, I put my sweatpants back on and shoved my feet into my sneakers, grabbed the jacket with the bracelet in the pocket, and rushed out of my room.

I had three things on my mind. One, I hoped the guard didn't see me on the cameras. Two, I hoped that door in the dining hall was still disconnected from the alarm. And three, I had to get out of here before the bus returned.

I was nearly at the stairs when Cheyenne walked out of the bathroom in the north wing. I hesitated, hoping she wouldn't look this way.

No such luck.

"Hey, I thought you were going right to bed," she said, her eyes dropping to the jacket hanging over my arm. Her eyes narrowed. "Where are you going?"

My lips pursed.

Cheyenne's eyes grew wide. "You're going after her, aren't you?"

"Yes," I answered. "And I have to go *now*."

"You can't go out there tonight. It's too dangerous." She looked afraid.

I was afraid too. But I wasn't going to let it stop me.

"I have to," I said and darted down the stairs before she could talk me out of it.

I slowed as I approached the first-floor landing. Thinking fast, I shrugged into my jacket and wrapped my arms in front of me.

Nick, the weekend guard, was stepping out of the security office as I rounded the corner.

He saw me and asked, “You cold?”

“Yeah, I can’t seem to get warm tonight,” I answered, feigning a shiver.

“It’s this weather,” he said as he headed toward the main entrance. “And it looks like the bus is on its way in, so this door is going to be open for a bit. You might not want to be standing here.”

“Okay, thanks,” I replied as he opened the door and stepped outside.

I rushed over and peeked at the screens in his office. One display showed two sets of headlights coming up the long driveway. Another display was blocked out with squiggly lines. I assumed it to be a view of the back gate of the courtyard, since the one next to it showed the courtyard from another angle. After a quick scan of the screens, I found the dining hall and planned my path to the door that would give me the least amount of exposure.

I pulled the hood of my jacket up over my head and hurried toward the dining hall. I had to get out while no one was watching the cameras.

The room was darker than it looked on the screen. I kept my head down and stayed close to the wall of windows on the left side. Reaching the outside door, I took a deep breath and pressed the push bar.

The door opened with silent ease, and I stepped out into the night. I caught a glimpse of Molly passing through the unopened gate, and I followed. Lowering my chin against the pelting rain, I raced across the courtyard and through the squeaky gate.

The tennis courts, which sat off to the left behind the gymnasium, were like a beacon, lit with spotlights hanging from posts along the surrounding fence. Though the light barely penetrated this side of the fencing, it helped direct me toward the Bear Forest Trail just beyond. I had a feeling that's where Molly was headed.

I was halfway to the tennis courts when something stopped me in my tracks. I thought I'd heard the gate squeak again. Was someone following me?

I spun around, the pounding of my heart echoing in my ears.

But no one was there. At least, not that I could see in the distant light. Although someone could be standing right next to me, and I might not know it.

I stuffed my hands in the pockets of my jacket and took off for the trail again, my footfalls slapping noisily on the saturated ground. The rain let up slightly as I entered the protection of the woods.

I slowed, lifting my chin, and wrapped my right hand around the bracelet in my pocket. "Molly? Are you here?"

"Yes," she said as she appeared in front of me, as a full-bodied apparition. I was taken aback—she'd never shown herself to me like this before. Never spoken so clearly before, either.

It was almost as if she were a hologram, powered by the rain. There was a vibrance about her, like she emitted light. And with each drop of rain that fell on her, it traced a path of clarity and focus. The more rain, the clearer the picture.

"I've been trying to put the pieces together. To remember what happened," Molly said, turning away pensively. She wandered a few feet and spun back. "I remember an argument. Right here." She splayed her arms.

"Do you remember who you were arguing with?"

"No," she cried, her hands shooting up and grabbing the sides of her head. The image of her flickered in and out. That had clearly upset her.

"Sorry. Just tell me what you remember, and maybe we can work it out together."

Molly calmed. Her image became stable again, and she continued, "I'd just returned from my sister's birthday party. I remember it was the first springlike day and a lot of people were outside taking advantage of it. I saw Will by the basketball court as I was getting out of the car."

My body tensed at his name, but I tried not to show it.

Molly's eyes lowered as if she were looking at her appearance. "He came over and told me that I looked pretty in a dress." She paused and thought for a moment. "Then we went for a walk—"

"Ronnie!"

The voice was far off, and even through the pounding rain, I recognized it.

Will.

My instinct was to run.

I took off deeper into the woods, following the hardpacked trail. Molly helped show me the way, appearing in twenty to thirty feet intervals.

"Ronnie!" he called again from well behind. I couldn't even tell if he was on the same path.

But then I heard the snap of a twig and froze. It came from my right and was much closer.

“This way,” Molly whispered, capturing my attention. She led me off the main trail, onto a narrow path that veered to the left. “Quiet, she’ll hear you.”

“She, who?” I shot back in a rough whisper, as I forced my legs to carry me faster.

This path—possibly a game trail—was much less traveled. Brush and saplings encroached. I held my arms up, in front of my face, shielding against the wayward branches while thorny vines grabbed at my clothing.

Suddenly, I could hear Molly’s thoughts in my head.

We were all fighting—the five of us—and I wasn’t sure our friendship would survive.

They wanted to get Mr. Santori fired. They’d been talking about it for days, were going to claim he’d acted inappropriately.

But he was a great teacher. He didn’t deserve to lose his job just because Greer couldn’t flirt her way out of a failing grade. She didn’t like rejection. But more than that, she didn’t like not getting her way.

I told them that was taking the Games way too far. And that if they went through with it, I’d go straight to Mrs. Brown.

I came to a stop, hunching over, my hands resting on my knees to keep me from collapsing as I tried to catch my breath.

“Is that why you threw out your bracelet?” I asked between heaving breaths, then brandishing the silver piece in my open palm.

“Yes,” she answered, appearing in front of me once

again, eyeing the bracelet sadly. After a beat, she looked off nervously. "You have to keep moving."

I clutched the bracelet tight in my fist and pushed myself forward. Slow at first, then faster as her voice filled my mind.

After Will and I parted, she told me to meet her by the trail in five minutes. I was irritated because it seemed like it was going to be another argument. Why else would she call for a secret rendezvous?

But all she did was lecture me.

Holding out her arm, displaying her bracelet—the one that matched mine—she said, "We made a pact, remember? We said these bound us together like family. But that unlike family we would never let each other down. We'd look out for each other, and we'd back each other no matter what."

I told her if being a member of their "so-called-family" meant going against what I think is right, then I didn't want to be a part of it anymore. I threw my bracelet into the woods and stomped off, leaving her standing near the trail entrance, while I walked farther into the woods. I needed time alone to cool off.

I didn't know that she'd followed me.

Molly's voice had become somber.

I knew this was it. We were coming to the moment of truth.

"Who is *she*, Molly?" I asked frantically. "Who are you talking about?"

We're almost there.

A sudden realization gripped my throat like icy cold fingers, constricting 'til I couldn't breathe.

Was Molly helping me escape the present danger? Or was she reliving her final moments?

I feared history was about to repeat itself.

****

Swiping a tree branch out of the way, I stepped into the open just as Molly appeared, standing not much more than an arm's length in front of me.

The light emanating from her revealed we stood mere feet from the end of the earth—only the dark abyss of the gorge valley lay beyond.

"This is where she caught up to me," Molly said, solemnly. Rain trickled down her face, bringing life to her two-dimensional features.

I narrowed my eyes, protecting them from the wind and the rain. Droplets fell from my lashes.

A loud snap had me spinning. I hadn't heard Will call my name for quite some time. I had a feeling I'd made a huge mistake running away from him. If only I'd known.

"Maybe we should go?" I suggested. This didn't seem like a safe place to be, given the circumstances.

Molly stood frozen, the look on her face as if she were deep in thought, reliving what would be her final moments. But I needed her. Without her, I'd never find my way out.

"Molly," I cried, trying to get her attention.

Her gaze met mine.

"I think we should go now," I said again.

But it was as if she couldn't hear me anymore.

"The look in her eye scared me," Molly said. "Her pupils had grown so big that her eyes looked black; it was like she was possessed. I asked her why she couldn't just leave me alone, but that seemed to anger her more.

"She said…she couldn't let me ruin what she had

here, at this school. And that the only way things would go back to normal was if I disappeared. She came at me, and we struggled, but I lost my footing." Molly's chin dropped to her shoulder, as she eyed the ragged edge behind.

"Loose dirt and rock crumbled beneath me as my foot started slipping. I tried to hold on—to latch onto something. Anything. Then she got on her knees and reached for me. I thought she was going to help pull me up, but…"

My body trembled. I felt the hopelessness in Molly's voice and the hesitation to go on. After a beat, she did.

"I cried and begged and tried to grab her hand…her sleeve…her arm…anything. And I did. I hooked my fingers around—" Molly's mouth snapped shut, and like a flip of the switch, she was gone.

A second later, I heard the voice behind me.

"You just couldn't leave it alone, could you?"

Suddenly, it all made sense.

"I'd been wondering what happened to *your* bracelet," I said calmly as I turned to face Eve. "It went into the gorge with Molly, didn't it?"

Wearing only a sweater, Eve was drenched from head to toe. Her wet bangs, hanging heavy and long, had been pushed to the sides, and she wore what appeared to be an old pair of glasses. The wire frames and narrow lenses seemed long out of date. She looked so different from the girl who'd always greeted me with a bubbly hello.

With her palms facing up, Eve lifted her shoulders and grimaced, sucking air noisily through her teeth. "That's why I can't let anyone find her…evidence, ya know."

My first and only thought was that I had to get away from the edge of the gorge. Eve and I were of similar builds, and without a weapon, I was fairly confident in my ability to hold my own in a fight.

Lowering the hood of my jacket to keep it from obstructing my view, I quickly darted to the left of Eve, giving her plenty of space. I was hoping to make it into the woods and possibly losing her.

I made it about two steps before I slipped in the mud. I went down hard, landing on my back and knocking the air out of me.

With no time to recover, I flipped onto my stomach and got to my hands and knees.

Eve slammed into me, throwing me off balance. We wrestled for dominance. Squirming. Rolling. Grabbing. And dragging. Fighting dirty, she yanked at my hair. I dug my nails into her hand in an attempt to get her to release. I'd lost sight of which way was up.

But a moment later I found out which way was down when we both went over the edge.

Chapter 27

Clinging to the craggy wall, my hands and feet searched for purchase. But made mostly of shale, the rock crumbled and gave way beneath me.

Still, I dug my shredded and bloody nails into the earth and fought to hang on. And while I slowly slid deeper, I knew that gravity would soon claim me, and with the river more than a hundred feet below, no matter how deep the water was, the fall would likely kill me.

Although the way my heart raced, it was possible a heart attack would take me first.

What about Eve? Other than a short, initial scream, I hadn't heard a thing from her. And since she was on top of me when we went over the side, I had little confidence she was still alive.

Something poked at my ribs.

A sapling.

Growing precariously on the cliff face, the young tree—not much taller than me and roughly as thick as my wrist—had caught on my jacket. The wood bent, slowing my descent until I was able to catch my feet on a ledge at its base.

The ledge was about the size of a cafeteria tray. But I managed to brace myself, squatting with my back pressed to the wall and arm locked around the tree trunk.

I finally took a breath.

And as the shock began to wear off, horror took its place.

In the darkness, I had no way of knowing how far I'd fallen. And until daylight, I had no way of knowing what my options of getting out of here were.

It wouldn't be light for at least five or six hours.

I tried to scream for help, but like a nightmare, nothing came out.

Or did it?

I tried again, pushing harder from my diaphragm. "Somebody help me!"

Faint and muffled, I realized it wasn't my voice that was the problem, but the wind and rain that carried it away. I could scream until my throat was raw, but it probably wouldn't do any good.

I closed my eyes and wept. My heart felt heavy as my brain delivered blow after blow.

Why didn't I try to call out to Will when I had the chance?

What are the odds of him finding me now?

I could be a half mile from the school. Even if the rain stops, no one will hear me.

My mind replayed the moments, counting all the ways I should have done things differently. Not just tonight but going back to that night in Greer's room.

I knew they didn't like me, so why did I stay? Why did I go along with something that I didn't feel comfortable with? Eve tried to put a stop to it…

Eve.

That was the blow that hurt most of all.

My closest friend since day one. I can't believe it, the girl who welcomed me to this school with open arms, encouraged me to come out of my shell, and went out of her way to make me feel included...tried to kill me.

She was a cold-blooded killer.

But she had everyone fooled.

My tears turned to sobs, the kind that were tiring and hard to control, and made everything from the chest up hurt. It didn't help that the muscles in my thighs burned, or that I was cold and wet.

Then my thoughts took a dark turn.

Maybe I deserve what I get.

A life for a life—punishment for my mother's death. Another night. Another bad decision.

My family would probably be better off. My dad wouldn't have to deal with me anymore, and he wouldn't have to pay to keep me away.

My legs trembled. Getting weaker by the moment, they were on the brink of giving out. I wasn't sure I cared anymore. I felt myself beginning to fade.

"What do you think you're doing?" I lifted my head, recognizing her voice. "You can't give up."

Sitting on the other side of the tree that anchored me, my mom's legs dangled casually off the ledge as if we were only a few feet off the ground.

"Mom…are you really here?" I managed.

"Where else would I be, silly?" She looked exactly as I remembered, untouched by the accident, or time, or even the falling rain. And wearing her favorite white nightgown, she looked angelic. A natural beauty, even with her dark, frizzy, unmanageable hair.

"But—" A sob constricted my throat, cutting off my words.

"But what?" Her voice was sweet and mellow.

"I've been with you the whole time, Veronica. Cheering you on through the good times and holding your hand when things were tough."

Mom reached over and placed her hand on my knee. The sensation was odd yet satisfying. At first, like a zap of static electricity, then a warm rush spreading out from there.

"There haven't been many good times," I said.

"It may not seem like it, but there have," she replied. "It's just going to take time—it'll get easier. You'll get through this."

"But what if I can't?"

"You're a strong, smart, beautiful girl with a really good heart. You can. I have faith in you."

"But what if I don't want to?" I confessed. "I miss you so much."

"It isn't your time yet," Mom said. "You have important things to do and people who love you and need you. You don't want Tori to grow up without her big sister, do you?"

"But Dad—"

"Dad needs you more than ever. He loves you so much."

"But I want to be with you," I cried.

"You will, someday. After you live a long and happy life." She moved her hand to my cheek. I tried to imagine the feel of her soft skin on mine.

"I'm sorry."

"I know you are," she whispered. "But it wasn't your fault, Veronica. It was an accident—plain and simple. Do you understand?"

Salty tears slid down my face and landed on my lips. "Mhm."

She lowered her hand. "Now, I need you to do something for me. Okay?"

"Okay," I answered.

"I need you to wake up."

I nodded.

"Veronica, wake up," she commanded.

Sucking in a sharp breath, my eyes sprang open, and I gripped the tree tighter.

Then I heard it, the voice in the distance.

"Ronnie!"

Oh my God. Will.

"I'm here!" I cried out. With a new burst of energy and my chin to the sky, I wouldn't give up. "I'm down here! Will…Will…I'm down here!"

Seconds later, a bright beam fractured the darkness overhead, showering me in light.

"Hang on." Using the light from his phone, he scanned the area around me, assessing the situation.

I did the same.

Basically, I was screwed. There was no way he was getting me out of here without help. Like, a lot of help.

Will moved the light to the side so I could see his face. I almost started to cry. I didn't think I'd ever see it again.

"Ronnie, I'm going to have to go for help." His voice was casual and smooth, as if to assure me. Although I detected a serious freaking-the-crap-out undertone. "But I'll be back in no time. Ten, fifteen minutes tops, I promise."

"Okay," I answered equally light and smooth, for his sake.

Then he flashed one of his goofy smiles and joked, "Don't go anywhere."

Shrouded in darkness once again, I felt a new calm come over me, and I realized the rain had stopped. No longer did I hear the constant patter. Silence, peaceful and serene, surrounded me. And with the clearing sky, the moon peeked out and cast the remainder of the clouds in a hazy glow.

I didn't see any stars, but I knew they were up there. And so was my mom, looking down on me.

Chapter 28

As promised, Will returned in no time.

"I'm back," he announced from a distance just before his light breached the edge above and he looked down. Then a second, stronger light shined down. I squinted against the brightness, and Will added, "I've got Nick with me."

"Emergency crews are already on the way," Nick said. I recognized his deep voice. "Are you hurt?"

"Umm." I dropped my gaze, mentally assessing my limbs, body, head. "I don't think so," I answered.

"Okay, good. Was anyone with you? Will said he thought he saw someone else heading into the woods ahead of him."

My chest tightened. "Eve was here. She went over too but…I don't think she made it."

The bright light circled the side and bottom of the gorge. If he saw anything, he didn't let on.

"Hang in there, kiddo." Nick and his light disappeared.

After a moment, Will peered down again, this time from his hands and knees. He'd set his phone down beside him, the beam shining straight up and washing him in light.

"Nick is going back to meet up with the emergency crews and lead them to our location. So for now, it's just you and me." He lowered himself and rested his chin on his arms crossed in front of him. With his elbows hanging over the edge, he looked as comfortable as if he were hanging out in his room and chatting with his roommate. "I'm sorry about Eve. I know she was your friend."

His words hit me harder than I expected. It was true. I lost a friend tonight. I felt sad and betrayed. And I didn't know how to explain to people what had happened out here. Not just tonight, but the night Molly disappeared.

"Did you find what you were looking for?" Will asked.

"Yes," I choked out so softly I wasn't sure he heard me.

He did. Not just what I'd said, but also what I didn't. I could tell by the way he responded. It was just one short word, but it was filled with shock and realization.

"Oh."

Now I had a question for him. "How did you know I was out here?"

"Cheyenne," Will answered. "She caught me as I was coming in the door. She was freaking out about you going out in the rain and the dark by yourself. And she was worried you'd get in trouble."

My neck had started to ache from looking up, so I lowered my head and looked out into the night. "But why did you come looking for me—risk getting in trouble yourself?"

"Because I was worried about you too."

Now I regretted ever second guessing his integrity.

"How was the movie?" I asked, needing the distraction.

"Pretty good," he answered casually. "Lots of action and laughs. And maybe a little too much popcorn," he finished with a dwindling laugh.

"Ooh, I love movie theater popcorn…with lots of melted butter."

"Yes, it has to be soaked in butter," he replied.

"I could really go for some popcorn right now."

"I think it'll be a while before I want any more. Like, at least not until tomorrow."

I laughed.

"Ooo, be right back."

"What?" I looked up. His light was still there, but he was gone.

A second later, he peered over the side again. "They're coming," he said with excitement. "Help is on the way, Ronnie! You'll be out of there soon."

A short time later, the forest above came alive with activity. Spotlights lit up the sky, and faces looked down on me as they strategized a plan.

Down here, things were still quiet.

Eventually, the crews lowered a man in a harness into the gorge. He came up beside me, a hardhat on and extra equipment clipped to his side.

"Hello there. I heard you might be in need of a lift," he said with a smile.

I was so happy to get off that ledge that I laughed at the lame dad joke. "You heard right."

After carefully attaching a harness to me and clipping it to his line, he gave the command.

"All clear. Bring us up!" Then to me, he added, "Hold on tight and don't look down."

They eased us up slowly, a few feet at a time.

As we reached topside, another man offered his

hand and pulled me over the lip of the gorge, while the man I was harnessed to pushed me from underneath.

Three crew members surrounded me the moment my feet were on solid ground. One on either side held me steady and walked me away from the edge, while the third undid the harnessing and freed me from my tether. I looked around, overwhelmed by all the emergency personnel, equipment, and lights. Beyond them and the forming crowd, the forest glowed red from the flares they'd placed marking their path.

My legs felt weak and wobbly. Not just from being in that position so long, but because I didn't like all this attention.

So many eyes on me.

Amongst them, Mrs. Brown. I wondered how much trouble I was in.

A paramedic swooped in and wrapped me in a blanket. Putting her arm around me, she steered me toward a place to sit down. An overturned tree made for a nice bench.

"Right over here. I want to keep you off the wet ground." I sat as she knelt in front of me. Another paramedic, a young guy, delivered a first aid bag to her side, then lingered over her shoulder to assist. "My name is Tracy, and this is Collin," she said, gesturing. "We just want to look you over for any trauma and check for hypothermia. Okay?"

I nodded, pushing the hair from my eyes as my gaze searched for Will.

Another man approached. "Hi, Veronica. I'm Kenny with Search and Rescue. I understand a second person may have gone over the edge in this area. Is that correct?"

My chest and throat tightened. There were too many people talking to me. Wanting answers. I closed my eyes and pressed my hands to my temples. I needed a minute to gather my thoughts.

He didn't give me but a second.

"Veronica, please, can you tell me what happened? Who else was out here?" the man pressed. "We need your help to locate that person."

I let out a deep breath and told him what he wanted to know.

"I was with Evelyn Gardner. She's a student at Evergreen and…" Tears pricked my eyes. I couldn't say it. I couldn't tell them the truth—that Eve tried to kill me and that she'd killed before. And at this point, did it really matter because there was no way Eve was still alive? She'd paid the ultimate price, and the truth would only make it harder for the families to heal.

So, I lied.

"It was an accident. We both slipped. I managed to grab onto something, but Eve wasn't so lucky."

"Do you remember what she was wearing?" Kenny asked.

"Jeans and a dark sweater."

"What were you two doing out here on a night like this?"

"A few weeks ago, a girl named Molly was reported missing from the school. She was thought to be a runaway…"

Kenny's brow wrinkled. "Yeah, I'm familiar with the case."

"The other day I found her bracelet not far from here and," I said with a pause, patting my pockets. *Shoot, I must've lost it in the scuffle.* "And I…I don't know how to describe it, but I had kind of a sixth sense that she'd fallen into the gorge. I just had to come out here and look." I lowered my eyes. "Eve was trying to stop me."

Kenny scratched his head.

"Molly is down there too," I said. "I'm sure of it."

Kenny patted my shoulder. "Thank you, Veronica. You've been very helpful." He shared a serious look with Tracy before he walked away.

Tracy met my gaze again.

"Can I go find my boyfriend now?"

"Is that the boy who found you?"

"Yes. His name is Will."

Tracy shot a look to Collin and gave a nod. When he took off, Tracy turned back.

"How long have you two been together?" Tracy clipped something to my finger and removed the stethoscope from her neck.

"Not long. It's really new."

"Well, I can tell he really cares for you." Tracy smiled as she placed the earpieces to her ears. "The poor kid was a wreck by the time Search and Rescue was on the scene. Nobody was moving fast enough for him."

My cheeks warmed.

"I'll try to make this quick and easy." She started by checking my pulse and listening to my heart and lungs. Then she removed the clamp from my finger. "Everything sounds good, and your oxygen levels look good. Are you in any pain?"

"No."

"Okay. Now I'm just going to run my hands over your body to check for any broken bones. You tell me if anything hurts."

She worked from my feet up, and other than a few bruises, I was fine.

"Okay, everything looks good."

No sooner had the words left her mouth when I saw Will. Wrapped in a blanket too, he broke through the crowd. I stood as he rushed toward me and pulled me into his arms.

I curled into his chest and closed my eyes.

"I'll give you two some privacy," Tracy said. "But don't go anywhere. I'm sure the police are going to want an official statement."

"Mm-hmm," I answered without moving.

"I'm so glad you're safe. I was so scared." Will stroked my hair and back.

His words—and more so, his actions—meant more to me than he'd ever know. It reminded me that there were people who would miss me if I were gone.

"I overheard them saying that there may be a second body down there," Will said. "Is it?"

I held him tight. My cheek brushed against his chest as I nodded.

"Molly told me everything. She was with me until Eve showed up." I felt a sadness creep in and slip out of my mouth, my lower lip quivering. "Then she abandoned me. I don't know where she went."

"I think I do," Will whispered with hesitation.

I pulled my head back and looked curiously into his eyes.

Will licked his lips. "Yeah," he admitted, though he seemed to be struggling. "She was, uh, with me."

My mouth fell open, and my breath escaped. "I don't understand."

"I don't either." He stuffed one hand into his pocket. "But it's the only explanation I have. I mean…I thought I was imagining it at first. It was like I could hear her voice in my head. Then my light reflected off something shiny." Will pulled Molly's bracelet from his pocket. "She didn't abandon you, Ronnie. She led me to you. Without Molly, I never would've found you."

A cold wave rushed over me, and I turned away from Will. Looking toward where the emergency crews still worked at the edge of the gorge and realizing how lucky I was to be standing here. Realizing how close I'd come to being just another body to be retrieved from the dangerous depths of the valley below.

That's when the tears came in a rush.

****

As daybreak neared, TV reporters arrived on the scene. Some even beating the families of the students involved.

The crowd was quiet and tense, waiting for news from the bottom.

While Eve's family remained hopeful, Molly's family seemed less so. They had been desperate for answers, but this was not the outcome they wanted. My heart hurt for them all.

There would be no happy endings for any of them.

I felt a little guilty about that as I stood amongst them, in my father's arms.

He hadn't let go of me since the moment he arrived. And though we never spoke, the catch in his breath and the way in which he squeezed me tight told me more than words could. We were going to be okay.

Earlier, a helicopter had done several sweeps up and down the gorge valley. Now it was back, hovering in one spot while two crew members stood in the open door; one directed a line braced to the side.

Nearby, crew members spoke on radios and pushed the onlookers back, clearing an opening.

Moments later, the helicopter lifted a stretcher out of the valley. It dangled over the land, slowly moving into place, and coming to rest in the opening. Crews worked quickly to release it from the line and wave the copter on.

The first thing I noticed was that the face was covered.

My gaze scanned the other families. One was about to be devastated.

Kenny, with Search and Rescue, called Mrs. Brown over. She nodded along as he spoke, then he lifted the cover. Mrs. Brown took one look at the body on the stretcher and gave another nod before turning away. Her gaze landed on Eve's mother, and the woman immediately broke into a sob. She knew. We all knew.

I was so focused on what was happening here that I hadn't noticed the helicopter was on its way back, another stretcher dangling beneath.

Molly's parents embraced, neither looking toward the stretcher as the crew released the line.

I passed a glance to Will, his teary eyes peeled to the body on the stretcher.

With my father's arm still wrapped around me, I looked up into his eye. "My friend needs me."

My father dropped his arm, and I turned from his embrace and into Will's, snaking my arms around his waist. I rested my head on his shoulder.

"I'm so sorry," I whispered.

Melting into my arms, Will rested his head on top of mine and broke down. His breath ragged, his body trembled. I squeezed him tighter and cried with him.

We'd been holding each other for several minutes when I thought I heard something.

I lifted my head and met his gaze. "Did you say something?"

"No." Will shook his head.

Then I heard it again. This time I made out the familiar voice. "Thank you."

Molly? My eyes wandered over the crowd.

"What is it, Ronnie?" Will asked.

I almost missed her at first. She looked so different—more like her picture. Her hair and clothes were no longer wet, and her skin had a pinkness about it. She was standing beside her parents.

When our eyes met, her lips curled into a smile.

"She's here," I answered, not taking my eyes off her. I smiled back. "And she looks so peaceful."

"Thank you," she said again. Even with the distance and commotion between us, and the thrum of the copter overhead, I heard her clearly.

I pressed my lips together and nodded.

"I'm not cold anymore." Molly passed a look to her parents and back. "And I'm finally going home."

Epilogue

Friday, May 28

It had been three weeks since the night I almost lost my life.

So much had changed. My father and I were talking regularly and working things out. Turned out, he never blamed me for what happened. What I had been interpreting as anger when he looked at me was actually sadness as I reminded him so much of his wife. She wasn't much older than me when they first met.

I even got to talk to Tori on the phone a few times.

Man, I missed that little dweeb.

I was excited that I was finally going to see her tomorrow. Dad was picking me up for the three-day holiday weekend. It would be my first time going home since I got to the school five weeks ago. Not only was I looking forward to seeing my room and spending time with family, but I also had a big decision to make.

In my session this week, Dr. Swan reported that I had made great progress in my short time at Evergreen. She said she'd spoken to my dad, as well as Mr. Kirkland, my old principal, and if I wanted, I could return home and finish the semester at my old school.

While it was awesome that my dad wanted me back home, it was a little scary. I had alienated all of my old friends. What if it was too soon?

Meanwhile, a lot had changed here at Evergreen too.

With the loss of two students, everyone came together to grieve. Even Sam, Amanda, and Greer.

And while the girls would never know the truth of everything that happened, I think they suspected. And *that* changed them.

****

It was just after eight p.m. when Will and I headed out to the courtyard.

The staff was throwing a Memorial weekend bonfire party. Jeremy was at the firepit, working on the fire. I stabbed it with the wrought iron poker. Bright orange embers floated up into the early night sky.

We passed a long table, where Kerry was busy setting out everything to make s'mores. At the other end of the table, Brandi was putting out stacks of cups and two-liter bottles of soda.

Will dropped my hand. "Find us seats. I'm getting stuff to make s'mores."

"Okay." I laughed and continued on without him to look for a place to sit.

At least thirty chairs had been pulled into a big circle around the stone pit. Maybe a quarter of them were occupied.

I grabbed the first two open seats and started to sit down, when a sharp voice stopped me.

"What the heck, Ronnie?"

I looked up to see Amanda eyeing me from across the way.

"I saved you guys a spot," she said, patting the seat beside her. "Aren't you gonna sit by me?"

Greer sat on the other side of her, whining, "Come

on, sit by us." She looked cute with her darker, natural hair color and new pixie cut.

"Sorry, I didn't see you guys over there," I said with a smile as I made my way to their side and sat in the chair next to Amanda.

No sooner had I sat down when Sam scooted past, giggling. "Oh my God, guys. It's finally happening." She plopped down on the other side of Greer and pointed toward the refreshment table. "Look. Look."

Cheyenne and Damian were standing next to each other at the s'more station.

We all watched their interaction with bated breath, but it was hard to tell from behind what was happening. Then we saw Damian reach for her hand.

In unison, the four of us sang out, "Awww."

"They're so cute," Greer said.

Sam put her hand to her chest. "I know, right?"

"Okay, girls, did you bring 'em?" Greer said in a tone that meant business.

I was confused, but Sam and Amanda knew what she was talking about.

"Yep," Sam replied.

"Uh-huh." Amanda nodded. "Let's do it."

"Come on, Ronnie," Greer said as they all stood. "You should be there too."

Curious, I joined them as they approached the firepit. Will and another kid stood on the opposite side, roasting marshmallows. Then Cheyenne noticed us and dragged Damian over.

"I'll go first," Amanda said with a melancholy expression as she pulled her silver bracelet from her pocket and dangled it over the fire. She hadn't worn it since the day after her old roommate was pulled up from the bottom of the gorge. "It's time to say goodbye to our old friends. May you rest in peace."

Sam held hers over the fire. "It's time to say goodbye to an era."

"Goodbye to our old friends, our old selves, and our old pact," Greer said. She released a noisy breath and dropped her bracelet into the flames.

Sam and Amanda did the same.

After a quiet moment of staring into the fire, Greer looked up and met my gaze.

"Here's to new friends," she said, a pensive grin tugging at the corners of her mouth. She turned to Cheyenne and added, "May they last forever."

"To friends," Sam cheered, pumping a fist in the air.

"To friends," the rest of us joined in unison, even Will and Damian and the other kid I didn't know. We all broke out in laughter.

A couple of minutes later, Will sidled up to me, putting an arm around my waist. In his other hand, he held a plate with two gooey s'mores.

"I made one for you too," he said, setting the plate down on the stone top surrounding the firepit.

"Aww, thank you." I wrapped my arms around him and squeezed. Lifting my chin, I gazed into his eyes and added, "That was so sweet."

Will leaned in, his lips meeting mine with a tender kiss.

My cheeks felt hot as he pulled away, and I noticed everyone's eyes on us.

"Damn, speaking of cute couples…" Amanda gushed.

Will's brow wrinkled. "What'd I miss?"

The girls laughed.

"Nothing," I snickered. "Just eat your s'more."

"You don't have to tell me twice," Will replied, grabbing it and taking a bite.

"You know," Greer started thoughtfully, "you two really do make a great couple."

From that moment on, the rest of the night was nothing but chocolatey, marshmallow goodness and laughs.

And as I looked around at my new group of friends, I knew I wouldn't need the weekend to decide.

This was where I needed to be.

A word about the author…

M.L. Stoughton is a YA author who loves abandoned houses and all things paranormal. She lives in upstate New York, with her husband, a super spoiled pup, and three kitty overlords. She is also the proud mom of two grown daughters and the unofficial neighborhood animal rescue. Her first novel, *Pleasantwick*, was a gold medal winner in the 2017 Readers' Favorite Awards.

Visit her at:

www.mlstoughton.com

Thank you for purchasing
this publication of The Wild Rose Press, Inc.

For questions or more information
contact us at
info@thewildrosepress.com.

The Wild Rose Press, Inc.
www.thewildrosepress.com

www.ingramcontent.com/pod-product-compliance
Lightning Source LLC
Chambersburg PA
CBHW070058030726
47506CB00002B/506

* 9 7 8 1 5 0 9 2 4 9 6 0 2 *